Hot Water Man

Deborah Moggach lives in Hampstead, north London, with a Hungarian painter and her two, almost grown-up children. She has written twelve other novels including *Seesaw, Porky, Driving In the Dark,* and *The Stand-In.* Her TV screenplays include *Stolen, Seesaw,* and the prize-winning *Goggle Eyes.* She also developed *Close Relations* as a five-part BBC serial.

Also by Deborah Moggach

You Must Be Sisters
Close to Home
A Quiet Drink
Porky
To Have and To Hold
Driving in the Dark
Smile and Other Stories
Stolen
The Stand-In
The Ex-Wives
Changing Babies
Seesaw
Close Relations

Hot Water Man

Deborah Moggach

ARROW

This edition published in the United Kingdom in 1999 by
Arrow Books

3 5 7 9 10 8 6 4

First published in the United Kingdom in 1982 by Jonathan Cape

Arrow Books Limited
Random House UK Limited
20 Vauxhall Bridge Road, London, SW1V 2SA

Random House Australia (Pty) Limited
20 Alfred Street, Milsons Point, Sydney, New South Wales 2061, Australia

Random House New Zealand Limited
18 Poland Road, Glenfield
Auckland 10, New Zealand

Random House South Africa (Pty) Limited
Endulini, 5a Jubilee Road, Parktown, 2193, South Africa

Random House UK Limited Reg. No. 954009

A CIP catalogue record for this book is available from the British Library

Papers used by Random House UK Limited are natural, recyclable products made from wood
grown in sustainable forests. The manufacturing processes conform to the environmental
regulations of the country of origin

Printed and bound in Norway by
AIT Trondheim AS

ISBN 0 7493 1261 0

To Enjum, with love

1

'TOO HOT for the ladies,' said his grandfather. 'Too blessed
hot. Had to send 'em away.'

Donald, who was ten, twisted his feet around one way
then the other. He wore grey socks darned by Granny.

'Send 'em into the hills.'

A sensible idea. Girls were no use, spoiling things and making
you feel foolish.

'Murree, Dehra Dun, Mussorie. Simla, of course. Good old
Simla, good old English flowers. Lupins, dahlias, you name
them.'

Donald could name nothing but he knew the noises so well.
Gandhi, Murree, this-wallah, that-wallah; sometimes he didn't
know which were people and which weren't. They were part of
the wallpaper of this house, its patterned carpet, the things
upon which he gazed as his grandfather spoke.

It was June 1955. Outside the day was hot, but not as hot as
India. The sun lay across the carpet, warming its weave. The
room was stuffy. Overhead a plane droned. He never noticed
the drone except in summer; it was part of the heat, like the
hum of the bees.

When he was younger he had thought all old people came
from India. Talk of natives and punkahs became, like blotchy
hands, part of the process of ageing. Perhaps you collected India
like a pension. Or perhaps the words were just in old people's

7

rooms, like Grandad's brass boxes and stuffed mongoose on the lounge shelves. He was ignorant then. Later of course he worked it out and separated his grandparents from the others. They were special. This made it more noteworthy, sitting here long after the tea had grown cold.

Grandad had forgotten his cup on the arm of his chair. Old people took so long. Outside it was all right; you could dawdle and explore, they did not make you hurry up because they were going so slowly themselves. Indoors it was different. But he did not like to get up, his mother and grandmother both being out.

They called him an obedient child. People were always patting his head. This was only because he lived with his grandparents (well, Mum too, but it was an old person's house). He couldn't be cheeky like he was to his mother, because they didn't catch on. He couldn't run off because they couldn't even start to find him. They probably hadn't even noticed he'd gone.

'When they'd gone, things shook down. Just the chaps together. Settled in for the summer, had to sweat it out didn't we. Not much choice about that one. Those days, you did your duty. Had some laughs too. Just the boys together—bit like you and me, eh, old chap?'

Donald nodded. But his mother and Granny were not up in the hills, they were down at the shops. They said they'd bring him back a Crunchie.

Donald fingered the rim of his comic. He had tucked it down the crack in the armchair. He had never met an Indian, though he had seen pictures of them in Grandad's books. They were different from Red Indians, he knew that much. But then he had never met Desperate Dan either, and he was real enough. When the women got back he would take *Beano* into the garden and sit in the bit nobody mowed behind the tool shed.

'And I'll tell you something else. Sweat it out's putting it mildly. The sun would go down and you'd still be standing in front of a blessed great fire. That's what it felt like. Women couldn't take it. Didn't have the constitution.'

8

Outside another plane droned overhead. Donald wiggled his feet. He loved Grandad. He was listening to Grandad's voice, and listening for the click of the gate.

2

MAY 1975, and Duke was driving his wife to the airport. It lay in the desert, nine miles from the centre of Karachi. The airport road was always busy; even at two a.m. he was overtaking taxicabs. Up in the sky a light winked; it was moving with them.

Is that my plane? He expected Minnie to ask this but she remained silent. She sat beside him, smoking, small and tense, her carton of Kent and her documents in her lap — her U.S. citizen's passport, her tickets in their plastic envelope he had prepared for her. She was already removed; she was in the plane, she was changing flights at Kennedy, she was greeting their boys. Already the abstraction of the traveller was upon her — she, Minnie, usually so close and anxious, clinging to his arm. He missed her already.

'Sahib?' They had arrived. Faces were pressed against the window. 'Remember me, sahib?' Porters pushed to the front, pointing to their badge numbers. These fellows were smart. They knew all the businessmen; after seven months they recognized him. One of them got the door open, shouting bossily at the others to keep away. Duke bellowed in his terrible Urdu and pointed to the luggage. Free enterprise: he who tries hardest reaps the rewards. This was his personal motto too.

The airport building was crowded day and night, bodies pressed against the glass to watch the drama of arrivals and depar-

10

tures, people standing on the roof watching the spotlit DC 10s being fed by tankers small as toys. Surrounded by scrubland and shabby suburbs, it was the big concrete theatre where everything happened. In the corridors families, waiting for local flights, slept in their bedrolls. Deep inside the building, within the smartened-up Transit Lounge, people sat in rows of chairs waiting to resume flights to Singapore and Hong Kong. To them, Pakistan was one hour of gazing at the closed tourist booth with its folk dolls — Sindhi, Baluch, Punjabi — sheathed in plastic.

Sitar-style Muzak played. They stood in the Departure Hall.

'Duke, I'm a little nervous.'

'Hey, hon, you'll be there soon.'

'That's what scares me.'

He took Minnie in his arms. Behind him the porter put down the suitcases. 'Hell, Min, I wish I could come.'

'That would be crazy. Besides, I've got the boys.'

Minnie was returning to Wichita to escape the summer heat, to look after the boys in their college vacation and to have her womb removed. She stood aside while he checked in her ticket. She looked like the smallest of his sons. So slight, she was, with her black cropped hair and tanned face. Through a cloud of smoke she was gazing gravely at her cases, moving away along the rubber belt. She wore the sleeveless pink pants suit that she had not worn since they had arrived here — her creaseless travelling gear. Soon she would be beyond his help, in limbo land the other side of the Departure Lounge door; she was now a Pan-Am passenger he was unable to follow, with a boarding card and passport ready for its stamp. Like a patient, injected now and ready to go through the double doors beyond which nobody else can enter.

He kissed her, holding her against him. He ran his hands up and down her thin, dry arms. Behind him the porter hawked and spat. He kissed her again, oblivious of the spectators. The buttons of her blouse pressed against his chest; behind the polyester, deep within her lay the mysterious place where his sons, now all over six foot, had lain growing.

11

'It'll be okay,' he whispered pointlessly.

He watched her leave, pause at the desk for her passport to be stamped, then disappear through frosted doors marked *Security: Ladies*. There she would stand, husbandless, while a P.I.A. girl, head modestly swathed in a dupatta, patted her front and rear, searching for weapons.

It was three a.m. but Duke was not tired. He was a big man, no beauty, strong as an ox. Prod him anywhere: muscle, all muscle. He believed in keeping trim. Soon when the sun rose he would be jogging, thudding along the dusty verges of K12 Housing Society. Pariah dogs would run out, yapping; they lived in the scrub of the empty plots. Past high white walls he would trot, past closed gates with their lozenge lights still bright though the sky was brighter. Gatemen would be sitting, propped up like dolls. No sound but his own feet, his own harsh breaths, and the murmur of air-conditioners outside closed bedroom windows. His business friends thought he was crazy; these Pakistanis did not take exercise. But he loved the early mornings, the distant loudspeaker calling from the mosque, and the air fresh before the heat closed in. He had urged Minnie to join him, these beautiful dawns. She seldom did. In the three months she had been in Karachi she had not settled; she could find nothing to say to the American wives and the slums reduced her to tears. In one small, uncomfortable way it was a relief she had gone. He had felt responsible for her, returning early from work when he had so much to do, trying to take on to his shoulders her burden of distress. Besides, she had missed their boys. He would ache for her but life would be simpler; without women it always was. This was what they used to do, apparently, out in these parts. Business did not stop for the heat.

Minnie was three dots in the sky. They disappeared. Up there she would be settling back on her pillow. A stewardess, blonde and comprehensible, would be passing round the blankets sealed in cellophane. Duke was standing on the roof. Even at this hour of the night, the concrete ledge was warm. Another jumbo, a British Airways 747, had landed; in the spotlight, toy people climbed down the steps and made their way to the bus. Some paused. He knew what they thought: that the heat came from the exhaust jets of the plane. Only when they moved away did they realize that this fire was not something you could leave behind so easily. It would last from May through September.

'Mr Hanson?'

Duke turned. It was Mr Samir from Cameron Chemicals. His bald head glistened. They shook hands.

'You have been seeing off your lady wife?'

'She was sorry to leave,' said Duke politely. 'She'd gotten to like your city.'

'We are all sorry too. But it is becoming so hot.'

Actually the heat was the one thing she could take. Duke said nothing, but nodded.

'She'll return in September?'

'Sure. I guess I know who you're meeting. Your English manager.'

'And his better half.'

'Kinda warm time to arrive. They been out here before?'

'I believe not. Mr Manley has only worked in London office. His tour here is two years.'

'I'll be seeing plenty of him.' Duke worked for the Translux Group. Their hotel project here would be taking out a large contract with Cameron's; interior fitments, paint. So far his hotel project was a flat stretch of scrub desert. These things took time. Here, they took time.

He accompanied Mr Samir down the steps. Around the Arrivals Hall the windows were full of faces but only those who knew their status had walked through the doors to greet the travellers – besuited Pakistani businessmen, Europeans in bush shirts. One of Mr Samir's colleagues was waiting, wanly at attention, in his hand a string of blossoms.

'I bet you find them inconvenient, these night flights,' said Duke. Aircraft usually landed in the small hours, destined to arrive at more attractive cities at a civilized time in the morning. To mention this would be tactless.

'No, no.' Mr Samir coughed. 'No trouble.'

Arrivals were trickling through. Roused from sleep, from the airline pillow against which, now, Minnie's head must surely be resting, each face looked blank under the strip light. They had travelled 3,500 miles; above black deserts they had eaten untimely meals sealed in foil. They did not look ready.

Duke spotted the English couple. They were younger than he had expected. The man, attempting casualness with his jacket over his arm, glanced back at the porter wheeling the luggage, then looked around at the faces. He was fair and freckled, pleasant-looking, softish. In this climate he would burn.

His wife walked a step ahead of him. She was the same height as her husband; she wore a crumpled embroidered blouse and jeans. Her fairish hair was frizzed, like the girls did nowadays; underneath it her face was radiant with an English glow. She turned back to speak to her husband; the spectators had their eyes fixed on her.

They met with much shaking of hands. 'Mr Donald Manley,' said Mr Samir to Duke. 'Our new Sales Manager. Mrs Christine Manley.'

'For us?' The girl ducked. The garland was placed over her head. Her face lifted, blushing. 'Do you always do this?'

'It is our custom', said Mr Samir, 'for honoured guests.'

'I feel such a mess. I've been asleep.' She touched the wilted flowers. On her upper arm, Duke saw the new inoculation plaster. 'They're so beautiful. What are they called?'

Mr Samir told her the name. Donald Manley said: 'I'm so pleased to be here. My grandfather served in Karachi, years ago. He was in the army.' The thread of the garland was tangled with his shoulder bag; he fumbled with it, twitching his arm up and down. 'He talked about it so much, I feel I'm coming home.'

There was a pause. The English couple, no doubt, were trying to think of something interesting to say about their first impression of Pakistan. The airport offered them a grey concrete interior, a crowd of men and the shuttered cubicle of a Habib Bank. And heat.

'Hot, isn't it,' said Mr Manley pleasantly.

3

MOHAMMED wore gymshoes. The reason for his silence as he passed from room to room, dusting, arranging, tidying up her mess, lay in his stealthy rubber soles. Lay also in his deference; his humble desire not to disturb, which of course disturbed Christine more. She reclined on her sun-couch, cocking her head sideways. She was a woman of leisure but she was not at ease.

Like the Cameron furniture, Mohammed came with the house. For two weeks she had lived with his attentions. Anything she did could be bettered by him; besides, it would offend him to take matters out of his hands. Yesterday she had picked some sprays of bougainvillaea from the garden; going into the kitchen she had met him, already arranging sprays of bougainvillaea in a glass of water, tinted pink. He had the feminine touch.

'But darling, you've always hated housework,' Donald had said last night. They were eating supper. 'You always said it was so demeaning, scrubbing away and nobody noticing. So thanklessly circular, you said.'

'I just feel silly sitting around. Lifting my feet while he sweeps the bit under them.'

'But you always said —' He stopped. The door was ajar; Mohammed stood in the kitchen, waiting to collect the empty plates. In his white uniform he could almost be felt.

15

'He can't understand English,' hissed Christine. 'Not that well.'

'All the same … '

'Can't we ever talk? For two years?'

Donald took his last mouthful. So did she. When he had finished chewing he cleared his throat. 'Mohammed.'

Plates were swiftly lifted. Mohammed emerged with a bowl of orange stuff. He was a slender young man, girlish and beautiful. He served them and disappeared back into the kitchen.

'Wages for Housewives,' said Donald in a low voice. 'He's only doing what those ghastly friends of yours were always going on about.'

'Don't be simplistic.'

'They were ghastly. They all had such bad skin.'

'Don't be sexist.'

'If only they ever laughed. They weren't good for you.'

'Anyway I wasn't just a housewife. I had a job.'

'Wages for Housewives.' Donald chuckled, spooning on the cream.

'Perhaps you should marry Mohammed. That Rosemary woman said all the Pathans are gay. Wives are just to have sons by.'

'Shh.'

Christine's dress stuck to her. She rearranged herself on the sun-couch. This should be the life. When Mohammed had retired for his afternoon nap she would strip down to her bikini, if she could bear to move out of the shade. He was upstairs. The window creaked as he opened it to air the bedroom. Now he would be making the bed upon which she and Donald had lain. She thought of last night; what Donald called That Department had these last months become something they were trying, by an unspoken pact, to treat casually. After all they had been married three years.

From here she had a view of the lawn, the hose lying across it like a snake. It was edged with dusty flowerbeds and enclosed by a high stucco wall. In the corner squatted the mali, an old man. The gates were open. Through them she could glimpse 4th East Street, K12 Housing Society. This was a new, already potholed strip of road backed by the white wall of the house opposite. Sometimes a car would pass. Sometimes a man would appear with his baskets and offer her something in a weird sing-song.

K12 was the choice place to live. She did not understand the name; there did not appear to be a K11 or a K anything else. It was one of these oriental mysteries. All the houses were modern; some were still being built. Theirs was large and functional. Behind her, beyond the sprung mosquito door that snapped shut, lay the living-room full of Cameron furniture – G-plan teak veneer, standard lamps and chairs passed from one manager to the next. Above the sofa hung a brass rubbing of a knightly couple, stiff and united. Their charcoal gaze followed her around the room.

She settled back. She had finished *A Passage to India*. She lit a cigarette. It was too hot; she stubbed it out. She moved herself forward so that her legs were in the sunlight. It was so hot that nobody sunbathed here. She scratched the mosquito bite on her shin. She wanted, more than anything, to hose the lawn. She had always wanted a garden. Before this they had lived in a two-roomed flat in Crouch End. But the mali was hosing the grass; he had moved forward, sunshine lit the spray. The grass was patchy green and khaki; puddled now. If she got rid of the mali she could squat there, her toes dabbling in the mud, and spray the foreign shrubs that grew against the wall, hearing the water patter on to .their leathery leaves. She could buy new plants and dig holes for them and press around their stems the beige, damp earth. But here, if you were grand enough to own a garden you were grand enough not to do it yourself. And if she sacked the mali he would be out of a job; when she had held her Urdu Primer and asked him how many – *kitne* – children he had, he counted eight on his fingers. Was it worth it, for her to drench the grass and feel part of this Pakistan?

'Can we go out?' she asked Donald later that evening.

17

'We are going out. By this new digital thing, in five minutes precisely if we're not going to be late.' He buttoned up his shirt. The dhobi, who visited twice a week, ironed it far better than she could ever do. 'Hardly been in, have we. Duke Hanson's on Monday, drinks at Charles and Rosemary Whatsit's last night. Bit of the old social whirls.'

'I mean into the real city. Out beyond all this.' She was standing at the window.

'Ah, the teeming millions and the local colour. Have you seen my keys?' He turned, smiling. She had never seen him happier than these last two weeks. He kept phoning from work to see if she was all right. She could tell by the tone of voice if somebody else was in his office. 'I feel so guilty, leaving you here all day. We'll go sightseeing this weekend. Remind me to get some film for my camera.'

'I don't just want to look at it. I want to get into it.'

He stood at the dressing-table, transferring keys and coins to the pockets of his new trousers. He was stocky, with blond fuzz on his arms. His face was blunt and regular; unmemorable unless you loved him. The question was: did she still? His nose was burnt red; so was hers. They resembled each other; people in the past had taken them for brother and sister.

We're alone now, she thought. A new country, a huge new sky. A stucco house with eight rooms and a flat roof. Its only familiarity was the decorated shawl she had fixed with masking tape to their bedroom wall. A trunkful of clothes, and themselves. Would this improve their marriage? It must change it.

Outside the sun was sinking. From this window you could see between the neighbouring houses. Way beyond, three miles away, lay the city; here and there blocks rose into the polluted evening sky. Turning to the left, you saw the last few houses of the suburb. Beyond lay the desert. Drab during the day, those scrub flats turned molten in the sunset. Future roads were already laid out, leading nowhere, and building plots were marked out with posts. The posts had turned pink in the light;

18

they stretched into the distance and made the landscape look shabby and temporary. Beyond them lay the silver thread of the Indian Ocean.

4

DONALD had grown up on the edge of the ocean. It was a tamed sea. Brinton, on the Kentish coast, was not far from Broadstairs. It was a holiday resort of pebble-dash semis, bus shelters and a windy esplanade. Old dears sat in the tea shops. Along Marine Drive the sea could be glimpsed, a grey strip between the parked cars.

It stretched for miles, bungalows and retirement homes, electric fires on throughout the year and chairs in crescents around the picture window. Between them and the sea were the amusements to keep people busy. There was a clock-golf course, Brinton Bowls Green with thoughtful men in braces, and the Happyland Caravan Park about which complaints were made.

Only regulars went. Brinton had not moved with the times. There were topless buses for brave souls and the Gaumont which showed *Carry On* pictures. Next door, the one-armed bandits were out of order. In winter the holidaymakers went and the gales blew the notices down. Donald loved it then. He loved it in all seasons, it was secure and yet there was the ocean to set him yearning. Along safe streets a van delivered bread, but above it clouds massed over a troubled Channel.

He lived with his mother and grandparents; his father had been killed in the war. His father was a photo on the mantelpiece, and sighed asides. He himself was the man of the family.

The responsibility had pleased him; as a boy he had grown up serious and adult for his age, out of step with his schoolfriends. He had always hurried home to Durradee.

And especially to Grandad. Grandad was like a father who was never too busy. He was always there, unchanging; he frequently told Donald that he took the same size in suits he had taken forty years before. Unlike Granny he never seemed to get older; unlike Mother, who was essential of course but usually out at work or preoccupied, he was always at hand. He was the only person who treated Donald as an adult, man to man. In fact he spoke to Donald as he spoke to nobody else in the household — proper conversations, just the two of them, while the women clattered in the kitchen. It was with Grandad that he did the things he remembered — the hikes along the cliffs, scurrying to keep up with Grandad's longer strides, tense with remembering the birds' names so he did not disappoint. By some unspoken family law, it was only himself who was allowed in the greenhouse where Grandad stooped, too tall for the roof, lifting the seedlings. Donald lifted them too, trying not to spill the earth. He had his father to live up to. His father had served in the R.A.F. Sometimes when a plane droned overhead Grandad paused, looking up through the glass.

He himself, though diligent, did badly at school. Grandad used to recite the names of famous men whose academic performance had been undistinguished. 'In the arena of life,' he said — meaning India — 'in the arena of life what disadvantage is that? There are more important things to be tested than *amo* and *amas*.' Donald had just failed his Latin 'O' level. Grandad was reassuring about that, shrinking it to its proper perspective. His gaze stretched beyond.

And Grandad had time. His Indian service had left him with a long retirement in the bungalow with the front porch, which he called the veranda, and its view over the sea. It faced the east. His life had dwindled to a lounge and those memories to which nobody else, Donald realized as he grew older, cared to listen. His brass objects were taken down, polished and put back again; they trapped the dust, Granny said. She hardly spoke of India. It

21

was not her life as it was his, she had only lived there for thirty years before returning thankfully to dear old Britain. In fact there was not a lot you could say to Granny; she just existed from moment to moment, making things comfy.

Yet there he sat, this noble man, enduring the inexplicable 1960s in which he seemed to be spending the last years of his life. He became more infirm. He just made it down to the esplanade. Teenagers giggled when he lifted his stick at the sea, mouthing words.

Donald felt he was protecting a worn god from the faithless. Here was a man who had done more than their narrow spirits could imagine. A man who had led three hundred men through Burma; who had marched through the Delhi streets during Independence. One of those personally asked by Mountbatten to postpone his return for three more years so that he could help train up the native officers. Grandad had been given a signed photograph of Jinnah. Though intensely proud of it, Donald had not brought it to school. Jinnah who? they would say.

He knew Christine long before he met her. He had seen her on the tennis courts. She was a summer visitor and wire mesh separated their games. She wore a white Aertex shirt and a pleated skirt; her honey-blonde hair was pulled back in a rubber band. She leapt for the ball. She was not that different from the others but he noticed her. She played high, soft, girl's strokes and pressed a hand to her mouth, grimacing. Afterwards she was more at ease, spreading out her legs at the café table, tipping back her chair and sucking Pepsi through a straw. That first summer she was sometimes with girls and sometimes with youths, their hair damp from their exertions. It was only later that she told him she did not know them well; her parents, groan groan, had forced them on her.

She told him this next summer when he talked to her for the first time. He had forgotten her during the winter. She was sitting on a wooden breakwater wearing what was to become the familiar blue-ribbed bathing suit. She swung her legs; she was alone; she was ready for anything. She was fifteen. Close

22

up her face was less perfect, with its chapped lips. She walked along the beach with him, stepping over the sunbathing adults who lay torpid as logs.

He splashed into the sea, showing off. She followed him with prancing, coltish steps, squealing. She floundered around; he impressed her with his manly crawl. Stepping out on to the beach she was bowed and shivering, her white legs goosepimpled. She looked thinner and smaller but he did not dare rub her dry. He longed to. Instead he whooped and they ran along the sand, jumping legs.

She was there with her parents and her sister Joyce. Each year they rented a bungalow. He hung around, gawkily seventeen. They walked along the cliff path; he grasped her hand over the tricky bits but relinquished it when they were safe. They swung on the children's swings; he was dizzy for her but he dared do nothing. To touch her would change her into his girlfriend; then at some point it must end. Presuming, indeed, that she would let him touch her in the first place.

They were too casual to write. The London Christine, wrapped in unknown woollies, was as arousing a thought to him as the swimsuited Christine must be to those urban rivals who had only seen her clothed. During the winter months he sat on the window seat at Durradee, his 'A' level economics book on his knee and the rain sliding down the glass. The next summer he saw her entering the sea-front newsagent's; she emerged with a cigarette between her lips.

That year he kissed her in the Aquarium. It was stuffy down there; half the tanks were empty. Wedged against the railing, he had kissed her dry lips, while behind them the eels coiled. After that they often embraced, but only in places like the cinema. They were sweethearts in the dark, but ordinary outside. He did not want to go further. Perhaps he was under-sexed. It was just that he did not want to spoil it.

The next year he went up to London to work, a Cameron's trainee. He met other girls but Christine was separate. That summer she returned but she seemed more inward, kicking stones along the beach and moaning about her parents. He was

23

part of her family by now; he felt included in this general complaint. She was going to university in the autumn. Their kisses were still fervent but chaste. He felt diffident and dull. Sometimes she snapped at him, and he was helpless. He wanted to grab her and take her by force but then he wanted to protect her, too, from people like himself. She had a secret life, kept from him as well as her parents. Sometimes he saw her on the back of motorbikes.

She did write; short scrawled notes full of *goshes*. Her writing stayed young and enthusiastic while she herself was changing. He wrote longer letters and more of them, ending them *lots of love*, carefully matched to the endings she put on hers. (Sometimes she put *much* love instead of *lots*.) He started seeing her in London; she wore make-up and tights, he took her to the Festival Hall and they made conversation. She went up to a new university, Nissen huts and bulldozed earth and a scattering of students who all knew each other.

One weekend he could no longer bear it; he went up to Warwick and made love to her. In the past he had plotted appropriate spots for this; he had made ardent mental bookings — the sand dunes, the creek where the bracken stood waist-high and you could hear the sea. In reality it happened on the narrow bed of her hall of residence during a sleepy Sunday afternoon, the Top Ten being played through the wall and somebody knocking on the door halfway through. They had clung; the footsteps had retreated.

He was far from being the first. She hinted that she was involved with someone else. But who else had known a Christine before she smoked; who else had seen her through three swimsuits? They did not know her sister Joyce, matronly at fourteen. He possessed years of Christine before she braided her hair into tiny plaits and questioned everything. She wore long Indian skirts and pale stuff over her healthy cheeks. She did not fool him. Her childhood was their secret.

It was four years before they married. She kept going off with other people and then coming back to him. He did not make a habit of this, himself. But then her father died. Soon afterwards

24

they married. They came together like a brother and sister who had been lost in the woods. They understood each other so well. Or so he thought.

They bought the Crouch End flat, second floor, nothing special except that it was theirs. She was training to be a teacher but she did not take it up.

When had things started changing? When she cut off her lovely, heavy blonde hair and frizzed it up; when she preferred to be known as Chris, and discovered it was oppressive to be supported by her husband? In certain moods he felt he was losing her to the seventies. She considered him the conventional one but it was she who followed so obediently the prevailing winds. But he could not blame it all on the decade, however much he would have liked to. He still could not put it into words. Here in Pakistan, perhaps, he could recapture the old Christine, and that time years ago when everything seemed possible.

And then there was that other difficulty. They did not talk about it much; though so outspoken about her woman's predicament in general, Christine was thankfully shy about mentioning this. To transfer oneself from one continent to another could hardly solve it; logically they were the same two people as before. But he no longer felt logical about this.

5

THE PARTY was held in the garden. The sun had sunk; even during twilight, however, the air felt centrally heated. Up above the crows banged about in the trees, disturbed by the social exclamations.

The film had not yet started. A blank screen hung against the wall. Spotlights were wired up amongst the bushes, pools of emerald leaves. People stood about chatting. Donald approved of dressing-up; nobody did it in England any more. Between the guests slid bearers holding trays of lukewarm gin and tonic. The Pakistani ladies drank Bubble-Up.

'This is the life,' he said to Christine, so they looked as if they were talking. He turned to the bearer. 'Thank you.'

'Thank you.' Christine took a glass. '*Shoukriah*.'

'You're much nicer to servants than you are to me,' he said. 'What?'

'Look, there's Shamime. She's the girl I was telling you about — does our public relations.'

Shamime turned. Tall and slim, she was one of those girls about whom you would say: She's not exactly beautiful. And keep wondering about it, unable to move your eyes from her face. Her nose was certainly too big. Her hair was looped in black coils. She wore a loose turquoise trouser suit with strings of gold chains. She looked somewhat like this in the Cameron office.

'Amazing dress.' She held out a slim brown arm to Christine. 'Where on earth did you get it?'

'In England. London,' said Christine. 'I worked in a dress shop. It sold second-hand clothes.'

'Trendy second-hand clothes,' added Donald. The dress was a floral thing from the forties, with padded shoulders. He had mixed feelings about this garment.

'Donald says I look like a charwoman.'

Shamime laughed. 'Where's the shop?'

'In a little passage where they sell antiques,' said Christine. 'At weekends they have stalls. It's rather like your bazaars, actually. You know, lots of people, no cars, covered arcades too, like in Karachi. Rather fun.'

'Sounds just like Camden Passage.'

Christine paused. 'So you've been there?'

'Adore it. I love Islington and Hampstead. I get so self-indulgent in those little shops.'

'I see. Do you go to London often?'

'When I run out of marmalade.' She laughed again. 'No, seriously, there are so many things you can't get here. It's impossible.'

'Which hotel do you stay at?'

'My cousin has a little house behind Harrods. But hasn't Harrods changed? Full of Arabs.'

In the pause that followed this remark Donald was aware of a general shifting. Chairs had been arranged; someone was fiddling with the projector. He sat down beside Christine. He leant towards her, then stopped. He would like to gossip with her about Shamime but his wife was turning out to be disappointing in this respect; invariably she was nicer about the Pakistanis than the English. This seemed like racial discrimination to him.

The guests had taken their seats now. The lights were switched off. Donald heard the scrape and whirr of crickets up in the bushes. Or were they tree-frogs? He had yet to learn. Forty years ago these streets were a wilderness of scrub. Karachi was a small sea-port then with a native bazaar and an English

27

cantonment; where two-lane carriageways now lay, Grandad had shot a tiger. Or perhaps that was somewhere else.

With a creak, Duke settled beside him. Donald had liked Duke from the start, when with commendable American frankness Duke had told him his wife was going to have a hysterectomy. Most people, himself included, would have steered murmuringly around the precise nature of her trouble. Christine leant across him.

'When's the op, Duke? Last time I saw you, you hadn't heard.'

'Saturday. I have faith in the guy – finest surgeon in Kansas.'

The whirring insects, or frogs, were reinforced by the whirr of the projector. People stopped talking. A pale, fluid shape appeared on the screen, flicking with numbers. It was an old picture, in black and white. Through a hoop the British Lion snarled, shaking its mane and growling. Showing its teeth, it resembled Grandad's tiger skin, now balding and stored in the attic.

Two people sat down in front. It was Shamime and her brother Aziz; they both turned around to smile. Aziz was as tall and as dazzling as his sister.

The film started. The hero wore R.A.F. uniform.

'We all have to do our bit, old girl.'

'Reggie darling. Each time I look up in the sky I'll think it's you.'

'Don't cry.'

'I'm crying because I'm so proud.'

The faces were familiar from scores of British films; they were smoother and younger here. Donald was absorbed. Shamime's piled-up hairstyle blocked his view; he tilted to the side. The scene changed to an airfield. Shamime was adjusting a pin in her hair; through the gap in her arm he glimpsed a Hurricane's wing. Reggie was talking to another pilot now. His voice came from her *coiffure*.

'Before you know it we'll be home. First one back at base sets up two pints.'

'I'm already saying cheers.'

In front, the two heads bent together. A muffled giggle;

28

Shamime whispered something to her brother. Donald stiffened. What were they laughing at?

A roar; the fighters were off the ground. Donald could almost smell the petrol. Through grey 35mm clouds, lit by the sunset, the Hurricanes sped. Voices crackled on the intercom.

'Can you hear me, Number Two? Over.'

A silence.

'I said, can you hear me?'

An explosion: streaks, flashes, the screen burst with fireworks.

Silence. Donald sat very still. Up in the black sky, a jet whined over Karachi. Its passengers were safe. On the screen, smoke plumed. A splash. Water settled; smoke drifted. Donald's throat tightened.

Beside him Christine shifted, rummaging in her handbag. But it was not for a handkerchief, it was for a cigarette. She leant towards him in a cloud of smoke.

'Dash it all, and it was his round.'

'What?'

'His turn', she said patiently, 'to buy the drinks.'

She sat back, crossing her legs so casually in her wartime dress. Donald grunted. He thought of his mother, a wartime sweetheart and so soon a wartime widow. She had worn a dress similar to Christine's but hers was not bra-less; underneath it she wore solid foundations. Christine seemed so untested. He was so untested. His father had braved the flak. How would he, his father's son, behave under enemy fire?

He would be called Don. At one period he had tried this name but nobody seemed to notice, so he went back to Donald. His life had been so safe; his father and thousands like him had made it secure. On the beach at Brinton there was a derelict bunker; *bang-bang* he had shouted to his friends, crouched in its interior which was littered with sweet wrappings.

'He was in a fighter squadron,' he told Duke after the film, another gin and tonic in his hand. 'But he wasn't killed on ops.' He stopped. 'Ops' seemed, in the circumstances, a poorly-chosen word. 'He was bombed in a train coming home on leave,

29

in 1945. So near the end of the war. Ironic really.'

But his father had been a hero, like Grandad. In Donald's sense of the word they both were. Men in the front line of action.

'You see, Duke ... ' He leant forward; alcohol had made him confiding. 'I come from a family of what you Americans would call achievers. I mean, not grand or anything like that. Rather the contrary; middling middle-class, quite ordinary really. But men who stretched themselves to the full and got things done.'

And whose women followed them, he added wordlessly, watching Christine wandering off in the direction of the french windows. How could he explain his need to protect her, and her corresponding urge to liberate herself from his manly support? Here in Pakistan he had a sales-force of thirty-five men; there were slums through which, as they walked, she must surely cling to his arm; there were signposts in Urdu script which neither of them could understand. She was no longer striding her known English streets. It was not subservience he wanted but some recognition, long lost, that he had skills to respect. He wanted to take care of her. He wanted no women friends around her, either, to raise their eyebrows pityingly at this concept. He wanted to recapture her. And if that was impossible, he wanted them to be lost together.

And another thing, he wanted to say. We don't seem to be having a child.

When he knew him better, surely he could confide in Duke. The man was like an oak, strong and weathered. He had lived but he was somehow innocent too, a big simple man. He looked fifty but he would look the same way for ever. And he could take his drink; Donald's head was already swimming. What had Christine said once? When you like someone you make them a hero; it's your short cut so you needn't work them out. Adding silently, no doubt: you like to build them up because you're so weak yourself.

Shamime approached. 'You'll all come to the beach on Saturday, won't you?'

'Saturday?' said Duke.

'We're having a few friends to our hovel.' She laid her hand on Duke's arm. 'We're not letting you pine away.'

'What's the hovel?' asked Donald.

'Our little beach hut. You must get a beach hut, Donald.'

Aziz appeared at her side with a plate of food. Oily spiced meats spread into egg mayonnaise; their British Council hosts laid on a multinational menu.

'We'll have some Scotch,' he said. 'The real McCoy.' With a charmingly quizzical smile he looked at his glass, which held the local stuff.

How did they get it, thought Donald, in this Muslim place? Connections, connections. Their uncle was a minister.

Shamime turned to Duke. 'I've found your perfect hotel receptionist. Aziz.' She pointed to her brother. 'He'd be wonderful. He looks gorgeous and he's such a dummy.'

Aziz smiled. The international type, he looked the part. He wore well-pressed slacks and a cotton sports shirt, the pocket jutting with his packet of Rothmans.

'It'd keep him out of mischief,' said Shamime. 'He spends all his time at the Club, or in his den fiddling with his veeseeyah.'

A pause. 'His what?' asked Donald. He pictured some local artifact, like a string of beads.

'V.C.R. Video.'

'Ah.'

'He's got some quite nice films. *Cabaret*, *Butch Cassidy*, that thing with Barbra Streisand in it.'

'A tiny bit more up-to-date', said Aziz, 'than the offerings of your kind British Council.' He speared a prawn.

Donald prickled. He thought of men like his grandfather risking their lives for this country. Keeping the peace, digging canals to bring fertility to what was then known as India, making laws that were still maintained as the arbiters of sense. All so the likes of Aziz – then considered a native – could now have a driver waiting outside in the Mercedes.

Shamime leant towards him. 'Do look at your wife,' she whispered. 'I think she's going native.'

Donald turned. Chairs had been arranged for eating. In one

31

group sat Mr Samir, his office manager, and Mr Samir's wife in a turquoise sari. They forked in the food, nodding and smiling. The third person was Christine. She looked large, pale and shabby. She alone was eating with her hand. To be precise, swabbing her plate with a folded flap of chapatti.

6

BY NOON Christine admitted defeat. She moved her idle paraphernalia — Nivea oil, cigarettes, damp, half-finished airletter to Joyce — into the one air-conditioned downstairs room, a small study. She clicked the switch; soon the air grew lukewarm, then almost fresh. On the dot of twelve-thirty there would be a tap on the door. There Mohammed would stand, her gin and tonic on a tray. She had a hangover but she did not dare tell him, as he was a Muslim.

The window looked on to the side wall. A strip of earth separated the front lawn from the back where Mohammed's quarters lay. This consisted of one room jutting from the kitchen, with its own curtained doorway. Unpainted concrete, it was stuck to the white building like a wasps' nest. From it came cooking smells and the sound of a radio. The front garden was empty but at the back it was always busy; chickens scratched around, but when they came up this side alley children ran out to shoo them back. She did not like to step around the back of the house; she felt shy. Mohammed's wife was a plump woman who was probably the same age as Christine; when she saw Christine she giggled and pulled her scarf across her face. Yesterday she had been sitting outside on a rug. She had looked approachable for once. It was in the heat of the day; the children were quiet. Christine had walked up, cleared her throat and said '*Salaam.*' The woman had lifted her head and bent

33

down. Oh heavens she was praying.

Once she knew she was coming out East Christine had started reading bits in the newspapers she would never normally have done — reports on the new order in the Middle East and articles called 'Behind the Veil'. By now she knew a little about women in Islamic countries. Behind the veil sounded gauzy and romantic, an enticement. But down in the streets she had seen women enveloped in grubby white sheets, a bit of crochet where their eyes were, stumbling along the pavement behind their husbands. She had been to a gathering at Mr Samir's house where chairs were lined against the wall and women sat in rows, pink sari, blue sari, glinting with jewels and drinking Fanta while from the next room came men's laughter. They had talked about somebody's wedding, speaking polite English for her sake. 'You have children?' the next lady asked her. 'No,' she had replied. And there the conversation had ended.

Last night after the film show she had asked Shamime about women here.

'Don't be fooled, it's a confederacy,' Shamime had said. 'We run the place really but we're too clever to show it.'

Christine thought of London and Roz, the girl who owned Rags Period Frocks. Roz, herself and some others had a kind of women's group, too informal to be given a name, just something that had evolved. They did not quite call each other 'sisters' but they felt like a sisterhood. A confederacy of women.

'Women rule', said Shamime, 'but subtly. We may not have much power but we've got influence. Far more effective, my girl. Women here are the real personalities. Every man I know is dominated by his mother. Just you wait and see. They're led by the nose. But we're cleverer than you; we don't let them realize it.'

In Shamime's nose was a jewel. There was something primitive as well as exotic about this; to pierce a nose seemed more shocking than piercing an ear. It looked like bondage. Led by the nose: who was leading whom?

'Do I have a pimple?'

'Sorry.' Christine blushed. 'I was just looking at that diamond. Who wears them here?'

'Who?'

'I mean — is it something to do with being unmarried, or grown-up ... ' She struggled with cultural images. Always it was the women who were marked — wedding rings, those red blobs Hindu women wore. Marks of ownership, sometimes by husbands and sometimes by God.

'Heaven knows.' Shamime laughed. 'I only had it done last month. A little man at the Intercontinental.'

'Ah.'

'You'd look lovely with one, but I think a sapphire with your skin. Shall I tell you his name?'

'Donald would have a fit.' Christine put her hand to her mouth. 'I mean, it looks gorgeous on you, but ... ' This was worse. But Shamime just laughed, her jewel winking.

Christine switched off the air-conditioner. It was lunchtime. Outside the window a midday breeze had found its way into the garden; in the silence branches scraped back and forth against the wall. Who was confining whom? She thought of her mother, back in the lounge at Mill Hill. She loved her mother with deep exasperation; these feelings were mutual. 'The Larches' was always home; a grassy bank separated it from the A1 dual carriageway, busy day and night. Signs led off in all directions, *Dover, Folkestone, Hatfield and the North*. During Christine's childhood the M1 was being built half a mile beyond the existing road; the giant legs of a flyover grew up with her over one autumn. When she was seventeen she took driving lessons.

Her mother had learnt to drive before Daddy died but she did it helplessly, gripping the wheel like a sinking woman. At first glance her mother was far from subjugated. She was slim, active and full of bright observations. She worked on the board of the local school, she brought up her daughters, she cleaned up before the cleaning lady arrived just as she, Christine, now hurried from room to room before Mohammed reached them. Yet she lived behind a purdah of the small and the personal. Setting the world to rights meant sorting out the sock drawer.

35

'Silly old me,' she would say, comfortably refusing to change. She invited indulgence; Christine's father fondly narrowed his topics when she took part in the conversation. If he had minded he never let it show. Wearied of confrontations Christine too had ended up by making allowances for her; in other words, by treating her as less. This had saddened her. Though easing the atmosphere her mother had noticed it too and treated Christine with the brightness of a hostess. She was settled in her domestic life, bound by her received ideas of what a wife and mother should be.

Christine had struggled free of all that. She had taken the M1 motorway up to university; she had travelled further. She had tried to escape what she had realized was the prison of her sex.

'What about the prison of mine?' Donald had asked once, mildly. 'All this lib thingy. Do they think I adore going to the office every day?' He had paused. 'I don't understand why women are such slaves. I mean, I am so you needn't be.'

'What?'

'I mean, I can't afford having a bash at being a teacher and then deciding I don't like it — wait a second, Chrissy — and then going into advertising and deciding it's too trivial, and then taking time off with all that yoga business, and then being a part-time waitress for one's experience of life with a capital L — wait a sec — then trying to write about life with a capital L but getting a lovely tan instead, then working in that clothes cupboard for a pittance. I mean, if I miss one repayment to the old Abbey National it goes down on a little file and if I miss any more they stop our mortgage.' He paused for breath. 'Somebody's got to have a nine-to-five mentality. I can't *afford* to find myself.'

'You're very hostile.'

'I'm not. It's just that I get a bit fed up when I come home and there's this tribe of them, all living off their husband's alimony and filling the kitchen with cigarette smoke. They look at me as if I've stepped into the wrong house.'

'It's only because you don't fancy any of them. You'd agree with them if they flattered you and had plunge necklines.'

36

'Now who's being sexist?' He took her in his arms. This seemed condescending; she struggled free. He said: 'You always say I'm conventional, darling, but you're just as bad.'

'Why do you only call me darling when you're getting at me?'

'You were much – well, freer, when you were younger. Sort of more original when you didn't mind about being ordinary. When you weren't worrying about any of this.'

'I wasn't married then. Sorry, sorry. It was just that I hadn't *thought* then.'

'Not thought – listened to other people.'

She had felt uncomfortable. Why did she remember this conversation so well?

She picked up her Urdu Primer and went into the kitchen. Last night, after the film show, Donald and herself had not learnt their Urdu together as planned; fired by alcohol and a tiff about her eating with her hands they had tried, doggedly, the bedsprings creaking, to conceive.

In contrast to the rest of the house the kitchen was primitive: stone sink, bare boards, a place memsahibs entered only to rub their finger along the surfaces and check the grocery list. Mohammed had finished washing-up the lunch. He was scrubbing the sink. The place smelt of cockroach powder. She leant casually against the wall, assuring him by her stance that she had not entered to inspect. 'Never trust the servants,' said that terrible Marjorie woman whose husband worked in Grindlays Bank.

'Mohammed, what's the name of that bazaar down in the old city?' She talked, of course, in English. A pause. '*Bazaar*.'

'Bohri Bazaar.'

'Not that one.' Everyone went to Bohri Bazaar. It was full of tourist knick-knacks; European women sailed through, the crowds opening like waves. Shopkeepers spoke in hectoring mid-Atlantic.

'No,' she said. 'Beginning with J, I think. In ... old ... city.' She spoke loudly, as if addressing the retarded. Donald did this too. She tried to find the word for 'old' in her Primer. It was full of words of a lost age, like 'inkwell' and 'cavalry', but no 'old'.

'Ah, Juna Bazaar. No good, memsahib.'

'I go.'

'Bad place, memsahib.'

'I go.'

'I go also.'

'No, no.' She prodded her chest. 'I go alone.'

She would not let him go out and find a taxi. He would get one quicker, of course. It awed her, the underworld that existed in K12 Housing Society. Bearer knew bearer, everyone was somebody else's cousin. Turn to your servant and snap your fingers for fish; in five minutes a man would appear out of nowhere with his damp basketful.

She stood for half an hour. Mohammed could not see her. It was his siesta time and besides she was standing some way down the street. The sky glared, whitely. She wore a sleeveless cotton dress; the wind blew from the far-off sea, blistering against her body. Down the road stretched stucco walls and half-built plots; dusty kittens played in the bushes. At last a rickshaw puttered into sight, trailing a cloud of exhaust.

'Juna Bazaar.'

She ducked under its plastic canopy. In a waggish moment Donald had called these things 'three-wheeled farts'. They were built-up on motor scooters and used by the humble. She gazed out from under its tassels; they were on the highway now, a dual carriageway that connected the Housing Society to the city. Beside the road stood petrol pumps and half-built blocks of flats; Karachi was growing so fast, soon it would be solid buildings from the Society to the centre.

They were in town now; the respectable business part. Under the jigging fringe she saw the rows of offices – Air France, Pakistan International Airlines, the Khyber Carpet Emporium Fully Air-Conditioned. Europeans strolled along the pavement; cars were parked outside the Intercontinental Hotel. They passed the Sind Club walls. Beyond them this lunchtime Donald had been sipping, no doubt, a bowl of Brown Windsor soup.

The rickshaw swerved; she clutched the metal frame. No safe

38

lunchtimes for her. Within touching distance sat her driver, his head bound up in a dirty cloth. Hunched in his rags he was her guide into the unknown. Her heart thumped; the meter clicked.

Down in the old city the streets were choked. She coughed with the exhaust smoke. The rickshaw pushed its way past camel carts and loaded buses with men hanging on to their windows. It stopped.

'*Baksheesh!*' Children crowded round. A mother pushed to the front, holding out her baby. The buildings here were yellowed and crumbling, their balconies draped with washing; between them ran alleys jammed with people. The stench was appalling. She climbed out.

She was in the spice bazaar. It was like drowning, being amongst all these people. You could not stop; the current swept you along. Bodies pressed against her. Someone pinched her arm. The booths' wooden shutters were open; men sat there weighing things on scales. Sacks stood in rows; they were filled with powder – dun, ochre and crimson. Cameron Chemicals had introduced cling-film to Karachi; this year they were launching their big marketing drive. If they had their way bazaars like this would be replaced by a supermarket full of packets. She had long arguments with Donald about this.

But she missed him now. She felt so exposed. Somebody pinched her buttock, hard. In this dress, too much of her body was bare. She could not stop to look at anything. When she did, people saw who she was. Then they struggled against the current to stop and watch her. A crowd had gathered. People nudged each other and stared. A woman shouted something at her. She tried to push on. She was damp. In passing, she glimpsed things she longed to stop and inspect – a man telling fortunes with parrots, tribal women grinning in grease-stiffened dresses. But she could not pause.

She reached a tea house – a pukka place with rooms behind dirty windows. She hurried inside and sat down at a table. She was breathless. I am enjoying myself, she told herself. The café was crowded but everyone had stopped talking. Without looking around, she knew there was not one woman in sight. The menu was a stained sheet of cardboard, with Urdu one side and English the other. Stembled Eggs, she could have, or Two Egg Boil. Alone, she could not smile at this. With some difficulty she managed to order a cup of tea. She kept her gaze on the tablecloth, the dented tin ashtray and the glass of tea like liquid toffee. Behind her, part of the café was curtained off. 'Family Rooms' said the sign. These were cubicles; beneath the hem of the curtain she saw women's feet. Men were looking at her and whispering; thank goodness she could not understand what they were saying. She could not take her tea into a cubicle; not now she was sitting here.

The curtains were a faded green. (The same colour as those of the clinic cubicles when she went in for her examination. Behind curtains like those she had lain on a paper sheet, her legs open. *Nothing wrong*, said Dr Ahmed, unpeeling his gloves. *Not as far as we can see. I would suggest that you and your husband keep trying.*

In an English hospital Pakistani fingers had explored her. *I'm going to live in Pakistan*, she told him as she dressed. *The company my husband works for, it makes the Pill there*. He did not smile at the irony. Because his finger had poked inside her, she had felt rebuffed as she pulled on her tights.)

Here in the café they were leaning in their seats and staring at her legs. Was it with desire or disgust? They nudged each other and gazed at her breasts. Stupid to have worn this dress. She could not look out of the window because it was now blocked with faces.

Outside they moved back to let her pass and closed in behind her. She walked briskly up an emptier alley, trying to look casual. The air smelt corrupt. Boys played beside an open drain; one of them threw a stone at her. Men were following her. She turned the corner. A beggar waved his arm at her; it was a brown stump, mottled with pink. She did not break into a run. She was lost in a maze of alleys like slits between the buildings. There were no stalls here, just beggars and footsteps following her. She must not panic.

She turned another corner and she was back in the cloth

bazaar. Pushing through the people she made her way to a booth. She climbed up the step and sat down in a chair, catching her breath.

It was empty except for the shopkeeper, a middle-aged man dressed in shirt and trousers rather than the loose pyjamas most of the other men wore. A crowd gathered at the entrance.

'Cloth,' she said, pointing to the shelves. 'Long.' She stretched out her arms.

'Ah yes.' He disappeared into the back of the shop and emerged with a tunic under his arm. Lime-green rayon, it was embroidered with fancy stitching. 'Tourist memsahib? American memsahib?' He held it up. 'Very good colour. All memsahibs like.'

'No, no. Cloth—long cloth.'

'All good cloths here.'

'Not clothes, *cloth*. Scarf, big scarf. *Purdah* cloth.'

She pointed to the shelves. He pulled out material, shaking the folded stuff loose. Finally she found what she wanted. It was a long pink scarf made of chiffon.

'Ah,' he said. '*Dupatta*.'

She had forgotten the word. Pakistani girls—the more liberated ones—wore dupattas modestly wrapped around their heads and breasts.

Some men were giggling. She wound it around her head and draped it over her shoulders. Pressing through the crowd, she held it against her mouth. It kept slipping off. If only she could cover herself completely but she had seen none of the full-length bourquas on sale. Besides, bourqua vendors would be bound not to understand English.

She tried to find her way back to the main road, hurrying down an alley, past stalls of dates sticky as sin. Flies stuck to her face. She wound the dupatta around her bare arms; the road was through here somewhere, she must not look as if she were panicking. What did I presume, coming here? She could not stop to try and remember the direction; she must keep walking.

She turned the corner. Music played and faces peered out between the shutters of the houses. Rosy light shone in the rooms. She hesitated. Up on a balcony, a woman laughed at her. There were faces in the doorways, she realized. She was just thinking that this seemed a friendlier place when she saw that all the faces were painted. One of them winked at her; she was fat and wearing a satin mini-dress.

Christine started trembling. She tried to back out and turn but the men were closing in. A man shouted at her. Through each of the doorways she glimpsed a bed. She must hurry through, there was no turning back. Leaning in the doorways, the women's rouged and powdered faces grinned at her; one called out in a deep voice. It was only then that she realized they were not women; they were men.

She was running like a rabbit. Three turnings; four. She was back at the main road and waving for a taxi.

It took some time for her to be able to speak. 'Adamjee Plaza,' she said at last. This was the building where Donald worked.

The driver adjusted his mirror to look at her, and shrugged.

'Intercontinental Hotel then,' she shouted. Everyone at Karachi knew this. He nodded and started the engine.

They drove through the streets. She wiped her face with her veil. She was sticking to the plastic seat.

'You English?' he asked.

She nodded.

'You in bazaar only?'

Only? He must mean 'alone'. She nodded.

He shook his head. 'No good,' he said, like Mohammed. 'You want marble maybe? You want carpets?'

She shook her head, politely. He seemed a nice man. He had saved her.

'My cousin, he is important man. He get marble, and air-conditioner if you are liking.' The man turned and passed her a card. It said *Sultan Rahim: Rahim Estates* and an address.

'You want beach hut? He fixes beach hut for Americans and Frenchies.'

'Beach hut?' She looked at the card. Her hand had stopped trembling now. She put the card in her handbag.

She relaxed only when they stopped outside the Intercon. A

42

cockaded doorman waited, his jacket bright with braid. The fountains dazzled her. Just last week she had told Donald how she despised the Intercon – plastic and American, she had said. Sealed off from the nasty smells and the real city.

She smiled at the doorman; for the first time she could meet somebody's eye. The grass was green and damp; through swing doors stepped blonde air-hostesses making for the pool. They all understood English. Fancy tongas waited for the tourists; between the shafts the horses were as polished as conkers, unlike the wretched creatures she had seen this afternoon, a mile away. Just a mile.

Inside the hotel it was cool. Businessmen strolled. A girl in the briefest sun-dress looked at postcards. Christine, heading for the Coffee Shop, unwound her dupatta and stuffed it into her handbag.

7

THIS country of yours needs our Translux Hotel. I'm speaking to you straight. It's a great country, this Pakistan. Leastways it can be great. You have the possibilities, you have great growth potential. Your businessmen have their heads screwed on. I've worked with Muslims – me, Duke Hanson, I'm what they call a field product development executive. I set up the deal, I find the site, I find the engineers and the architects and the designers, I'm here to see they come up to Translux standards, we have a 500-page manual specifying Translux standards right down to the hemstitch on the bed-linen. We see that these standards apply to each one of our hotels across the globe, in Africa, in Japan, you name it. Our motto is *You've Never Left Home*. We have it on our napkins, our menus, we have it stitched on to the uniforms of our staff; each bellhop is a reminder that our service is the finest American service and that means it's the finest you can find. It don't matter if outside the windows it's the Gobi Desert. Inside it's Translux.

Look at it this way. To get the business you need the businessmen, and to get the businessmen you need to get the hotels. And that means hotels of international class. That means telex and telephones that work. Laundry, room service – put it like this: only when you don't notice the service is it a hotel with calibre. Here in Karachi you have one five-star hotel, the Inter-

44

continental — high-class shopping arcade, banquet and conference facilities, block-bookings for the airline crews. You have three more coming up, the Hilton, Sheraton and Holiday Inn, that airport highway is one big building site. Fine sites, fine hotels, but they have one thing in common. They're downtown. Sure, downtown's where the business gets done but even Karachi's biggest fan — and that's me, there's something about this place, I love it — even he can't call this place the most beautiful city in the world. Like it doesn't have too many tourist sights. They travel thousands of miles, they arrive and what do they see? There's a couple of old mosques, there's the Monument to Islamic Progress, there's your quaint Bohri Bazaar. But it's kind of dirty, it's crowded and it's full of traffic. That's what development means, sure — the new buildings coming up, the industrial growth. But you have to have the relaxation facilities too, if you're going to keep your businessmen happy. A refreshed man works harder the next day. He's more committed to the country. He can bring his wife out to join him. And you have to get the tourists. As you say, tourism's your big growth industry. That's where the Translux comes in.

Sure, I've worked with Muslims. Eighteen months in Kuwait I lived out of a suitcase, I left my family back home, did I miss them, but now the Kuwait Translux is a hotel all nations can be proud to enter. When that happens my job's done. I like it out here. I like the heat; I like to sweat it out. My wife calls me a puritan and that way she's correct. I like it tough; the more I sweat the more I achieve. There's something about the air here and the big dry spaces; the potential. The American West was like this once. I come from the West; there are still the big wide spaces but now they're yellow with corn. We've farmed them and made them function.

And I respect your Islam. It's a clean religion. No mumbo-jumbo, no incense and plaster figurines cluttering up your heart. I step inside your mosques and I see water faucets and white tiles, and in your holiest place what do I see? A blankness. A niche. I'm a religious man myself, Baptist born and bred. Our chapels are bare too. Our God speaks direct to us; we've always been God-fearers as you yourselves are – a spare, fighting religion, nothing soft and easy about it. It's the same hot white sun up there and the same God; we're not so different from you, we believe in plain living, in rigour and denial. I've seen your Ramadans, with simple men flagging from thirst; fasting in the heat as they lay the highways across Saudi. It's always the simple men.

'It's not tea leaves, you know.'

'Uh?'

'You're staring into it so intently,' said Shamime. 'And it's only milk. Do you want me to read your future? You'd have to believe me because I'm brown. There are some advantages. Can I sit down? I came here to see a client but he hasn't turned up.' She sat down on the other side of the table. 'So unreliable. You must find us maddening.'

Duke mumbled something polite. He was sitting in the 24-hour Coffee Shop at the Intercontinental. Only place you could get a glass of milk in Karachi.

'I enjoyed that party last night,' she went on. 'That sweetie British Council couple, straight out of Somerset Maugham. I hadn't really talked to you before. I see you coming into the office and disappearing into Frank's room, now Donald's room. I suppose it's not really my department.'

'It's nobody's department yet. I mean to say, nothing's happening.'

'Still?'

'I won't trouble you with it.'

'Go on.' She leant forward, chin resting in her hands. In this light her skin was greeny-brown. She was wearing a multi-coloured blouse; she looked like a dusky butterfly. Each time he met her she unnerved him. 'Bore me.'

'We have the site, we have the plans drawn up, the tourist board is right behind our project one hundred per cent. It's just what this place needs, a leisure centre just a half-hour from the city. We've done the soil tests, we've ordered the materials, we've fixed the tenders for the electrics – yesterday I completed that.' He stopped. He could not discuss cement contracts with

46

this girl with a jewel in her nose. 'You've nothing to drink.'

'Know what I crave? An ice cream.' She lifted up the menu. The sleeve fell back from her arm.

Duke took a menu. *Tempt Yourself*, it said. *Our Ice Creams Are Full of Eastern Promise.*

'I mustn't,' he said.

Shamime was gazing at the menu. Today her hair was loose. She pushed a strand behind her ear. 'Sheik Charmer,' she read. 'Mango Ripple Water-Ice Drenched in Sun-Kissed Orange Sauce.'

'I'm dieting,' he said. 'I'm watching my weight.'

She smiled over the rim of her menu. 'I'm not.' Idly she scratched her arm; the bangles clinked. 'I'll have a Knicker-bocker Glory. I'll be American.' She read out: 'Veiled Mysteries. Can You Resist Our Surprise Dessert? Go on. I'll feel so greedy all alone. Try a Monsoon Mousse. They're out of sight.'

He controlled himself. 'I'll join you in another glass of milk.'

Her ice arrived, heaped up in a tall glass. She dipped her spoon into it. Duke did not really want this second glass of milk but he must be polite. He thought of the kitchen back home, when the boys were younger. The freeze box was always cram-med with those big family tubs — Strawberry, Rum 'n' Raisin. Chester had his own tub of Pistachio because that was his favourite. When Minnie came back with the groceries the boys would crowd round, jumping up like puppies.

Shamime was licking a blob from her finger. *Turkissed Delight: Smooth Dark Chocolate* ... He and Duke Jnr, his eldest; they had a weakness for chocolate. The Hershey Bars the two of them got through. He'd always kept a supply in the glove compartment of the Buick. Age three, Duke Jnr knew. No flies on Duke Jnr.

'Go on,' said Shamime. She was holding out the spoon. 'I've saved you the cherry.' She leant over; he opened his mouth.

'So what happens next?'

Duke stopped. 'Happens?'

'Or doesn't happen. You've got the equipment ... ' She took another mouthful. 'You've got the site.'

'Sure we've got the land, though we haven't signed the

contract yet. That's just a formality. But we're still waiting for the planning permission to come through. It should be a formality too. Trouble is, seems to be something holding us up. There's big money involved. Things can be made difficult. Like you know, there's power fighting going on – these politician guys have their fingers in all kinds of pies. And you know how unsettled it is now, up at the top. There's people being replaced for no reason. One word in an ear and overnight it's all changed.'

'Whose ear? Who's doing your whispering?'

'Pardon me?'

'Who's your fixer?'

'Ma'am, I have no fixer.'

'Oh Duke, don't look so stiff.' She laughed. 'You know what I mean. The man who knows the right people. Heavens, you didn't arrive here yesterday. And haven't you been out in the Gulf?'

'Sure. Kuwait.'

'Well, you built a hotel. Don't tell me that got set up without a crate or two of Scotch.'

'Ma'am, it did not.' He moved in his seat. The Coffee Shop was styled in laminates, all easy-wipe. Tables screwed to the floor, plastic seating soldered firmly in place. Solid American workmanship.

Shamime pushed back her hair. That greeny brow. When she moved, her blouse changed colour; it was made of some thin, shifting stuff. It disturbed him. You could not pin anyone down in this shifting country, they trickled like water through your fingers. 'Sure I know what happens,' he said. 'Some guy's car gets its import licence, some other guy gets an air-conditioner permission through, things are made easier for someone close to the top.'

'You have to know the right people.'

'Sure. I know the right people. They walk through this hotel lobby each day. They're in the Boat Club and the Sind Club. I know them but not, with respect, the way you mean.'

'I'll have a word with Bobby.'

'Bobby?'

'My uncle.'

That was the minister. 'No sir.'

'He's an awful ninny but he'll do anything for me. And he likes his tipple.'

'Ma'am, I don't like to offend, but ... '

'Just tell me exactly what needs to be done, so I can tell him.'

'I won't. Thank you all the same.' He looked down. *Tempting, Tempting* said the menu. 'Myself, I don't work like that. Nope.'

Shamime looked amused. She scraped out her glass. She had the most delicate hands he had ever seen.

'Tell me about your father,' she said.

'My father? You want to know about him?'

'I want to know about you.'

Duke paused. 'He owned a laundromat. He was a religious man. He was honest. He worked his way up in the business till he had a place of his own. Nothing fancy — eight front-loaders, nickels in the slot. We had an apartment above it. My mother came downstairs for the service washes.'

'Service?'

'The customer left the clothes and she loaded them. Plenty of working wives did that and collected them in the evening. My mother took a pride in it. They called it the cleanest laundromat in Topeka. Something you don't need here, a laundromat.'

'You mean because of the dhobies?'

'You live with your parents?'

She nodded.

'I guess you have plenty of servants.'

She started to count her red fingernails. ' ... six, seven ... ' She gave up. 'They were proud of you? They gave you such an aristocratic name.'

He nodded. 'My father was a lay preacher, a Baptist. Say, you don't want to listen to this.'

'I do want to listen to this. It's fascinating.'

'He preached in the chapel around the corner, evenings. He was a well-respected man. The family came from Scotland, way back.'

'Washing the clothes clean by day and the souls clean by night. Tough job.'

Duke laughed. 'Hadn't struck me like that.'

'And you worked your way out of that, through college. America, land of opportunity. Newspaper-sellers give birth to Presidents.'

Was she laughing at him? He rubbed his nose.

She paused. 'And your wife?'

'Minnie? She worked as a stenographer the first place I went to. An engineering corporation. We met at the dance.'

Shamime was lighting a cigarette. Duke felt awkward. He could see no reason why she should want to talk to him; besides, shouldn't she be back at work? She took her job so casually, yet she ran rings around them at Cameron's, she was so smart.

The conversation came to an end. He had not talked like this for some time; not personal talk. Since Minnie left he had spent his days trying to make himself understood down the telephone and trying to contact government agencies. He was a man of action not words. Besides, nobody talked much about the past here because they came from all over the world. Even the Pakistanis — most of them came from India, their past was over there beyond the closed border. Shamime stood up, her black hair swinging.

'You haven't forgotten tomorrow? The beach.'

He shook his head, and she left. Tomorrow was Minnie's day. Minnie was taking it badly; she had kept saying, 'It's the end of an era.' She read books on subjects like that — coming to terms with middle-age, growing kids, her digestive tract. Here in Pakistan you accepted things; you had to. But in the States all the wives read these books, dense pages of print to consolidate their anxieties. New publications announced new topics for self-doubt. He was proud of her command of the terms but worried that she seemed to need them. Surely a hug could solve most everything. I wish you were here, he thought. He would book a call tonight, to reassure her. He had spent so long telling her it made no difference and that thousands of women a year

50

had it done that he had not stopped to wonder if he himself minded.

He walked past the tables. Young people sat around. Shamime was so young; he was old enough to be her father. She had scraped out her ice cream like a child.

Christine Manley sat there, writing postcards. She looked sunburnt; kind of flushed.

'You been doing some sightseeing?' he asked.

She paused. 'I've seen some sights,' she said, with a little smile.

There was so much for her to see. Like Shamime, her era was just beginning. She would have babies. *The end of an era*, Minnie had said. He felt old and confused. It must be that darned contract.

8

CAMERON Chambers was built of heavy stone, brown as liver. It inspired confidence. Constructed in 1890 it was Karachi's finest monument to Indian Gothic. It was Bradford Central Railway Station; it was Leeds Town Hall. Then you looked again at the straw blinds and those dusty palms. Strong convictions had built it; it might have stood there for centuries and it could last for centuries more. Donald considered it just right. It belonged. New stuff rose up all around – the I.B.M. building, the Habib Bank skyscraper – but they looked bland and flimsy. They paid lip service to the country, with their plywood Moghul arches, but they were imports. That Cameron's itself had supplied their paints and plastics was business, and business was in the head, not the heart.

Adam Cameron had been a Scot and a strong Methodist, a man of character. He had built up his company from a corner shop and in the 1880s brought it out East. In common with several other British concerns, Cameron's became a name connected with the subcontinent. In those days they manufactured soaps, paints, mosquito repellents and Cameron's Tonic Wine, based on a secret glycero-phosphate formula. Old Man Cameron was the best advertisement for his own pick-me-up; his bewhiskered face was printed upon every bottle. Despite the beard there was some resemblance, in Donald's mind, to Duke Hanson. The same straight gaze; frontiersmen both, men of belief. In the old days the Tonic Wine had been sold in Britain too. From his childhood Donald remembered the Brinton corner shop (always behind the times) whose wall had carried the metal plaque beside the Bovril and Lipton's Tea. Rusted with age, it showed the famous face and a scrolled list of all the ailments from which the drinker would gain immediate relief. Production had stopped in 1950 and the only plaque he had recently seen was upon the kitchen wall of one of Christine's friends. 'For Nervous Spasms,' she had said, laughing, 'Lassitude and Wind.'

Cameron's had manufactured and sold through the big emporiums: the Army and Navy of Calcutta, Bentalls of Bombay. Much of their trade had been with the army — shirt stiffeners in particular. Donald's own grandfather, Lieutenant-Colonel Manley, had no doubt appeared more formidable thanks to Cameron's Hot Season Starch. *Don't Let the Troops Droop.*

But the starch had gone and with it the British. India had changed; this part was Pakistan now. Cameron's had changed. It was Cameron Chemicals now and had expanded into plastics and fertilizer, with its own pharmaceutical division. It had other international interests. There were branches in Australia and Hong Kong. They were the important ones now. Even Bombay branch was larger than this. Here in Pakistan the English had been squeezed out; nowadays, with the government's policy of native managers and nationalization, Donald himself was the only European and he was not the top dog — only Sales Manager, with a Pakistani Director and Chairman above him. In his office hung the old photographs, rows of faces as at school; behind them the blurred sepia arches of Cameron Chambers. Each year the white faces were reduced in number, and now there was only one.

And Cameron Chambers had been taken over as government offices. Ten years ago Cameron's had moved to Adamjee Plaza, a functional block with a rubber plant in the foyer and rows of rusting windows. Cameron Chemicals occupied four floors. By leaning back in his chair Donald could glimpse one turret of the old building several streets away. It pointed into the blue sky. Otherwise it was obscured by newly-erected office blocks on the same lines as Adamjee Plaza, 1950s style and already shabby. Opposite his window was a hoarding attached to one of these buildings. Upon it was painted a large oriental lady's face, cocked coyly and holding up a bar of Tibet Soap. Manufactured, it said below, by the Karachi Sanitary Corporation. In idle moments he caught her eye. She seemed to be asking him a question.

It was noon. Outside the buildings looked blanched in the heat. Inside there was the rattle and hum of the air-conditioner. Saturday; in a few moments the office would be closing down for the weekend. Back home Mohammed would be finishing his morning duties and retiring to his quarters; Saturdays he left out cold cuts. He himself ought to be returning home and making love to Christine. The unusual time of day, siesta hour, might make the whole thing more spontaneous than usual.

A tap on the door. Mr Samir came in.

'Figures, Mr Manley, for the fertilizer plant.'

'Ah, thank you.' Part of him wished to be called Donald. After all, Mr Samir was his second-in-command. Yet this formality flattered him too. With the exception of Shamime he was treated with grave respect by all his staff, most of whom had double his age and experience.

Mr Samir took a seat while Donald flicked through the papers. Should he perhaps set the precedent by calling him Ayub? A new fertilizer factory had recently been opened up-country, in Upper Sind.

'Do you know what Shamime told me yesterday?' said Donald. 'That the British are to blame for this state of affairs.'

'I am sorry?'

'That our – that British canals were responsible for the salinity of this whole province. Something about the drainage leaving a salt sediment.'

'I am most surprised.' Mr Samir frowned, probably not because of the facts but because he disapproved of Shamime. 'I think that it was a most barren region before the British arrived.

54

I think that it is due to the British that there is any sort of fertility at all.'

There was silence; but a relaxed one, as it was the end of the week.

'What was my predecessor like? The famous Mr Smythe?' Perhaps Mr Samir had called him Frank. Donald could not bear it if he had.

'A very charming gentleman. Most athletic and respected. Something of a sportsman, as was his lady wife.'

'She was chairman of the British Wives' Association, wasn't she?'

'She was most active in those spheres. Mrs Manley, she belongs to the Association?'

Donald paused. 'She hasn't quite got around to it yet.' He refrained from mentioning Christine's vow never to set foot in the place. *I came to Pakistan*, she had said, *not Tunbridge Wells*.

'It is primarily for the kiddies, I believe,' said Mr Samir. 'There is swimming pool and social facilities, and kiddies' parties. That was told to me by Mrs Smythe.'

'Well, that counts us out,' he gave a little laugh, 'so far.'

'We have a saying: there is no time that is better than next year. You have no doubt seen that this applies to business. Above all, perhaps, in the case of offspring.'

Donald rubbed his nose. With a little smile he asked: 'How many do you have, er, Ayub? Your wife told me once.'

'More than sufficient, you might say. Three boys and two girls.' Mr Samir cast his eyes down, perhaps out of modesty. This small man, in his shiny suit, had produced five children.

They both gave another little laugh. Donald turned his attention to the fertilizer figures. The factory in Sukkur produced 1,200 tons of nitrogen-based compounds per month. He, Donald, was responsible for the selling and distribution of enough soil enricher for 500 square miles of otherwise barren desert. Remaining, apparently, unable to fertilize his wife.

He looked at his watch and closed the file. 'Half-past twelve. Um, Ayub, do you know where Fotheringay Road is? I've been searching all over the place. People keep giving me the wrong directions. I don't think anyone knows, but they don't seem to care to say so.' Mr Samir stroked his bald head. 'It's where my grandfather lived. Somewhere near the old Military Lines.'

'The majority of them have been knocked down. You have asked me this before. And then the names have been changed.'

'That's what makes it so tricky. Sorry to go on about it. My wife and I drove round last weekend. No one seems to make any maps.' Not adding: the British were the last who did.

'The city has multiplied so much and so fast. Each year the maps must be changed.' He shrugged, like an Italian waiter saying the restaurant is closed. 'So we have no maps.'

Indeed, in Frank Smythe's business address book, written in that familiar, confident hand, most of the places said Behind this, or Opposite that, or Two Blocks from the Paradise Picture House. There were so few street names. No doubt it had all made sense to Frank.

Mr Samir had excused himself and left. In a few moments he returned.

'I had a little brainwave,' he said. 'Our eldest peon has been living in that district for many years. I have asked him your question and he has come up with the answer. He thinks it might be now named Ajazuddin Road.'

When the office closed Donald drove off. He would have one last try before he went home. Though interested during their first couple of searches, Christine now presumed 56 Fotheringay Road to be extinct and had rather fallen off in her support. At some point she had seemed to stop searching with him and start looking at him instead. In recent months she had grown so swiftly critical of what he did. Unfortunately, a change of country did not seem to be altering that. She probably thought that his anxiety for roots stemmed from some basic lack of identity. No doubt at some point she would want to talk this through.

He slowed down behind a donkey cart. Other cars hooted their horns and swerved to pass. The driving here alarmed him. This was the main business street, once called Inverarity Street and now re-named I.I. Chundrigar Road. It was filled with exhaust fumes and hectic Toyota taxis. At every crossroads policemen stood on plinths, waving their batons and swivelling as if they were conducting an orchestra.

Was he weak, to look back to this city's past and prefer the crumbling buildings sagging between the office blocks? Christine, artistic and romantic, preferred them too, but then muddled it all up with Raj Oppression, British Imperialism, all that stuff. That made it difficult to talk. Clichés kept popping up and blocking the conversation, her expression changed, her pupils shrank when she talked like that.

Cameron Chambers loomed up on his left. Solid dark stone. Above the door had been fixed a placard saying *Government of Sind: Division 3*. However, above each first-floor window was still carved the double C, knotted with stone foliage; the building could not rub away its old identity so easily. It was a landmark; in an address book you would write *Two Blocks from ...* Once he had overheard a man say: 'We will make a rendezvous outside see-see.' It had taken him a moment to realize, with a twitch of loyalty, that the man meant C.C.

On the pavement, scribes were packing up their typewriters; the offices were closed now for the weekend. During the week men would squat there dictating letters and petitions to be delivered inside. Within the building, no doubt, those letters would be piled up from years back, wedged in dusty corners. Bureaucratic red tape was something you had to come to terms with, here. He was discovering this, his cabinets silting up with official forms; Duke, too, appeared to be suffering considerable difficulties in getting his Translux off the ground. Doubtless Christine would blame this, too, on the British.

He slowed down behind a bus. It belched fumes; men clung to its sides, their clothes flapping. It looked like some extinct beast burdened with wings. His heart beat faster in this detective search. Wisps of half-remembered conversations hung most strangely around these foreign streets. One or two things, like those horse-driven tongas, were similar enough to click together with the past. But most of the city had changed too much to be recognizable. This had made him more determined, much to Christine's surprise. But he could at least do this for his

57

grandfather. He had loved Grandad but he had never said so; he had been too self-conscious for that. He felt guilty for all the times he had not listened, and for being up in London when Grandad had died and asked for him. When he had arrived it was too late.

Of course it was too late now. Much good this would do anyone. But then the rituals at a funeral did not help the dead one, did they? It was the living who were eased.

He knew some facts, having copied them into a notebook before he arrived in Karachi. Prior to Independence Grandad had served in Quetta, Karachi, then Cawnpore and somewhere outside Allahabad in what was to become India. Granny had come out to Karachi; they had married here in the church. He himself had visited it, of course. The place looked neglected now; children played ball games in the dust of the compound.

It was Karachi that Grandad had mentioned most often. 'Happened on my Karachi tour,' he would say. But Donald was so young then, lying on the hearthrug and counting the tiles on the gas-fire surround. Karachi was the caged pinkish glow in the fire, somewhere far off. What else had Grandad said? It had mostly dissolved. We presume that when we speak we communicate; we have to believe this, otherwise what would we do? Donald could remember some chuckles about this or that, colonel somebody coming a cropper. He could not even distinguish if the setting was army quarters in India or England, where Grandad served for the last few years, they sounded so similar. The same talk, if he could remember any of it, and the same jokes.

He drove down past the cantonment station, with its tea houses and the squalid hotels where the hippies stayed. This was the sort of place Christine liked, its fruit stalls black with flies. Around it lay the old residential quarter, or what was left of it. This area, with its station, Anglican church and Military Lines, was where the British used to live if they did not live in Clifton, a mile away. One thing he did remember was Granny complaining that the shunting trains used to keep her awake.

Meadow Road. The name was carved in a corner wall. This

sounded familiar but then he had searched along here before. At a junction stood the newer, metal sign: Ajazuddin Road.

He must have passed it on several occasions; due to the name he had not driven that way. It was another wide street, with old bungalows on either side. Built by the British for themselves, they had now been taken over: the brass plaques said *Alliance Française* and *Dubai Commercial Division*. These buildings looked mellow compared to his own raw house in K12. Ahead, the road curved round a corner.

He slowed down. Now he was here he hardly dared arrive. What would he do: ring the bell and ask to look around? There were no cars about. Chowkidars, seated at the gates, watched him without interest. Little did they know. These large trees were younger then, mere saplings when Grandad had walked this street fifty years ago. Otherwise it must have been the same. Grandad would recognize it now, house for house.

And so what? Christine would say. She was always there, a hum in his head. *Look at what's happening, not at what happened.* He drove round the corner.

The street stopped abruptly. The houses had been demolished.

Donald halted the car and gazed through the windscreen. Ahead of him lay bulldozers and rubble. The stench was strong; he wound up the window. A milky creek ran under the road. The whole place was one vast building site. In front of him, a banner drooped from a half-completed block: *Ahmed Prestige Apartments*. On the ground floor were the empty concrete boxes where the shops would be. Electrical wires hung, knotted, from their ceilings. *Coming Soon: Orient Photocopy*. Beyond this, stretches of vacant dust, more construction in progress and further still the highway leading to K12 Housing Society. Scaffolding stuck up into the treacherous blue sky.

Donald sat still, the engine running. He waited for his breathing to settle. Christine had been right, of course; it was foolish to have hoped. Overhead buzzards drifted. In front of him the road was blocked with a row of oil drums.

He turned the car and drove back slowly. Black birds stood

around in the street as if they owned it. He wanted to rev up and run them down. At the junction he turned left and then stopped the car.

He looked at those carved letters: Meadow Road. He switched off the engine. Meadow Road. Was it just because he had seen it five minutes earlier, and several times before that, or was it an older memory? He gazed at the cracked pavement, trying to concentrate. At this moment it sounded so very familiar.

Above him a tree had shed black pods. Must be a tamarind. The pods lay scattered; some were squashed. Ahead lay the sleepy afternoon street. Meadow ... Fields. (A most unmeadowy road.) Something was stirring. He closed his eyes. In the clenched blackness he tried to remember. Deep within his head it was echoing.

Afternoons in the lounge, stuffy upholstery, stuffy as this car interior, and sunlight outside. Fields ... Gracie Fields ... Forces' Favourites. *Forces' Favourites?* He screwed up his face.

It did not work. He opened his eyes and gazed at the dashboard dials, all at 0. He had got nowhere. It was nothing useful. He had just remembered the wireless programmes. It was simply the old breath of his childhood air. Sounds and cooking smells coming from the kitchen.

He started the car and crawled along, glancing at the gatepost plates. *New Zealand High Commission ... Maj. A. D. Khalid (Retd).* Some were almost illegible; they held the mild, impersonal interest of old tombstones. The lettering on number 17 was painted on to a glass panel set into the post; it had partly peeled off. He read: 17A *Mrs I. B. Gracie.*

The car jerked to a stop. He had done that. It stalled.

The gates were open. In fact they looked so broken they probably could not be closed now. Beyond stood a dilapidated house. It was enormous. There was no sign of life.

Gracie.

9

CHRISTINE'S chart was Sellotaped to the inside of the wardrobe door. Here it could be met casually. Pencilled asterisks indicated the days of the month when, as it were, it was All Systems Go. Donald had never seen her pencilling these in, though Christine with a thermometer in her mouth was as familiar, in the bathroom each morning, as Christine brushing her teeth. Also uncommented on, and only too familiar, was the Tampax tube in the lavatory bowl each month. It never seemed to flush away first time; it would float in the water, uncurling gently and with regret. She had kept the chart for over six months now. He doubted whether she had told anyone about this. It was his secret with her, though they seldom mentioned it and were as shy about it as newly-weds.

She had fixed the paper crookedly, with one strip of Sellotape; it flapped when the wardrobe door was opened. The margins were wavy, the writing as usual loopy and careless. It appeared so casual but this fooled neither of them. They must pretend not to adjust their embraces, like a clock, to the ticking of Christine's internal rhythm. They did, of course. Twice a day Donald opened the wardrobe to get his clothes, once in the morning and once after work when he had showered. As he foraged amongst the hangers, out of the corner of his eye he saw the paper shift. Her womb was part of the business of dressing. Below the hanging space a drawer held his rolled-up socks. He

61

had grown superstitious about which he chose: black today, or the dark ones with the wavy red thread down the side?

Some time ago, when they had cleared their throats and admitted that there might be a problem, they had both been to the clinic. Medical expertise had informed them that nothing seemed to be the matter with either of them. This had been a relief, of course. It had been preceded by his own sperm-count, itself preceded by a solitary exercise so flushed and stubborn that he had only been able to describe it to Christine in joke form, papering the cubicle with Playboy centrefolds and introducing topless nursing staff. So luridly had he coloured it that later he could almost believe it himself.

When he arrived home Mohammed had already retired to his quarters. Christine was standing in the kitchen, the *Guardian Weekly* spread out on the working surface. The ceiling fan spun; the *Guardian* lifted and rustled like tissue paper. They had been away from England three weeks now; already the news items, though read by them with the quickening pulse of exiles, seemed quaint and distant. Lacking the bearer the kitchen seemed larger; it belonged to them now.

'Hungry?' He stood behind her, resting his head on her shoulder. She had washed her hair; the frizz, fragrant today, tickled his cheek.

'Too hot.'

'Let's not bother with lunch,' he said boldly. A record-breaking heatwave was forecast in Britain, he read.

He remained behind her, his chin supported. Today had a pencilled cross against it. Did she know he remembered? Mohammed's grey cloth was folded on the draining board; the cups were stacked. Everything was ready.

Neither of them moved. Due to her sunburn, he did not rest the full weight on her shoulder. He looked at the photograph of deck chairs in St James's Park. She appeared to be reading too. Donald felt as if he hardly knew her. Tilting his head he could see his watch: 2 o'clock. Mohammed would not come back indoors until five.

'And they call *that* hot,' said Christine.

They stayed rigid. A fly crawled up the window screen. Donald cleared his throat.

'Let's mosey along,' he said in poor American, 'and have ourselves a little siesta.'

In the bedroom he drew the curtains, yawning loudly. He stretched. Christine yawned too and lay down on the bed. He took off his clothes and closed the door. He walked around the room, delaying things. In the gloom his wife was a pale blur. He heard her yawn again. Perhaps she was actually going to sleep. Five asterisks already; that meant that tomorrow, Sunday, the operative period would be over. He climbed on to the bed.

'Ouch!'

'Sorry.'

'It's my sunburn. Sorry.'

'You were mad to go out in the middle of the day. That bazaar place.'

'I know.'

'At least you bought a shawl thing.'

'What?'

'To protect you from the sun.'

'Ah. Yes. That's right.'

'I'd better not touch you.'

'Oh please do. Just not here, and here.'

'That all right? I'll be very careful.'

'Mmm. Ouch! It's a bit tender there.'

Suddenly he wanted her so much. Now he should not touch her, his blood rose. She was so feminine, shrinking like this. He would take care of her: his hurt, burning girl. He laid his careful hands on her face.

Afterwards she went to sleep. He leant over and switched on the World Service, softly. She shifted away from him, hunched up. So reckless when awake, during sleep she covered herself with her hands, pressing them against her little pointed breasts. He felt as sad as he usually did; only he had been moved. *Radio Newsreel* began, with its massed bands. Oompah, it went—the tune was called 'Imperial Echoes'. Beside him Christine stirred and hunched herself up more tightly. He lay there, damp and wistful.

Usually he presumed that it was himself who was barren. But sometimes he thought: had she ceased being fertile when she had called herself Chris? Her new opinions had made her criticize him and explain away the mysteries. Nowadays he could not reach her. More deft, her lovemaking, but no longer innocent. When she cried out it was not for him; it was for herself and, it seemed, for womankind.

Oompah, oompah. Outside in the street a car hooted. When people returned from work they sounded their horn to get the chowkidar to open the gates.

Christine sat up.

'What's the time?'

He told her.

'Must get dressed. I'm taking Mohammed out.' She climbed off the bed and switched on the light.

'What?'

'And his wife. We're going to the doctor.'

'Are they ill?'

'We're going to Dr Farooq to get her fitted up.'

Christine was rummaging in the wardrobe. She was naked; for the first time he saw her sunburn, a pink square between the shoulder-blades.

'I had a long conversation with him this morning. You see, he's got four children already. He doesn't want any more.' Her voice grew muffled as she rummaged. 'He seemed never to have heard of birth control. I read somewhere that the doctors give them condoms and they give them to their children for balloons.' Deep in the wardrobe she mumbled: 'Seems his problem's rather the opposite of ours.' From the back, her pink patch looked inflamed, as if it blushed.

Donald remained on the bed. Then he thought: and I haven't even told her about Mrs Gracie.

10

THE FIRST time that Mohammed, with his baskets, has accompanied memsahib Manley to the bazaar, she opens front door of the car and indicates him to step in. Front door, not back. This has put him in some confusion. This has not, of course, been the custom of memsahib Smythe; this has not been the custom of any memsahib. Mohammed is sorry to see memsahib Smythe quit his country. She is fine lady, always spick and span, he has been proud to accompany her around the Empress Market. The vegetable-wallahs treat her with respect, with her fine outfits and voice that carries far. Mohammed himself, of course, has been treated with a corresponding respect not only by food-wallahs but by the other drivers and bearers of his acquaintance, even those who serve the diplomatic. Memsahib Smythe has the highest standards, turning the mangoes in her hands, rejecting those that are being inferior and demanding the lowest price. If still unsatisfied she moves to adjacent stall. She is seldom unsatisfied however for soon the food-wallahs learn that she only expects the best and accordingly keep for her their choicest fruits. Mohammed has been feeling personally their approbation.

Memsahib Manley, she is a very different kettle of fishes. For one point, there is her garments. Upon her feet she wears the common chappals, costing only three rupees and worn by the humblest coolie. But it is the upper portions which disturb.

Upon them she wears garments suitable for beggarladies or else, more inflaming, more offending, the most figure-hugging jean-slacks through which can be observed the contours of her form. She walks with little shame. If he is not her cook-bearer but lolling at ease against some street corner, he would keep his eyes on the said form, even although her bosom, so visible, is of poor size. As it is he keeps his eyes averted when in bungalow. He has seen others, of course. He is man of the world. There are the hippie persons wandering hither and thither, lowest of the low. There are also the tourist ladies from the Intercontinental Hotel but those persons are guests of his country for only some days, perhaps not respecting Muslim ways but confined to the major thoroughfares and government shops. In addition, for the cost of one half-week's salary a man of the world can purchase the *Penthouse* magazine or similar from Mr Khan who is keeping the *pan* kiosk backside of Reptile Handbag Emporium. But a memsahib is different matter. At large, his standing it is lowered.

And there is one other point. They are already making two journeys to provision bazaar, once in car and once in taxicab when sahib is in office. But though she asks his advice the first occasion she now prefers to purchase alone and she is topful with delight whatsoever she is buying, never bargaining over the cost — in what respect do the vegetable-wallahs hold him now? She also carries a basket herself while he follows with another: is he not a man with strength in his arms? Is he not paid Rs 275 a month? She walks with lightest heart into the dirty alleys, venturing into places he is shamed that a British memsahib must be seeing, and where the shop-wallahs are knowing no English turn of phrase. This makes him look even smaller bearer. And now she is making the habit of going out alone with her baskets, summoning a rickshaw like a Pakistani clerk's wife and dispensing with his services.

It is not as he is expecting. He is thirty years old. First he works for Pakistani lady but he is rising in the world since that time. He is now at sixes and sevens. The very second day, memsahib Manley she is entering his kitchen — not, as is memsahib

Smythe's custom, summoning him to lounge or, if entering kitchen, giving loud warning, such politeness being secondary nature to such a memsahib. Memsahib Manley she is entering kitchen quiet as a mouse, she creeps around residence, her feet nude like beggarwoman, he not knowing where she is next popping up. She points her finger to his uniform. Swiftly he explains small mark on jacket caused by tomatoes ketchup. No it is not that. Complicated talking follows, his English words not so good in speech as in his mind, and her Urdu no good. The final result is she is asking him if he is not more happy wearing no uniform but own personal garments.

He can make no reply. His cousin Jalauddin, who is dursi to many residences, among them German Consulate, has himself admired the double-stitching and superior cloth. The jacket bears CC of Cameron, formed in green. His own garments? He has one bush-shirt and slacks, and three shalwar-kemise; when wearing them what is to be distinguishing him from the many other men occupied in the most menial manner, or with no occupation at all? Not to mention bearers of inferior Pakistani households; bearers who cannot cook the potato chips the European style.

That is another point. Memsahib Smythe is giving him most inestimable training not only in the English customs but also in the English cooking. After six months his Apple Charlotte is more superior, memsahib Smythe say, than even back in Wimbledon, England, where her residence lies. (She kindly sends him snapshot, already, with greetings from little Karen and Jamie, that scallywag.) For the first dinner for Manley-sahibs he is cooking his finest meal, that most beloved of the Smythe-sahibs, the fish and chips followed by the guava mould and custard — for this he has purchased tin of Bird's Custard coming all the way from Britain, its price being twelve rupees but then quality goods, say memsahib Smythe, they are being the most expensive. But then memsahib Manley she is taking him aside and say him that she is wanting to learn the Pakistani cooking, and is this green chillis more heated than red? He say Smythe-sahibs they are eating curry one time each week. She

67

say she want more. She is eating it much in Britain, she say, and she talks of restaurants and Vindaloos. He is thinking: this is Bengali food, I am not Bengali man, she is thinking that all Pakistanis are the same?

And there is yet another point. Memsahib Smythe, she is taking pride in his work. She runs the finger along picture top, for her he works his best. He is eager to improve and learn. But memsahib Manley she does no such actions; he escorts her around bungalow and she is not looking but all smiles and everything tickitiboo. Manley-sahib, he is more good in this respect.

And there is one further point. Manley-sahib, for whom he has plenty more respect, who understands the Pakistani customs, at one time he is ringing little bell during dinner that tells Mohammed the moment for re-entering with dessert. With such a bell Mohammed is at his ease in kitchen, he feels little restraint in smoking his cigarette. He has the freedom. But memsahib Manley, with outrage and mirth, is consigning little bell into the cupboard and now he must wait most anxiously, listening to noise of knives and forks, again at sixes and sevens. Nowadays, it is clear, nothing is comfortable for him, memsahib Manley treating him like brother not cook-bearer. The most pleasant time is now at breakfast, if only Manley-sahib eating and memsahib is still sleeping, when equilibrium is order of day.

This Saturday himself, Mohammed, is seated in back of conveyance. Reena follows him, bending to enter, her dupatta pulled across her face. She is shy; she is unaccustomed to cars. They are passing down National Highway and now past Sind Club and offices of Saudi Airlines. His brother Yusaf, he is working as labourer in Saudi; his cousin is working Dubai-side. His family is from Peshawar. The Middle East it is topful of Pathans, these are strongest men. Sometimes they are living twelve in one room but they are sending home plenty of cash. When Yusuf is returning the last time, during Eid, he is carrying as gift transistor radio. Mohammed is wanting, too, job in Middle East. Even though he is cook-bearer to English family with knowledge of English language, it is not he who is big man in family now, but his brother Yusuf. He himself cannot buy Sony Transistor with cassette built-in.

The doctor's office is backside of Gymkhana Club; outside there is brass sign. Memsahib is parking the car. Mohammed has only been to doctor at Jinnah Hospital, where he is standing in queue for one morning, and then one morning more. He walks up the stairs, his wife following but at a distance; she is brimful of fear. He tells her to hurry quick and not keep memsahib waiting. She is country girl, from Tatta; she is not townsperson like himself. Her skin is dark, in common with the Sindhi peoples, but she is good wife and plump, no bones sticking out like memsahib Manley. Besides country girls are best, everybody is in agreement over this, they have no bold city habits; they have no family to chatter with all day long, even upon the subject of their husbands. His wife, she has just one disadvantage, but this will soon be remedied by Dr Farooq.

Within this waiting-room there are no queues; in fact there are no other persons present. There are fine carpets on the floor. For moneyed persons, everything takes no time. Already Dr Farooq is conversing with memsahib. He himself stands, to show that he is at his ease; he even is lighting a cigarette. He cannot in truth understand the conversation, but now memsahib is smiling and talking to his wife. He hears the word 'easy'.

If so easy, he wonders more persons in his position do not have it performed to their wives. He is still unsure of exact method but does not like to speak and show ignorance. He presumes that Dr Farooq has new wonder-drug from the United States of America, or will perhaps be performing some small surgery. Mohammed strolls from one side of room to the other. After he is working in Saudi, he also will afford this Dr Farooq.

Dr Farooq turns to himself, Mohammed, and says in Urdu: 'Please wait a few moments while I take your wife into the surgery.'

He nods his head, man of the world, and puts ash into brass ashtray large as dinner plate. The door closes.

Memsahib smiles at him, seats herself and is opening magazine. He too sits down on settee. This is costing memsahib, no doubt, two hundred or even three hundred rupees. He is proud that his wife is coming here rather than offering prayers at shrine of the Pir. He is also pleased that memsahib, who has not been seeming to understand the Pakistani customs, has so truthfully seen into his own heart. He lights one more cigarette and picks up a magazine, looking at the pictures.

He hears voices through the door. His wife is suddenly speaking loud and fast, this is most unlike her. He cannot hear the words. Dr Farooq is speaking louder too, and then he is laughing.

There is more loud talking and then the door opens. His wife is hastening out and is whispering something in his ear. He tells her to be quiet; memsahib is speaking with Dr Farooq. Without doubt his wife is disgracing him in this place.

Dr Farooq is laughing. His wife pulls his sleeve. This time he is hearing one of her words. Now he listens. He does not move.

For a moment every person is silent. Memsahib has red face; it is now covered with her hands. She is laughing with a high noise. Dr Farooq is smiling also. His wife has covered her face with her dupatta.

Dr Farooq is talking with him now in Urdu, as if Mohammed is small child. 'I think there's been a little misunderstanding,' he says, still smiling, 'between yourself and Mrs Manley. You were sending your wife here because you already have four girl children, I'm right? And your wife is three months pregnant. Your wife seemed to imagine I could give her some pill or something to remedy this next time, so that she could give birth to a boy. This is correct?'

Mohammed cannot speak. He moves his head.

'Mrs Manley seemed to understand something rather different. She thought that you wanted to ensure some method of birth control.'

Mohammed is keeping his eyes on carpet. He is no longer man of the world. He is fool. He feels humiliation of the deepest kind. What man is he, that he cannot understand? That he is

70

causing this Dr Farooq such high amusement? This night Dr Farooq will be saying to his rich friends: 'Today a very simple man came to see me. Let me tell you what happened.'

They are now in the street. Memsahib herself is looking all at sixes and sevens now. Mohammed enters back seat of the car; his wife follows him. He wants to strike her; he wants to strike himself. Mostly he wants to strike Dr Farooq.

Now they are driving down highway. At crossroads they are stopping for policeman. Memsahib is turning around. Her face is still red colour.

'I'm *sorry*,' she is saying, and something else he does not understand.

He is trying to make conversation. He finds some words. 'Pakistani womens,' he says slowly, 'more better ... boy childs.'

'I know.' She is hitting her head: she points to it. 'Idiot.'

He is trying to find the words to explain. Memsahib is waiting for explanation. He must oblige. How there are prayers and the brown liquid to drink, that make ill some women. His own wife has been lying on charpoy three days, the last time she is drinking it. And still she is bearing baby girl after that. He is trying now to explain other method to ensure the baby boy.

'Bus,' he says. '*Vroom*. Rickshaw. Make journey to shrine — holy Pir.'

'Pir's shrine? Where?'

He counts on his fingers. 'Some miles from Karachi.' He is making his fingers wiggle. 'Water. *Garum pani*. Hot water.' Coming out of the earth, he is wanting to say. 'Also womens ... no childs ... want baby. Making journey.'

The policeman is now waving them onwards. But she does not make a move.

'No children?' she says. 'No baby?'

'*Tikka*.' He spreads his hands and shakes his head. 'No baby.'

'Yes. I see.'

The taxicab behind them is making loud hooting. The policeman he is blowing on his whistle.

'They go to Pir,' he says. He is trying to find the words. 'To hot

71

water man.'
   'A hot water man?'
   'For praying, to make child.'

11

I T WAS sunset before Duke got away. It had been a Saturday
of crossed lines and frustration. He had sat in his office above
Khyber Carpet Emporium, he had bellowed down the
phone. The room was small and hot, he had paced from side to
side, knocking his shin against the desk. He could not get
through to the Planning Department, he could not get through
to Minnie though he had booked the call yesterday. 'Make a
friend at the central switchboard,' someone had advised him.
'You won't find any problem then.' He wanted to hear Minnie's
thin, far voice. He wanted her to hear his. The operation was
taking place at midnight tonight, Karachi time.

The beach lay ten miles south of the city, through the slums
that nobody passed unless they were going to the seaside. K12
Housing Society, the offices, hotels and prime locations all lay to
the north. He drove down the road. To one side lay the salt
marsh; drained land. To the other stood the slum blocks with
washing hanging from their windows. They were new but
already dingy, rising out of the dust. In this city nothing ever
seemed finished. Nearly, but not quite. Nobody applied the last
coat of paint; nobody cleared the debris. The apartment blocks
stood gaunt amongst stagnant creeks and subsiding huts. Chickens wandered into their doorless entrances. Country buses,
grey with dust, were jammed at all angles in any available
parking space. Nothing was planned in this frenetic, but torpid

73

city. Projects were started with hectic speed then what happened? They kind of dissolved, defeated. He should have gotten used to it by now. He would sit in some guy's office, progress being made or so he would believe. Then, halfway through, the man's eyes would have that far-away look and he starts on about the nature of temporal phenomena. It all subsides, like those new buildings nobody has quite finished. There's the smallest hitch – a perfectly understandable setback – and suddenly everyone gives up. It's the will of Allah. But his Translux was planned, and when it was built it would be landscaped, down to the last damn flowerbed.

Evening prayers were starting. In the little plaster mosques the muezzins were calling; green neon lights shone in the minarets. Men squatted in rows watching the passing trucks; humble, public evenings. Despite his frustration, this place got to him. The highway branched. One route led through the industrial sector out towards the site where his Translux would be built. In that direction stood the pink pasteboard hills of Baluchistan. They glowed in the evening light, they seemed near enough to touch. It was a trick of the sunset. His hotel seemed so near but so far. Could he trust anything in this baffling country?

He branched to the left, towards the sea. The cluttered city was behind him now. He speeded across the cracked, grey desert. Ahead glinted the water but each pool was a mirage. When he approached it disappeared and another further ahead took its place. See, you never arrived. But beyond that lay the true silver strip of the Indian Ocean. The beach huts stood like teeth stretching from one side of the horizon to the other. There were hundreds of them, most of them owned but seldom used. They stretched from one side all the way to where the Baluchi hills met the sea, where the power station stood. Way beyond that, the sensitive Afghan border was closed to civilians.

What he, Duke Hanson, could do with a place like this. The city of four million was growing day by day and this beach was its natural resort. Down near the shore the Tourism Development Corporation had made some kind of effort. The guys had

74

tried. They had built a little roundabout; on account of the power station they had named the highway Reactor Road. On either side, shrubs drooped from smartly-painted oil drums. He had arrived now. The placard saying *Welcome to Hotel Splendide* had collapsed in the sand; it had lain there ever since he had arrived months before. The hotel was a larger version of the concrete beach huts that lay to either side. It resembled a derelict public convenience; he had never seen a sign of life there.

Cars passed him travelling in the opposite direction, back to the city after a Saturday at the beach: cars crammed with men and crates of Pepsi; sometimes a family car, the men sitting in front and the women in the back. But few people came here; not enough. The only entertainment this place offered was riding on skinny horses and camels, the Pakistani girls squealing as the animals jogged. The beach huts were shuttered. They were recently built, like most everything else, but already they were cracked and pitted. Their broken steps led into the sand.

Outside Shamime and Aziz's hut, however, several cars were parked. He climbed out. The hills had faded to the softest mauve. Beside him a palm tree shed, with a thud, a slab of rind. He heard the laughter of young folk. Beyond the roof of the hut, smoke drifted up into the luminous evening sky. The hills were changing colour as he looked at them. Jesus the evenings were so beautiful here.

Aziz was still wearing his swimming trunks. He and his friends had obviously made a day of it; they had all the time in the world. Aziz roared with laughter as he did in the Sind Club. Shamime must be in the hut. Duke would like to tell somebody about the barbecues he made back home in Wichita, his boys' faces laughing in the light of the flames, but they would not find that too interesting.

Christine Manley approached. 'Isn't it lovely here. I've never been to the beach before. I don't feel watched here.'

He put down his boxful of contributions. He wished he could have built up the fire. That was something he could do.

'We're going to try and find a beach hut,' said Christine.

75

'Duke, do you know this man?' She rummaged in her shoulder bag and held out a card. 'Sultan Rahim.'

He shook his head. 'It's kind of hard to find a hut. They all belong to families who never use them. Perhaps this guy will fix you up.'

'His cousin's a taxi driver. He says this Rahim man will fix anything.'

'That's the way they work.'

'Of course, it's not right. I mean, it's a barricade of huts. Ordinary people have to creep through the gaps to get down to the sea.' She looked along the beach at the other buildings, murky in the dusk. Outside this hut the fire blazed.

'I'd do it different,' said Duke, 'if I had my way. I could develop this place. I'd open it up.'

'It reminds me of a beach in Kent where I used to go for my summer holidays. The bunkers looked just like these. But that was to keep the Germans out.'

Aziz put his hand on Duke's shoulder. 'A drink, old chap? Let's go into the hovel and find Sammy.'

Inside, spirit lamps glared. It was a bare concrete place, furnished with a few chairs; a place to act out the simple life. Shamime was giving instructions to a bearer. Her hair was loose, as it had been at the Coffee Shop the day before, but tangled now. She wore green clothes the colour of seaweed. She hurried over, smiling.

'You shouldn't have. We didn't ask for any more.' She looked at the cold box. 'You're just like Father Christmas.'

'Just a few things from the Commissary.'

'Ah, your super-exclusive American supermarket. You look like a Christmas present yourself, in your jolly shirt.'

'You don't like it?' He looked down. 'I bought it in Hawaii.'

'It's great fun.' She peered closer. 'All those little palm trees. You're a walking tropical paradise.'

But it was she who looked exotic. She glowed; the jewel winked. He unclipped the box.

'Ah, pumpernickel,' she breathed. 'Californian wine, cold beer ... ' She lifted them out one by one. He was not Father

76

Christmas, he was her father. He loved seeing her face.

Christine came up. Shamime turned to her. 'At school my English friends called me Piggy. Me, a Muslim. One of them came out once and stayed with us. My parents nearly died when she called out *Breakfast time, Piggybins*.'

The two girls were sitting on the floor. 'Just tell me what you want,' said Duke. 'Either of you, of course. It's all flown in fresh.'

Christine said: 'American woman do their teeth with soda water, don't they, so they won't get contaminated.'

He looked down at the fuzzy head. He did not reply: *Minnie did too*. Christine squatted in her embroidered tunic. Her bare feet looked more nude than Shamime's brown ones. He liked Christine's husband but he had not figured out Christine yet. Her pink face looked confused; Shamime's walnut skin looked closed and sure: mysterious.

'So you went to school in England,' said Christine.

'Some boring suburb,' said Shamime. 'Nobody knows how to educate their girls here. Not the bright ones. They send them to university in England and France but they think it's only sort of mental flower-arranging. Then the girls come back and find their marriage has been arranged for them.'

'The double standards.' The frizz nodded.

'My best friend from Karachi – she went to Oxford and had a wild affair with her tutor. She went on to do a Ph.D. in London. She had thousands of job offers. She had another affair, with an East End painter. And then she came back to Karachi.'

'And what happened?' asked Christine.

'She married the son of her father's business partner. She changed, just like that. She sat at her wedding, all obedient on her little chair, covered in tinsel and rupee notes, her eyes lowered like a good virgin.'

'Gift-wrapped,' said Christine.

Shamime laughed. 'I'll take you to a wedding, Chrissy. They're something else. They go on for weeks. The bride and groom don't speak, they're just decorated and shunted from place to place.' She touched the garment Christine was wear-

77

ing. Duke thought it had seen better days. 'Your kurta, that was made for a wedding — a poor, country wedding. Her mother and her sisters would have been at it for months, stitching that. The more stitching, the more status for their daughter.'

Christine's head bent to gaze at it. 'I never realized. A garment of bondage. It *is* a bit tight under the arms.' She paused. 'And you?'

'We've had stiff little tea parties when the two mothers excuse themselves halfway through. Ministers' sons, businessmen's sons. The son of the chief of customs, now there's a useful lad. Pity he only reaches to my elbow.' She lifted her head. It glowed below Duke. 'What about you, up there? We've only got to know each other since the Manleys came. Do you have a daughter?'

'I have three sons. Chester's in his college football team, they call themselves the Rangers. Johnny's in his last year and Duke Junior's in business, he's an executive with I.B.M.'

'Lucky you,' said Shamime. 'Who wants daughters? Out here, anyway.'

'I didn't realize till this afternoon ... ' Christine stopped, gazing at a can of beer. They waited but she said nothing more.

Duke was silent. Minnie had in fact borne a girl, a miscarriage at six months. His daughter would have been the same age as these two girls at his feet. She too might have rummaged through the gifts he had brought her. Yet these girls seemed older than that, too: they discussed things better than he did, with their educations behind them. But that was why you made children: to improve upon yourself. There was no point in working, otherwise.

He did not mention this, or the surgical termination of Minnie's possibilities way beyond these black hills, out in the afternoon sunshine of Wichita, U.S.A.

'We breed like rabbits here,' laughed Shamime.

Duke gnawed a chicken bone. He did not feel he had much to offer conversations like these, but he leant forward to listen. Beside him Shamime was talking to Donald.

'I don't fit here any more,' she was saying. 'I'm a hybrid. I've

78

seen too much. My parents didn't realize what they were doing, sending me abroad. They thought I was just learning some French verbs.'

'I didn't learn much at school either,' said Donald, gazing at the embers. 'I think I'm only starting to learn out here.'

'Donald darling, your lot have never come to learn. You've come here to take things away. Your ancestors used high-minded words but they had sound commercial interests at heart. They just liked to disguise it to themselves.' She laughed. 'We're just as bad. But at least we're straightforward about it. No waffling self-justification. We go to England to get what we can out of it. Like money.'

'Rather successfully too. You know, the Asians. But what do they want to learn about Britain?'

'Only the bare necessities. Don't you see, I'm on neither side. Or both. That's my trouble. I'm in the right line of business, I can do a lousy P.R. job on anything. I can slither around either way. Aziz looks like me but he's not. He's like all the young men here – he's a real Pakistani. He's got everything the way he wants it, so why should he change?'

Duke wanted her to go on, but Donald said: 'That's not quite fair, you know. People like my grandfather were lost without this place. He didn't know what to do in England. He'd left himself out here.'

'I'm not speaking personally about him. I'm sure he was a marvellous man. But I still think they came out to find what *they* wanted. It was called Imperialism but it hasn't really changed. You come to pillage us for the good of your country or your bank balance or else your experience of life. It was called cotton or territory then. But it's still the same thing. You take home your snapshots and your whiffs of oriental mysticism. You're still getting off on your own thing. But you can't get to us, not really. We look so welcoming but we can't be touched. Take Karachi. It looks so modern. But just look closer.'

She threw her bone into the embers. It sizzled. Donald threw his, but it landed in the sand.

'Now Duke here, at least he's honest,' she said. 'He doesn't disguise it. No traditions or preconceptions behind him. Nobody's told him what to find. He's come to develop us. Haven't you.' She swung round to smile at Duke, and turned back. 'At least he thinks he has. But you can't start from scratch here; it's not like the Middle East. He wants to stick his hotel in the desert because commercial sense tells him that's where it should be. I'm not saying we don't need it. But it won't change anything.'

Long after that night, after everything had been changed, Duke remembered her turning to him and laying her hand on his arm.

'As I said, at least you're honest about it.'

Despite the intellectual talk this seemed the last moment of simplicity. The three of them mopping up their salad, people moving around, and the shadows leaping against the wall of the hut.

Eleven o'clock, and the barbecues lay there, three cool tins. The servants were packing up. Many of the guests had left; Aziz and some of his friends were off to the Excelsior Night Spot. There were cries of 'cheerio' and *wala ale'icum*. These youngsters never needed sleep. Himself, Duke: he was tired. Beyond the hut he heard engines revving. Headlights swung over the beach as the cars turned.

A spirit lamp lit the trampled sand. A flashbulb popped.

'I only just remembered,' said Donald. 'Trust me to be too late for the main event. The story of my life.' Donald, like Duke, had drunk a good deal of Aziz's excellent Scotch.

The music had stopped. Duke could hear the waves now, and the barking of dogs further down the beach where the fishing village lay. In the States there was true wilderness but this country was inhabited, every inch.

Shamime was sitting next to him. She leant over.

'I thought Uncle Bobby was coming. He thrives on this sort of thing. He thinks he's so young at heart. It's a shame; you could've met him.'

Duke was uncertain whether or not it was a shame. He had

his principles, hadn't he? He raised his head to the vaulted sky. The stars made him dizzy. He could usually take his liquor. He could usually take being alone too. But tonight was worse than usual. He could not work out if he was missing Minnie, or lonely because he wasn't. He shook his head, trying to clear it, and gazed at his gaudy chest.

Shamime was pushing the sand with her finger. He looked at her profile. With the clarity of drunkenness he realized it was far from perfect: her strong bumpy nose and her full lips. Her feet moved him. They were small-boned and fine as a bird's, so delicate. He turned his head away. He wondered which of those young men, driving back to town, was her beau.

Another flash. 'Sorry,' said Donald. 'Kept not working. Shamime put a jinx on it, talking like that about snapshots.'

Christine hugged her knees tighter. 'Remember at that mosque? By the time old Cartier-Bresson had fixed his exposure, all the tastefully tattered beggars had gone.'

'Not gone. Come.' He bent over the lens. 'Up to me, to get some money.'

'Except the women who covered their faces.'

'I won't cover mine,' said Shamime, pushing back her hair and smiling. Duke looked away and the bulb flashed.

'At least you're not the home-movies type,' said Shamime. 'I don't think I could take any more ayahs pushing blurred little Habibs in front of the camera.'

Duke was silent. In fact he happened to be something of a 16mm expert himself. Back home he had a cupboard full of reels: Chester's sixth birthday, John-John in his cowboy suit shooting the camera. That vacation stop at the Grand Canyon, his little family standing, tense, near the drop. Below them, nothingness. He had stopped the film and called out, 'Get back from there!' But there had been no danger, had there?

'Duke, could you drive me home?'

Duke paused. 'Sure.'

'Aziz has taken his car, and the bearers have taken the things back in mine.' She paused. 'You look doubtful.'

'No,' he said. 'Fine. Sure.'

He climbed to his feet, heavily. The other guests rose. Sha-mime gathered her sandals. They collected the last glasses and extinguished the lamp, while Shamime locked up the hut.

The moon had risen. In its light they could see their way around the corner of the hut, stepping over the tussocks of grass. The others drove off. Duke put the rest of the party debris into the trunk.

They climbed into the car. Duke switched on the headlamps. They lit up the back wall of the hut. He started the engine. Beneath the wheels there was a grinding and spinning. The Datsun did not move. He revved the engine. More spinning.

'We're just getting deeper.' He switched off the engine.

They sat still for a moment, then they climbed out. The wheels were sunk into the sand, right over the hubcaps. In the moonlight the automobile looked like some stranded creature, just crawled from the sea on his own damnfool demand. He should not have come here.

'Heck.'

'Perhaps we could get some help. There's always somebody around.'

'I'm getting us out,' he said.

'Anyway, I don't fancy creeping about this place at night.' The dog barked again. She shivered.

'Could you sit in the driver's seat?' asked Duke. 'And I'll push.'

She climbed in. 'I'll try.'

He leant over and showed her the starter. 'Put your foot on the clutch, here.' He bent and patted the pedal. She moved her sandalled foot.

'I've never driven a Datsun.'

'Press the clutch. I'll put it into gear.' He leant over, careful not to touch her, and eased the gear-shift into position. 'When I say *Now*. Okay?'

He went over to the front bumper. She peered out of the window, watching for when he would push. She was so slim, the car felt no heavier with her inside it.

'*Now*.'

She revved. He pushed, willing every muscle in his body to move the automobile. His feet dug into the sand. His shirt stuck to his chest.

'*Now.*'

She revved again. He pushed, grunting. The wheels spun.

'*Now.*' She revved. He moaned.

He rested a moment, leaning against the warm hood. The air was full of exhaust smoke. She was leaning out of the window, coughing with the fumes. He wanted to protect her.

'Again?' she asked.

Groaning, he pushed against the car. He must get this girl delivered home.

The door slammed. She was beside him.

'I've put it into neutral,' she said. 'Shall I push from here?'

She, too, was breathless. She pulled up her sleeves; they fell back again. They put their hands against the hood. He could smell her perfume and warm sweat.

He took a deep breath. '*Now.*'

They pushed together. Her breath rasped beside his. His head swam with perfume and exhaust. The wheels spun. They stopped. He looked up at the spinning stars.

'I think there are some ... planks ... in the hut.' She caught her breath. 'From when we had the shutters replaced.'

'I'll go.'

'No. I know where they are. But please come with me.' She looked around. 'I know it's stupid ... '

He reached through the window to get her pocketbook. The illuminated clock stood at ten after twelve. Something was supposed to be happening at midnight but he could not remember what.

Shamime crossed the headlights, making her way round the hut. He had no torch to help her. The wind had risen and the moon clouded over.

A sharp cry.

'Shamime?'

He stumbled forward and bumped into her. She was climbing to her feet. He put his arms around her and helped her up.

83

'Just a can,' she said, her voice shaking. 'Probably one of ours.'

He was still holding her. She was thinner than she seemed. 'Pardon me.' Quickly he let her go and took the can, inspecting its label as if his life depended on it. She stood near, looking at it too.

'Root Beer. I thought we'd cleared them up. Sure you're okay?'

'Fine, I think. I should've worn my shoes.' She lifted one bare foot, holding his shoulder for balance. The wind blew her hair, whipping his cheek.

Along the beach, a loose shutter banged. She searched her pocketbook and found the key.

'Let me do it.' He felt his way to the hut door and unpadlocked it. He stepped in. The party seemed to have happened a week ago. 'You wait here,' he said. 'You have some matches?'

She did not wait outside; she came into the hut. She was walking around, holding out her flickering lighter. The flame lit her tilted face and that bumpy nose. 'I'm sure they're here somewhere.' Indoors her voice was smaller. 'Somewhere around.' She sounded unsure. 'There must be some candles. They leave the candles by the sink ... I thought they did.'

'I'll feel around.'

Like a blind man he ran his hands along the wall. Outside the waves were roaring. Shamime's face was flickering the other side of the hut.

'Can't find the candles,' she said. 'Perhaps they took them back.' She was lost without her servants.

This end of the hut it was pitch dark. He continued his search. The walls were rough and warm. He felt the floor. It was gritty with sand. His fingers felt the debris swept into the corner – a weightless cigarette carton, more sand. Waving to the right, his hand brushed the webbed back of an armchair. He felt down its wooden leg.

'I don't think they're here at all,' said Shamime's voice.

He looked up. The light caught her face as it turned. She should be safely back home. His hand met another leg, the next

84

chair. He was old and clumsy. He should be back home too. His fingers felt the wall again; in places it was cracked.

'You've searched your side?' her voice asked.

He was near her now. He straightened up.

'What shall we do?' she said. 'I don't know where they leave things.' She held up the lighter. Her hair was messed by the wind. His heart lurched. The small flame illuminated her face; her eyes were filled with tears.

'What will my parents think?'

He had never seen her like this. The dog barked again, nearer. The wind slammed the door shut. The flame blew out. He felt her jump like a deer.

A shaky laugh. 'This is silly,' she said. 'You see, I'm terrified of the dark. Duke, are you there?'

'I'm here.'

'When I was little . . .'

Her hand touched his chest. 'Duke, don't leave me alone.'

12

A s SHE entered the door, Christine was already writing the letter to Roz. Part of the reason she had come here, in fact, was to produce something amusing for Roz to flatten out on her desk at Rags. She imagined Roz laughing in that cubbyhole full of other women's lace. (Her own sister Joyce would not see the joke; Christine's letters to her were fond enough, but travelogue in tone.)

The British Wives' Association is over the other side of our modern suburb. Cars parked down the street outside. I had walked. I only came to see if somebody wanted a gardener so I could find mine another job. Chintzy curtains; loud women in loud prints. Tins of Nescafé and plates of biscuits, a Coffee Mornings atmosphere. Oh, remember our coffee nights? I miss the way we talked.

Everything nice and safe. Furnishings preserved, Weybridge circa 1956. A room from my own childhood. Wars might rage, Pakistan be gripped by Russians invading through Afghanistan, the crooked Prime Minister overthrown; outside there might be famines and floods, but here inside there will be honey still for tea.

Large woman called Anthea introduced me. Everyone started praising Ann Smythe, my predecessor, what a brick she was, didn't know how they'd manage without her. Doubtful looks at my potential as replacement. Children everywhere. A.S. had two.

Besides children, main topics of conversation: parties and servants. High jinks, like young blood from Consulate throwing someone's wife into swimming pool. A Fancy Dress do — 'Look Who's Wearing The Trousers' — where men dressed as women and vice versa. Men simpering, with rouged cheeks, and asking for Little Girls' Room. Daring stuff. Remember my last letter about transvestites down in the bazaar? Felt tempted to contribute this item.

'It's not like England,' said one woman. 'We have to make our own entertainments here.' Another one asked, 'You're not one of those Women's Libbers are you?' Tried to explain about our group. 'Sounds just like us,' she said, 'but fewer laughs.'

Servants discussed at length, mainly complaints. Servants are like second-hand cars — cheap to buy but performance to be distrusted. Not considered human being at all, let alone friend. Marjorie Somebody said: 'Ibrahim made Nicky a birthday cake, with five candles and H-A-P-Y B-U-R-thday on it. Still, Nicky can't spell either.'

Behind the armchairs, shelves of lending-library books — Agatha Christie, Catherine Cookson etc. Not a single book about this country except Indian Horticultural Association Tips for the Tropics, *printed 1935. Charming tinted illustrations of dahlias etc., with background of bending servants. Curious how much more palatable old pictures are of this subject.*

Had to sign up for B.W.A. in order to borrow book. Also to leave notice. Beside french window noticeboard is fixed with lists of members' names, ages of their children etc. Plus announcement of films at Consulate and amateur production of Salad Days *at British Council. Plus Mrs Wilmot's recipe for marmalade, posted up by public demand. Plus small ads for cook-bearers and fridges. Thought of replacing, at nightfall, with small ads from our café, how I miss that place — cards for Tai Ch'I and inner growth.*

'Here's a pin.'

Anthea was standing beside her. With a smile she passed Christine a drawing pin. She was a middle-aged woman with a wide, pink, placid face, as if any questions it had once felt had long been settled. Her hair, dried coarse and yellow by the climate, was fixed into permanent waves. *Like a thatched aunt,* Christine would write.

'I'm seeing if somebody would like my mali.'

'Thanks for your subscription. Welcome to the B.W.A.

Wouldn't you like one of these?'

'Er no thanks, I like smoking these.'

'The subscription money all goes to charity, you know.'

'I see. Who?'

'There are still some old folk living here—mostly widows, whose husbands served here.' She scratched the straw. 'They've no place in Britain now, so they've just stayed. And there's a couple of schoolmistresses from the old British Grammar school.' She pointed to the list.

Christine re-lit her cigarette. These Pakistani ones kept going out. She looked at the names. 'Mrs Iona Gracie, how wonderful. Sounds like the heroine of one of those books.' She pointed across at the cloth-bound romances.

'By all accounts she looked like one, long ago. She's a bit eccentric now. Quite a character. You must meet her.'

Christine thought: I don't want to meet English people. 'Do you have any Pakistanis?'

'Goodness no.' Anthea laughed. 'Pakistanis keep their old folk in the family. They take care of them better than we do.'

How many Pakistanis do you know? thought Christine.

'We also do practical work,' said Anthea. 'Visiting hospitals, fund-raising, that sort of thing.'

Christine thought: I don't want to go around like Lady Bountiful with my basket. I don't want to give them, as a gift, my idea of what they should want. She sucked her cigarette back to life.

The room felt enclosed and hot, with its portrait of the Queen above the bookshelves. In the garden, safe inside the high white walls, children played on the grass. With the temperature in the nineties, they were fully clothed. No doubt Anthea had children, driven from house to house, never stepping foot on the dusty road between. *I thought of your children, Roz, running bare under a lukewarm English sun.*

'We're visiting Jinnah Orphanage next week,' said Anthea. 'Would you like to come? We collect our spare toys. It's a bit upsetting. Some of the babies are very young.'

Christine paused. 'I'll think about it.'

'Heavens, I've forgotten to sign up myself.' Anthea took out a biro. 'After all my cajoling.' She wrote her name on the list of volunteers. *Anthea Siddiqi.*

For a moment Christine did not understand. The word looked vaguely foreign.

'What an unusual surname,' she said. 'Is it Italian?'

Anthea roared with laughter. 'Good God no. Looked in the phone book? It's as common as Khan.'

'Ah.'

Christine felt her face heating up. To hide it, she turned and put out her cigarette in somebody else's saucer. The stub hissed in the brown puddle.

Her mental letter to Roz ceased. Anthea had moved away to talk to someone else. Christine felt irked and unsettled, in her flimsy ethnic blouse. Everyone else was talking, probably about their children. There were about fifteen women here, four of them visibly pregnant.

'Another card,' said Anthea.

'No, it's not for pinning up. I just wondered if you knew where this place was.' She spoke to Anthea with more respect now. As if in confirmation of her own stupidity, a brown-skinned girl was now sidling against Anthea's slacks, rubbing her cheek against the linen.

'Sultan Rahim Estates.' She read the address and thought for a moment. 'Nazimabad's miles. Right the other side of Karachi.' She explained the location.

Outside it was noon, and very hot. Somebody — Margaret or Marjorie — offered her a lift but Christine refused. None of these women would live in Nazimabad. It was the sort of place that one only read about in newspaper reports of riots.

She waited some time for a rickshaw, her feet scuffling the dust like a refugee.

'Nazimabad?' The man repeated the word without interest.

'East Nazimabad, Street 13b.' Bending down, she repeated the words again, louder. She could not tell if he understood. If he did, he did not care to indicate so. Was he waiting for her to get in? She felt the usual irritation rising. It was like fighting cotton wool. They stared when you were trying to be alone; they gazed way beyond, uninterested, when you actually wanted an answer.

A car stopped beside her.

'Can I help?' It was Anthea.

She took the card and explained, in fluent Urdu. The man still looked bored but he understood, wrapping his turban more tightly around his head.

Time Is Golden, Do Not Fritter Away. The placards bounced past. The rickshaw bumped along the highway, showing off with its European lady passenger. The driver had tilted his mirror to get a better view of her face. She expected this now. She wished she had worn her dupatta, as much for the dust as for modesty. They passed miles of suburban slums. The highway was lined with hoardings—big painted women's faces taken from the magazines. They held up talcum powder and soap. One showed Julie Christie, repainted in bolder style, with *Dr Zhivago* printed beneath. Only a month before, these faces had loomed out of the dark. She had sat in the Cameron car, the air ripe with her crushed garland, and wondered at it all. She had laughed at her first sight of a rickshaw. Now she sat, sticky on the plastic seat, her feet dusty in their rubber chappals, swaying with its movements.

It took a long time to get there. Karachi had grown so huge. Donald had told her the exact figures: it doubled in size every three years, or was it five? He was the one for facts. Now they were arriving at what must be the commercial centre of Nazimabad, though there were no signs. Europeans did not come to a place like this. The rickshaw stopped. Beside the road stood a block of offices; white, stained concrete like the Adamjee Plaza where Donald worked. Signs, bleached by the sun, were fixed on various floors of the building to indicate the different businesses within. *Sultan Rahim Estates.* She felt a rush of excitement. Donald presumed her to be clinking tea-cups with British mums.

The interior of the building was as sweltering as the street.

She walked up the stairs. The walls were spattered red from betel spit. A peon in a dirty uniform was coming downstairs with a tray of tea-cups. Clerks were walking down, talking together; it was lunch time. They fell silent and stopped to let her pass. But they worked in an office; they did not jostle her like the men in Juna Bazaar. Perhaps Mr Rahim had gone out for a meal too.

She had pictured a suite of rooms and people typing. In fact it was a small cell with one desk and a man rising from his chair.

'Please to enter. Come in, come in.'

'But you're on the phone.'

'No importance.' He gabbled some Urdu and put back the receiver. 'This is my pleasure.'

He shook her hand, drew out a chair, hurried to the door and yelled down the corridor.

'That is the tea,' he said. 'You have understanding of our language? No? You are recent arrival?'

'Very recent.' She sat down. 'I should've phoned really. I came on impulse.'

'You are a lady of impulses. Already I can tell. I too work from the heart.' He sat down at his desk and put his hand to his chest. 'All good business is done not from the head,' he shook his head, 'but from the feelings.'

A peon came in with a tin tray. Mr Rahim took out a grimy note and sent him away.

'You are liking our Pakistani tea?'

'Very much,' she lied. She inspected him over the rim of the cup. He was plump, perhaps forty years old; his hair was sleek with oil. He was perspiring — as, indeed, was she. His skin was dark, almost purple; he looked like a ripe plum in his nylon shirt.

'I heard about you through your cousin, the taxi driver.'

'He carries my recommendation. I tell you, Mrs ... '

'Manley.'

'Mrs Manley, I am coming from nothing. I can speak with frankness, I am not proud. I am self-made man. With my own energies I build my business. Now I do dealings with all the bigwig persons. You will see my cards.'

He pulled out a drawer and handed them to her. 'Here is Vice-Chairman of Philips Electrical, a most pleasant gentleman from your own fair country that I myself have visited one time. Sure, I have visited London town. This man, he holds Pepsi-Cola agency, he has three fine kiddies, I have been guest in his residence. And this — he is head person of Toyota Spare Parts. I find them all beautiful bungalows with their secluded compounds.'

She looked at the cards. Deep down she felt a twitch of reassurance, that he knew such people.

'I have many letters ... ' He was opening the drawer again.

'No, please don't bother. Actually I didn't come about a house. I have one, in K12.'

'Ah, the tiptop location, most exclusive. Please, some biscuits.'

'No thank you.'

'It hurts me, here.' Again he put his hand to his heart. 'You are not liking my biscuits?'

She ate one. The phone rang and he spoke lown it. She seemed to have been eating biscuits all morning. But how different this room was from the other. No Queen on the wall; instead, a tinted print of Jinnah. No chintz curtains to draw against this foreign sky. Outside stood a block of flats topped with a water tank. Buzzards lazed in the air, ready to swoop and scavenge from the street. Down there, television sets were being unloaded from a camel cart and carried into a shop. Further along two men squatted, their backs to the street, and relieved themselves against the concrete wall. These Muslim men did it so discreetly in their loose pyjamas, rising to knot the cord.

'It's nice to look at a street without them seeing me,' she said when he put down the phone. 'This is like a purdah window, up here. The only place I can sit looking out is at home, but then all I can see is the garden wall.'

'Ah, in K12 the compounds are so beautiful. It is no wonder you are preferring the looking there.'

'I don't mean that.' She stopped.

'Let us talk heart to heart.' He leant forward. 'That is what I say when I am meaning speaking business. Maybe you need air-conditioner.'

'Yes, your cousin said—'

'I have many threads to my bows. I have many friends, many contacts. My very dear friend, he works in the import agency. You want it, I find it. Sultan Rahim, he say, Sultan Rahim, he is never sitting still on his backside.'

'Actually, I wanted a beach hut.'

'No problem. I find you the beautiful beach hut quick as a flash.'

'You can? I've heard it's difficult.'

'Everything is possible. You put your trust in Sultan Rahim.'

They fell silent. She looked around the room. It was bare, but for the desk and two filing cabinets. Mr Rahim was rearranging the papers on his desk.

'There are some?' she asked.

'Yes?'

'Beach huts? You have some on your files?'

'The little home-from-home beside the ocean. It is what, in his heart, is the dream of every person. I am right?'

She nodded. Another pause.

She looked at the filing cabinets. Still he made no move. Outside the window the buzzards wheeled round and round. They never moved their wings, coasting on the heat.

She drained the syrupy tea. 'Do you have any?'

'We have the saying: All things they are arriving to he who is wishing them.' He rose. 'Come. We will visit my very good friend. He too has visited your city of London.'

'So he has one?'

'With Sultan Rahim, there is not any questioning of have and haven't. My conveyance is waiting outside.'

She followed him down the stairs. She had lost track of time. His shiny, blue-black hair bobbed below.

'This is very kind of you.' Her voice echoed in the stair well. She hurried down, her rubber chappals flapping.

His conveyance was a small, smart Fiat. She must stop these questions. She settled into the furry passenger-seat. A doll hung above the dashboard. It was a ballerina; it jigged as he started the engine.

They arrived at the highway. To one side stood the Baluchi hills, white as bone in the heat. They turned the other way, towards the city centre. He reached forward and pushed in a cassette. Gunfire rattled. An American voice spoke, hoarsely. Galloping hooves and then music.

'What's that?'

'The Clint Eastwood movie. You are liking these Wild Westerns?'

She nodded. They loved the movies here. The newspapers were full of ads — 'Don't Miss It. It is a Wonderful Exciting Picture of Lust. An Unforgettable Experience for Young Hearts.'

'I suppose you import V.C.R.s?' she asked.

'I fix it. You are wishing one?'

'No.' She looked out of the window. It was real life she wanted, not cassettes.

He was a manic driver, blowing his horn at every crossroads. It was a police siren, he explained.

'You are liking our city?'

'Oh yes.' She paused. 'It's not, perhaps, quite as old-fashioned and ... well, picturesque as I'd imagined.'

'Due to expansion Karachi is now big business centre. Myself and my brother Muslims, we are not like our Hindus over the border, we are energetic businessmens. Karachi is once little fishing village, as Dubai once little fishing village.'

'And you're in the right business.' She pointed at the building sites they were passing. She thought of Duke, another self-made man, building his hotel somewhere outside Karachi. By the time it was finished, perhaps it would be engulfed by the city.

She wanted to ask Mr Rahim so many things. He might know about that hot water man. He would know why the lorries were painted like children's picture books, and why people knotted their clothes this way, or that way. They passed a vacant plot.

94

Washing lines were strung across it; purple sheets hung from them. Hundreds more lay on the ground, drying in the sun.

She pointed. 'What are they for?' Perhaps they were special robes for some religious festival where everyone dressed in purple. Hindu priests wore orange, or was that Buddhist? Widows, she knew, wore white.

Mr Rahim looked over his shoulder. 'Those cloths? They are for the exports.'

She paused. 'Exports?'

'That is big colour this fall, the violet. I know this, as my cousin has shop in your Kensington Market. All your British dolly-birds, they buys his clothes. He also is having other shops, short lease in prime location like your Piccadilly Circus, he keep them open until eleven o'clock in the night-time. After movies, night-owls come to buy his kurtas.'

'I see.' The gauze skirt of the ballerina floated up and down. 'I worked in a clothes shop, actually, back in London.'

'How I am loving your Bond Street. Mr Manley, he is in garment business?'

'No, *I* worked there.' She stopped. Perhaps she would not tell him about the old clothes. He might not understand. He might hold her in lower esteem, and he was taking such trouble for her now. I am learning, she thought.

He drove into the centre and stopped outside Bohri Bazaar. The pavement was spread with sunglasses and bootlaces. Even in this early-afternoon heat, the place was busy. To one side of the street were alleys hung with saris and embroidered tourist clothes. On the other side stood a covered emporium full of stalls. She had been here several times. Outside sat a young, pale European in dirty Pakistani clothes. He was doing nothing; just sitting in the sun.

Unlike Kensington Market men tried to waylay her, but in friendlier fashion than Juna Bazaar. 'Yes madam you step this side?'

She shook her head. She was no tourist. She was a resident, on business. Sultan Rahim was already seated in a large stall full of hideous brass objects. A chair was produced for her. A young man gave her a cup of tea.

'He's here?' she asked Sultan. 'Your friend?'

'He is returning in five minutes, his nephew say me. We will drink some tea.'

Minutes ticked by. She thumbed through her library book. Now nobody was looking she need not finish her tea. She wondered vaguely about lunch; her stomach was full of syrup. There was no worry about Mohammed because she had told him that henceforth she would get the lunch herself; she had felt so foolish sitting there with her jaws working. Sultan Rahim was telling some long story to the nephew, a pock-marked youth with a weak chin. She seemed to have been forgotten. Opposite was a booth stacked with sober suitings, greys and blues; on the floor sat an elderly tailor at his sewing machine. Further down the passage was a doorway. Beside it lay a collection of men's shoes. It was a mosque in there; she had been along this passage before. Just inside the doorway she glimpsed a row of taps for the ablutions of the faithful. She remembered something Duke had said about commerce and religion existing together here; there had been approval in his voice.

More minutes passed. The brass coffee sets reminded her of Brinton. Donald's grandparents' bungalow had been full of the things. Then, too, she had felt obliged to sip sweet tea and eat too many biscuits. Their lounge had been suffocatingly hot. But outside the window, a glimpse of sea.

Who owned this beach hut—Sultan's friend, or a friend of his friend? Networks of men speaking heart to heart, business to business, holding hands as they did here and bending side by side in the little mosque, placed adjacent to the cash desk.

Two women passed, their faces veiled; they wore black sateen raincoats. No doubt Sultan Rahim had a wife tucked away somewhere. Perhaps she, too, was obliged to dress in black when she went out of the house. He was a different class from the Pakistanis she usually met.

She scratched her leg. She felt sticky in her jeans. What did

Sultan's very good friend think of Kensington Market, with its bold girls meeting his stare? Did he eye their skimpy clothes with only a professional interest? She looked at Sultan, slapping his thigh at something the nephew said. By now she felt quite bound with him, she seemed to have been in his company for hours. She thought of him as Sultan now. But she felt fidgety too.

'When did you say he was coming back?'

Sultan spread his hands. 'Five minutes, ten minutes, one hour.'

'But you said five minutes before.'

'Who is knowing?'

She must relax and slip into the tempo of this place. That was what the hippie did outside, sitting on the pavement and experiencing.

She wriggled her toes. She thought of the biro'd list at the B.W.A., times fixed, promises kept. *Time Is Golden, Do Not Fritter Away.* She felt a rare pang for Donald, who did things when he said he would. To the dot.

Here the brass shone timelessly; the tailor stitched. But back at Sultan's office the phone must be ringing for nobody. Didn't he have anything else to do? Was it such an honour, having an English girl as companion, that he was sacrificing his business hours? Perhaps he was just being kind. He drove with such frenzy, then he just sat here, swopping desultory jokes. She looked at her watch.

He said: 'You have other place to go?'

'Actually, not really. I suppose I could spend all day sitting here, come to think of it.' She paused. 'It's odd, not having a job.' All she had planned to do was to go home and read her *Tips for the Tropics*. Even then she couldn't do any gardening because she still had a mali. 'I wish I had a job, but my husband says foreign wives can't work. It's against government policy or something. They can only do voluntary things.'

'You want job? Leave it to me.'

'Can you really help? It's only supposed to be something a Pakistani girl couldn't do.'

He smiled, pointing to his head. 'Here, there is idea. Yes.' He paused, still smiling. 'Mrs Manley, I have many surprises up my sleeves.'

13

T HEY recognized him at the Sind Club now. When he approached the bar, Iman (yes, he had learnt his name) — Iman would pour out a small Scotch without Donald saying a word. When his chit arrived and he signed it, the bearer said, 'Thank you, Mr Manley.' In the Reading Room the chap there nodded too, with muted but unmistakable acknowledgment, and sat down again.

It was the fairest building in Karachi, built by the British of yellow stone with arched verandas along its length. More graceful than Cameron Chambers, it was made for the pleasure that follows business. The lawns were watered daily. Mature palm trees stood guard around its walls. During this hot season the flowerbeds were bare. In winter however, according to that Rosemary woman, they would be fragrant with English flowers. At closer glance the building was perhaps shabbier than in the old prints but at a distance it looked exactly the same. Indeed, it was joked at the bar that the servants seemed as if they had been there since the place was built.

Outside, too, the sounds had hardly changed. Beyond the walls came the noise of traffic and horses, and the shrill blasts of the policeman's whistle. But through the palms could be glimpsed the scaffolding of the Holiday Inn, an ugly skeleton, due for completion next year. And transistor radios could be heard from the little park next door, where office clerks sat at lunchtime.

And inside, the Club had been partly modernized. Thank goodness they had left intact the Reading Room, and the Billiards Room with its cracked leather sofas and *Wait For The Stroke* above the door. (They had removed, apparently, the sign halfway along the veranda saying *No Women and Dogs Beyond This Point*; he had told this to Christine and watched the reaction.) The Billiards Room remained, with its dusty ceiling fans, shrouded tables and wooden plaques commemorating past champions, long since in their graves. He had searched down the list of golden boys but amongst the Cottons and Sotherby-Smiths he had found no Manley. But he had at least found his grandfather in the ledger.

They had made an effort, however, in the bar—turquoise armchairs and fake veneer—and in the Dining Room with its portable partitioning and its huge, lurid, abstract painting. This was disappointing. There was a small bandstand with microphone and amplifiers for Saturday nights. The room was permanently twilit, with the blinds down and the hooded wall-lamps casting cones of light towards the ceiling.

Today he had just finished a business luncheon, he must watch his weight—tomato soup, fish cutlet and then a curry, even he could not manage a dessert. As usual there were few diners, but the room was full of turbaned bearers, waiting. 'Like extras in some obscure pantomime', Christine had said, half-amused, 'that nobody knows how to finish.' He had brought her here one evening when the place was even emptier and she had kept giggling.

After coffee he shook hands with his guests, three reps from upcountry. Thank goodness they had not hung around. He must remember their names, these Pakistani ones seemed so interchangeable—Khan this and Khan that and something else Khan. The men left before he did. He signed the chit.

He wanted to hurry. Before he returned to his seat—this word came quite naturally to him now, like 'on tour' and 'bungalow', it was the way everyone spoke—before then he was going back to Meadow Road. It was only a couple of streets

100

away, in this old residential area that spread around the cantonment station and the Sind Club. She was probably a wild goose chase, this Mrs Gracie; though excited last Saturday when his memory stirred, by the time he had thought of telling Christine reason had set in and so he had postponed it. There was probably nothing to tell.

He left the air-conditioning for the blast and blaze of the sunshine outside. He walked down the road. Large trees stood on either side; apart from Clifton, the other old residential quarter, and the Parsee area downtown, there were few mature trees in Karachi. It was only a few hundred yards; a short distance for his grandfather to saunter, spick and span, from Club to quarters those many years ago. A tonga clopped past, heading for the cantonment station. When Grandad had sat at the window back home, hour after hour, taking off his glasses and rubbing them as if that would make it all come clearer, was this street amongst those he remembered? Donald's eyeballs ached in the sun.

The residence looked as closed as before. Today, however, a car stood in the courtyard. It was a large, dirty Humber with its boot open.

He went up to the door. The bell-pull had rusted. He was about to tap with his knuckles when the door was opened. He stood aside as an elderly bearer made his way down the steps, dragging a basket of carrots. Seeing Donald the man put down the basket, salaamed, and went back into the house.

He reappeared. 'One minute,' he said.

He went down the steps and picked up his basket. A handle broke and carrots rolled into the dust.

'Oh Lord, oh Lord.'

An old woman came out of the house, hurrying down the steps. '*Iqbal*. They couldn't possibly eat them now.' She turned to Donald. 'Do excuse me. Crisis time.'

'Can I help?'

'Gallant young man.'

The three of them picked up the carrots and started putting

101

them back into the basket.

'Dear boy.' She put a hand on his shoulder as they stood up. 'You're a gift from heaven. It will be one of those days.' She leant closer. He smelt eau-de-Cologne. 'Between you and I, Iqbal's a teensy bit past this sort of thing. One has to pretend to load him up. But we don't want to let on, do we.' She paused. 'We'll have to give them a good wash.'

The carrots were back in the basket. 'Please let me,' said Donald.

He hitched the basket under his arm and followed her towards the house. There were dirt-smears on his lightweight trousers but he did not care. He felt charmed by their need. How had these two managed without him all this time?

'Careful of the step,' she sang out, addressing the house. 'And the rail's broken.' From the back she could have been twenty years old, in her straw hat, white blouse and elasticated trousers like Donald's own mother used to wear, the kind with straps under the feet. She was slim and walked like a girl.

In the gloom the hall looked enormous. He could make out a good deal of unidentified clutter, amongst it some armchairs waiting for someone to sit on them. It must have been years since anyone did. His eyes grew accustomed to the dark. Everything was covered with dust.

The kitchen was stony and primitive, like most kitchens here, but squalid. Cats came mewling out and brushed against his legs. On the floor stood empty saucers ringed with yellow. Donald tipped the carrots into the sink.

'Iqbal will take for ever,' she said. 'He has rheumatism.'

'I'll wash them.'

'You see, they won't eat them otherwise. They have their standards.'

It seemed curious to be washing the carrots when everything else was so dirty. Donald turned on the tap and rolled and rubbed the carrots in the water.

'Who's they?'

'My little friends, my lovely little donks.' She was taking out the carrots one by one and putting them back in the basket.

'Angelic boy. I can't thank you enough.'

'Where do you get the carrots?'

'There's a charming little fellow at the cantonment stalls. I grub around. Iqbal helps me. They know me there.'

'Where are these donkeys?' Through the torn mosquito screen he saw the back regions — undergrowth and some collapsing servants' quarters.

'I know I can interest you in my Sanctuary. Yes, my dear boy, I can see you're going to be one of our *supports*.'

She was gazing at him. She must have been beautiful once. In fact she still was, though the skin was stretched over the fine bones. She must be sixty, but her hair was a cheerful orange. Her eyes were blue but vague, and she wore crimson lipstick shakily applied. She looked like somebody very respectable painted by that Lautrec chap. He could imagine her dabbing at her mouth in front of some mirror miles upstairs in this enormous house. Perhaps she hummed to herself. He had forgotten why he had come.

'A Sanctuary?' he said. 'Where is it?'

'It only takes half an hour. I'm tootling off now. Do come with us.'

'But ... '

'You have such an honest face, so very open. I took to you right from the start. I'm like that. I always trust my instincts.'

'Can I make a phone call?'

He went into the hall and phoned the office. He was detained, he told Mary, his Goanese secretary. He was Sales Manager now, he need give no reason. This was a bold, new feeling. In a month he had not felt so managerial. He phoned home. There was no answer. Christine must have met up with somebody at the B.W.A. He drew squiggles on the dusty table while the phone went on ringing. He joined them up neatly. This was a promising sign. Only after some persuasion had she agreed to give the B.W.A. a try. It would supply her with friends; it would broaden her horizons. He fingered in some stars. She was so dismissive about the Brits, bundling them together with a shudder. Shouldn't travel broaden the mind?

He rubbed his dusty forefinger in his handkerchief. So far Christine had not really settled in. She was restless. Yet for once she had room to move, and the freedom of the spacious house he could at last afford to give her. Not quite as large as this one, perhaps, but a good deal cleaner. In England she had always grumbled at housework; well, she did not have to do it now. He wanted so much, when he returned from work, to find her happy with comprehensible satisfactions.

He hitched the basket under his arm and went outside. For a month now, he realized, he had done no lifting or carrying. He loaded the carrots into the boot of the Humber. The back seat was already piled with hay.

'Is there room?' He peered into the front seats.

'Do you know, I haven't the first idea of your name. There I was prattling.'

'Donald.' He climbed in next to Iqbal. She climbed in next to him.

'Iona Gracie.' Cramped, she hunched herself to shake his hand. Her hand was as he had expected, thin and dry, all bones, and knobbly with rings. He remembered now why he had come. He presumed one was not introduced formally to Iqbal, though he was wedged next to him – wedged between them, in fact, one frail body on either side. Iqbal had the shrunken look of one who for many years has obeyed the most bemusing of orders. Perhaps once he had questioned them. Donald did not know whether to mutely sympathize with him for the squalid house, or blame him for not making sure it was cleaner. The old couple obviously had some understanding; Iqbal had probably been her servant for decades. Donald looked down at his two thighs; they looked large in their fawn trousers. Sitting like this his stomach bulged over the waistband, but whose wouldn't, all hunched up? He felt young and plump compared to these two old birds. He felt ready for anything.

Iqbal drove in a leisurely manner as if behind the wheel of a limousine. Perhaps he had been, once. At crossroads he disregarded policemen, passing them like royalty. Behind them the policemen waved their arms, though Donald was too wedged to turn. Pakistanis always drove too slowly, Donald considered, or maniacally fast. One always noticed *how* they drove. Englishmen just drove. Mrs Gracie was peering from side to side.

'Slow down. Shame, shame.'

A donkey cart passed. It was loaded with oil drums; the driver stood up like a charioteer. The donkey trotted by on its stiff, furred legs.

'It's disgraceful, Ronald, the suffering.'

'How do you get the donkeys?'

'Confiscate them. I have a boy with a van, a Christian, quite keen really. He's my full-time officer. Whenever we see them badly-treated or whenever they look too thin. Poor little mites.'

'But what do the owners do?'

'These Muslims, they treat their animals so dreadfully. The pitiful sights I've seen, Ronald, the sores. They drive them flat out until they're worn through.'

'Like cars,' said Donald. 'Never servicing them.' He was going to expand upon the subject of immediate gratification, so noticeable to newcomers here. Duke's postman who had apparently sliced through the veranda screen because he could not see a letter-box. Donald, however, fell silent. This might be too lengthy for her, and Iqbal might be offended.

'Let me tell you something, Ronald. I simply can't bear suffering. Can't bear it.'

They were passing a creek. Naked children sat in the puddles. A boy pulled along a trolley, on which sat a legless man.

'Dumb animals. They're God's creatures, Ronald, they didn't choose to be harnessed between shafts. They're born into slavery.'

Iqbal had driven past the slums. They were passing the industrial sector. Factories stood on either side of the road. Ahead lay the Baluchi hills, blanched in the afternoon glare.

'What do the people do, when you've taken their donkeys?'

'We'd like to prosecute, but that isn't easy. But we invite them to the Sanctuary and give them a lesson in proper management. We try to tell them it's sound business sense. I say, "What is the use of an ill-maintained machine?" That gets to them.'

'Do you give the donkeys back?'

'By all means, Ronald, if they recover. But we make regular checks, flying visits when they're least expecting it. You should see their faces when they spot our little van. We like to keep them on their toes.'

Half-charmed by this, Donald watched the road ahead. They had left the factories behind and Iqbal accelerated a little. It was suffocatingly hot. The highway was empty. Were only English-women mad enough to brave the afternoon sun? He thought of Emily Eden and Fanny Parkes in the last century, riding out on their horses to the amazement of the natives. He had their books back home. He liked resourceful ladies. No doubt he was weak himself, that was why. He admired them. Strong-minded, but feminine, like Mrs Gracie with her bright curls. Women who did things without minding the comment they aroused, unlike Christine's friends who thought themselves so strong-minded, with their patched woollies and lank locks.

They must have driven ten miles or more. Iqbal slowed down the Humber. The desert seemed empty, but for a sign pointing to *Karachi Asbestos Company*; a track led from the road to a hideous concrete factory, jellied in the heat. Ahead lay some scrub bushes and a tree or two.

'That's a shrine,' said Mrs Gracie. 'We turn off now.'

They bumped along a track just beyond the factory. They turned a corner. Ahead lay a low, yellow-stone place built like a fort. Iqbal sounded his horn and the gates were opened by a sleepy youth in creased pyjamas.

Inside, the walls were broken in places. Wooden pens had been built around them; through the bars he could see dozing donkeys and horses too. There was a pukka stone office set against the wall, with the youth's rope bed in its shadow.

'This is Emmanuel,' said Mrs Gracie. 'He's a Christian like us, he understands about animals.' She always spoke as if the native were not there. But then had she registered Donald – no, Ronald? She knew nothing except that he was English like herself. In her, however, such self-absorption was appealing.

Flies buzzed around the donkeys' ears. She stretched out a hand, sparkling with rings, and rubbed their fur.

'This is Bosie. I always ask their names first. If they don't have one, I make it up.'

The air was ripe with dung. 'And their owners do visit?'

'Not utterly and precisely to visit. They come to get them back. A lot of them come anyway to that shrine up the road. It's the place to go if you want babies.'

'Babies?'

'If they're barren. There's a dead saint there, a *pir*. They throw money into a tank and pray for a baby.' She paused, re-tying the ribbon under her hat. 'I was just wondering, would you like to adopt one?'

Donald stood still. 'Adopt?'

'It's a scheme I have. I keep you in touch with his or her progress. You donate twenty-five rupees a month. That covers feed, ointment and lice powder.'

'Ah.' He paused. 'A donkey.'

'That's the way we tick along. I've applied for money, of course, but ... ' She lowered her voice. ' ... don't want the donks to hear. But all they want to give it to is the blessed humans. Priority number one, they say. Silly asses.'

Donald started to laugh. 'Asses – donkeys ... '

But she was looking beyond him. 'Emmanuel!'

He came running up. She pointed to the wall near the office. 'Who knocked those bricks off? It wasn't like this yesterday.'

'Please memsahib, I am hearing this noise in the night. The dog is shouting. So I shoot my shotgun into the air.'

'And they went?'

He nodded. 'I listen to the car.'

She sighed, and turned to Donald. 'Sometimes I wish dear Manny would aim a little lower.'

Emmanuel went off and started unloading the feed. 'Actually, if it was only them we wouldn't worry. Most of them are too clueless to break into a paper bag. But see those hills?' Donald nodded. 'The wild Baluch. How long have you been here, Ronald?'

'A month.'

'You'll hear all sorts of stories about them.'

He was going to say that he already had, from Grandad. But he did not know how to introduce this and she went on: 'Horse-obsessed. Rather a romantic bunch but a filthy nuisance. When I was a gel we'd make up all sorts of games about them.'

'You've been here since then?'

'More years than you could remember, I daresay.' She touched his arm. 'So nice to see a fresh young English face. It takes me back. This place used to be full of boys like you. Now there're just a few old tabbies like me.'

Through the broken wall he looked at the ridge. It lay many miles away, he knew this, and Afghanistan lay the other side, but in this deceptive light it seemed to be close behind the wall.

On that unsettled border even the British could not control the wild Baluch and Pathan, but had had to settle for political agents roaming huge areas. He had always found that romantic. Bang-bang, he shouted in the shrubbery, when he was a boy, while from the kitchen the wireless murmured. Baluchi territory then was the big grey sky, and the washing flapping. But out here it had never been a game.

'Funny you should say Baluchis ... '

'Seven, eight ... 'Carrots fell into a tin bowl. 'We're fighters, this little team, Ronald. And those loathsome Yanks won't win either. Fifteen, sixteen ... '

She straightened up, with a sigh, and tucked her blouse into her slacks. 'I shall go into the office and check the medicines.'

He followed her. 'What Yanks?'

'Haven't I told you our latest saga?'

Inside the office it was even stuffier. She looked so fresh; with her matt white skin she seemed inviolate to heat. His shirt stuck to him, front and back now.

'We will stand firm,' she said. 'I rent this land from the Government of Sind. They will bulldoze us over my dead body.' She started opening cupboards and checking bottles.

'Who are they?'

'I don't know, Ronald, and I don't care to know. Some ghastly conundrum — no, conglomerate. Faceless international money-men, no doubt. Not like you or I, Ronald. If necessary my faithful servants and myself will man the barricades. I can handle a gun. I'm not senile yet.'

He imagined her crouched in the office, barrel pointing through the window, eyes narrowed under her dotty boater. It seemed so wonderfully English, this place. Crumbling walls erected against the mutinous natives one side and mid-Atlantic mediocrity the other. Holding out, holding on.

'That's what they're after.' She pointed through the window, down to the right. Leaning over, he could see the bushes. 'The shrine with the warm springs. Did I tell you about it?'

He nodded.

'They're turning it — correction, they're *trying* to turn it, over my dead body — into some vast — what do they call it in the letter? A Leisure Complex. I presume they're trying to say hotel.'

Donald paused, his hand on the windowsill. Studying the tacked-on mesh, he did not turn round.

'You mean that shrine is Ginntho Pir?' He kept his voice conversational.

'That's right. What's Manny done with that iodine?'

He had not realized. Ginntho Pir was the proposed Translux site. There were no signs to tell him. In a few days he would have known, because Duke was planning to bring him here on a visit.

There was a silence, broken by the clunk of bottles as she moved them, and the whirr of the table fan behind him. He gazed at the windowsill. Dead flies lay with their legs in the air. He tried to remember Duke's words. *She's an old dame, Don, one of these recluse-types. Must be crazy to be out here. We've gotten her this beautiful site a couple miles outside town, piped water, bigger too. The works.*

He did not know how he could speak to her. What had she called his face — frank and open? He turned round. 'Here, do let me help. And, by the way, what does one do about this adoption scheme?'

109

14

THERE was no shade to speak of out at Ginntho Pir, under that gauzy blue sky. Duke had parked his automobile on the verge, beside the highway that led from Karachi. He sat inside, the engine and the air-conditioner running. You had to keep the one going for the benefit of the other and today, boy did you need the other. Through the window stood some thorn bushes, furred with dust. Buses and rickshaws passed this way. They parked down the road behind him, where the path led up to the shrine and the old mausoleum.

It was a small place, kind of shabby and kind of likeable. There was no part you could call a village, as such; just a few huts the other side of the mound. This side, the pathway up to the shrine was lined with tea stalls, food stalls and men selling religious offerings. Around them, the scrub. It was real insanitary, with its excrement and scavenging dogs. These people had to use whatever place they could find, on account of there being no toilet facilities. He remembered Walter V. Hirschman, Translux Chief Executive, stepping round the place and lifting his feet. And that was way back in December when the odours were not so apparent.

Today, Tuesday, Duke had the windows closed. He could not hear the sounds outside because of his cassette playing. It was one of his Nashville tapes.

'You're swe-e-et as blueberry pie,

You've broken my heart, my Rosalie ...'

Back home they teased him about these tunes, calling him sentimental. His boys were reared in the rock 'n' roll generation. But this old country-and-western it spoke to him, straight to the heart. Through three continents he had grunted along with the words, driving down a hundred freeways.

'Your hair black as a raven's wi-i-ing ...'

He would not think about her hair. Instead he fixed his concentration on the dashboard clock. 3.30. Soon Don would be here with Mr Chowdry, Under-Manager of the Lahore Translux. From this position Duke could see the highway leading back toward the city, straight as a ribbon but wobbling in the heat.

He was looking forward to showing Don the place. Don had this enthusiasm. You wouldn't think it first time you met him; seemed that his wife did all the talking. But just get him on to his favourite subjects. In fact Don knew more about this place, from his old books, than most of the Pakistani businessmen and sub-contractors Duke had spoken to, and more than Duke himself but that wouldn't be so hard. When he was at their home for dinner Don had gotten out these tomes. He had spent a long time thumbing through and reading stuff out, the bearer waiting with the liquor and Don not noticing. They were these travellers' tales, when the British were the real explorers, riding on horseback hundreds of miles in this heat to chart the frontiers and manage this place. Don had read out about Ginntho Pir and the history of the name, how it had changed from some old Hindu word when the place was India. No doubt he would be informed of more facts today. He, Duke, wanted to know; in this respect — in fact in every respect — he was uneducated. He remembered one sentence: *The Sind Desert is a land of sepulchres and dust* and somesuch, full of *holy shams and holy humbugs*. And some more about dating the tombs and shrines and how they were scattered everywhere, but in this region of intense heat, *dreary aspect*, sure that was it, and shifting river-beds, it was impossible even for the British to chart all the antiquities. See, this place shifted; you never got quite where you wanted. He

111

himself was realizing this. Then something about the warm springs being a remarkable feature, but the big Moghul-type mausoleum (in better repair, for sure, when the book was written) and the small new shrine being nothing so special, architecture-wise. You saw wayside shrines in all these parts, whitewashed tombs with rags stuck on sticks. Sometimes little buildings around them for the important guys. No, it was the hot springs and this particular *pir* who was unique. Seemed that the belief here was more exceptional than the surroundings.

Duke opened his cold box and took out a can of Coke. He pulled the tab; it hissed. 3.45 and still the road was empty. You couldn't trust the cold drinks up in those stalls there. People had gotten dysentery from them. Or visitors thought they would, so they brought their own. And then there were the beggars and the staring; worse for a female, of course. That was the trouble with this place, Karachi. They had their one or two monuments: fine. They had their beach: fine. Period. You saw them and then what? You could hardly take a stroll out into the desert. Not even in the more fertile land upcountry because it would be somebody's little plot and you were tramping on their corn. There was nowhere just to sit and relax, with a drink you could trust, with somebody serving you who spoke your language. It wasn't open to people. As he told the tourism guy, how could a country get itself up off its ass, well he hadn't put it like that. How could a country develop, if when folks came they just wanted to do what business they'd come for and hightail it out of there? Christine Manley, she said the same thing but in a different way. You couldn't really get into a country, not really understand it and want to stay, if all you could do was sit in your automobile and drink your own Coke.

He slid in another cassette.

'It's okay by me, it's ok-a-ay ...'

He tipped the can. Icy, it pressed against his lips. He drank from the sharp hole. *Ok-a-ay by me.* Okay, was it? How was she? How could either of them be okay, since Saturday night? Say he was under the anaesthetic, like Minnie. Say he dreamed. If only he had.

Far down the highway a blob shimmered. As it drew nearer it whitened: the Cameron car. It was Don he wanted to see. He kidded himself that he just wanted old history. Any other day he would want it. But Don worked in the next room to hers. Through the wall today he must have heard the rattle of her typing. Did it ever pause? Mr Chowdry he had met before – a nice guy, but there were no questions he wanted to ask Mr Chowdry. Like what was she wearing this morning. Had she twisted up her hair or did it lie like a raven's wing against her cheek? Her cheek had lain on his chest. Had she acted different on Monday? He could not bear her to have to act anything. He would give anything in the world for it not to have happened.

The car drew nearer. Duke switched off the engine. He snapped shut the cold box. He could not be devious; he did not know the method. He would just ask Don a straight question, like was she in the office today? He would bring up her name casually. But he did not know these techniques. Long ago, perhaps, when he was a young man. No, he guessed not even then. He had always said things direct, but then there had been nothing to hide.

The Cameron car stopped on the other side of the road. The driver climbed out and held open the back door. Duke reached forward to eject his cassette, then stopped. Mr Chowdry stepped out, and then Shamime.

He could not move. His tape played on with twangy guitars. She was saying something to the driver, nodding her head and indicating her wristwatch. She was wearing traditional shalwar pyjamas, dark-blue and plain as if she was in mourning. She had a dark dupatta wrapped around her face. She was walking towards his car.

He fumbled with the door catch. His fingers had gone flabby. Big useless hands. He ejected the tape, climbed outside and managed to greet her. He shook hands with Mr Chowdry.

'I'm so sorry about our colleague,' said Mr Chowdry. She was a dark blur beside him.

'He hadn't come back from lunch,' said the blur. Duke turned. Her voice was bright but muffled by the dupatta.

'Apparently he phoned Mary and said he'd be late. Mary forgot to remind him we'd switched it to today.'

Mr Chowdry waved it away with his hand. 'It is not important. Miss Fazli kindly consented to be my escort.'

In fact it was not too important, that part of it. Mr Chowdry's visit was purely a courtesy call; after all there was nothing much to see at this point. Besides, Translux was a turn-key operation; once built and ready for occupation the hotel was out of their hands. Individual managements then took them over. 'And you ride off into the sunset,' Shamime had once said, smiling.

'Let's start this way, with the tomb and shrine,' said Duke and they crossed the highway. Why did she hold the dupatta across her mouth — to protect herself from something? Only the dust?

He started leading them the wrong way, down towards the water — himself, Duke, who forty times had paced this site with architects and engineers.

'Pardon me.' They retraced their tracks between the bushes. He held the thorns aside for his guests to pass. He wanted his hands to be scratched. More than anything he needed to speak to her alone. They arrived at the pathway that sloped uphill. She was walking behind them. She seemed so withheld, swathed darkly and following them like a village wife. He had tried to phone her these past two days but it was always her sister or mother who answered; she had never been at home. And no way could he speak on something so personal by phoning her at the office. Had her mother told her he'd phoned? He felt adolescent, waiting at home for his own phone to ring; jumpy, wandering about the rooms. He felt very old.

They walked up the path. At the top of the mound, ahead of them, stood the mausoleum. It was a heavy, pitted building, eight-sided, made of weathered brick with a domed roof. It had arched doorways each side in the Moghul style, a common feature. Closer you could see the decoration. It was built for some minor ruler four hundred years ago, what was his name, he needed to tell Mr Chowdry, there wasn't much else to tell him — Mir Ali Beg or Mir Ali Khan. Behind it, with just its edge jutting out, stood the saint's shrine.

They walked up through the bazaar. There were stalls full of garlands for the faithful, sticky candy and roasted nuts. The hawkers sat in the shade of the bushes. The place buzzed with flies; there were few people about this sleepy afternoon – a mullah; cripples of all ages come to get cured. Along here Minnie had gripped his hand, squeezing it in her anguish. There were plenty of beggars. These Muslims, for the good of their souls, gave away their small change in the holy places. The beggars who could do it clambered to their feet; the ones who couldn't leant forward rattling their tin bowls. 'Sahib, sahib.' They recognized Duke because he was in the habit of giving five-rupee notes; it had gotten to be embarrassing, walking up here. He guessed the reason might be that soon these stalls would be Translux car park. Mr Chowdry threw little paisa pieces. He looked neat and urbane, with his grey suit and grey hair. Maybe he was superstitious; maybe he was devout.

He tried to concentrate on Mr Chowdry. She was not catching them up. 'You been here before?'

'Ah no, though I have visited many places like this. I'm a Punjab man. Lahore for me. We have so many tombs up there.'

'Plenty of tourists too, lucky fella.' Up in the north of the country the Lahore Translux stood in the centre of town, surrounded by gardens, historic monuments, museums and Kim's cannon. In addition to its natural advantages, tourists passed through on their way to India.

Mr Chowdry glanced around. 'Certainly a new departure for Translux.' He stepped over a piece of dog dirt. He wore shiny pointed shoes, very small.

Lahore had that kind of old-world Raj atmosphere. It was like India up there. Down here it was just desert, an international airport, a port and a big city full of slums with the multi-storey blocks coming up.

'This is where the action is, business-wise,' said Duke. 'So the place is wide open for us. We have to develop the potential, Mr Chowdry, wherever we can find it.' He pointed at the tomb ahead. 'Make a feature of whatever we can grab.'

Behind them Shamime said: 'We had a picnic here once,

when I was a child. Under that tree up there beside the tomb.'

Duke's throat constricted. She moved no nearer them.

'My ayah told me about the *pir*. His head found the place first and his body followed after. Down in the pool the fishes always swim with their heads facing him, never their tails.' She paused. 'It wasn't so run-down then. Nowadays the young bloods don't come here. They hang out at Nazimabad Happyland. That's where the action is.' Her voice was bright and social but still she did not move in beside them, though they had slowed down. 'Lots of slot machines. The car park's full of studs, ten to a Toyota, revving their engines.'

They reached the top of the hill and paused in the shadow of the old mausoleum. It was quiet. There were some trees up here. Shamime stood a little apart from Duke, facing the breeze. The dupatta blew against her mouth.

Duke turned away. Down there lay patchy scrub, the highway and the asbestos works, surrounded by a wire fence. A truck was bumping along in a cloud of dust. Way beyond was the smudged sky where the city lay.

Beside him Mr Chowdry took out a handkerchief and mopped his face. They sat down on the step. Duke pointed out the site below them: the place where the screened-off staff quarters would be, the tennis courts over there, where the animals' home lay at present. The gardens and steps leading up here to the tomb, where they sat.

Minnie had had to sit down here. She said it was the heat; in fact he knew it was the damaged pilgrims who had upset her; the hopelessness of their case. He knew Minnie. She did not want to spoil things for him, when he was so keen. She had tried to show interest in his site. He remembered her efforts to be chatty, all the while her hands clenching. He wished he could shield her from them. From everything else besides.

He tried to show interest in his site, now. He tried to picture it down there amongst the bushes, for Mr Chowdry's sake. 'Steps up to this boundary will have fancy railings in rendered concrete, Moghul-style, ending with a pre-fabricated archway.'

A little apart, Shamime lit a cigarette. Her gold lighter flashed in the sun. He smelt the smoke but he did not dare turn his head. She must despise him; a man twice her age. But she gave no clues, acting as if nothing had happened. Maybe she felt humiliated. He could not bear this. Maybe she felt indifferent. He could not bear this either, but that's what he should be hoping for.

He tried to think of something to say to Mr Chowdry. He turned round and pointed at the doorway behind them. It was set in a larger arch, and the intervening space filled in with honeycombed granite – kind of decorative Islamic ventilation. This patterning, he told Mr Chowdry, was going to be the main personality motif of the Translux, found in the screening of the car park and staff quarters. But mainly, of course, in the hotel proper, both externally and internally: in the latter case, in rigid plastic. Mr Chowdry was wiping his neck with his handkerchief, turning his head from side to side. He had not loosened his tie.

His shirt was unbuttoned. Her neat fingers had done it. 'You're like a grizzly bear,' she had said, stroking his chest. 'Wall-to-wall fur.' She had laid her head against it. She had rubbed her nose in his hairs. 'Are they grey? I can't see in the dark.'

'Pardon me?'

'I was saying, just how will you incorporate this tomb and the shrine behind?' asked Mr Chowdry.

'They remain on public property,' said Duke. 'The Translux land is all to the front of them. There will still be public access from the rear. But even in the public sector, the tourist authorities have undertaken to smarten the place up.'

'The tomb looks vandalized,' said Mr Chowdry. 'People always steal, when monuments are unsupervised. Pieces of marble and mosaic tiles; they sell them to the dealers. Another few years and there would be nothing left. We rely on yourselves, as foreigners, Mr Hanson, to preserve our heritage.'

'Should be a cleaner place for everyone, whether they're Translux guests or not.' He paused, trying to remember what to mention next. Shamime was scratching her leg; the nylon stuff rustled.

Mr Chowdry lit a cigarette. Like most Pakistanis he had beautiful hands. On either side of Duke, Mr Chowdry and Shamime smoked in silence. Duke's hands looked coarse and hairy; freckled slabs. They lay heavily, one on each knee. He felt large and hot and foreign. Perhaps they were bored. How alien was this place to them? After all, they were both Muslims.

Shamime scrunched out her cigarette with her foot. Already he felt protective about her smoking. He wanted to pull her hair loose, where it was caught in her dupatta. He wanted to care for her without being allowed ever to touch her. He wanted to speak to her and explain that it had never happened before, couldn't she tell? And that he hadn't been drunk, no, not that. He had been intoxicated. He was out of his depth. He would die if he never saw her again.

Mr Chowdry cleared his throat. 'You have had good news, I trust, from Mrs Hanson?'

Duke paused. 'Sure, I spoke to her last night. She's recovering fine. Two of the boys are with her.' Shamime was bent forward, gazing at her feet. 'A little discomfort, of course, on account of the stitches.'

Duke scratched his mosquito bites. A small boy approached, barefoot along the platform. Yoked over his shoulders were two pans of nuts. He stepped with care to balance them; they swayed with him.

'*Gram*, sahib?' He held out a paper cone.

'They are in the vicinity, your sons?'

'Sure. One's at college just six blocks away. That's Chester. He'll be graduating in two years.'

The boy stood in front of them, his face sombre. He was wearing shirt and shorts; he had skinny legs, grey and dusty. Chester had been a skinny boy once, before he shot up and filled out. Now he was six feet two, one of the tallest freshmen in his year.

'He's majoring in business studies.'

'Two *annas*, sahib.'

'Sure.' Duke bought three cones, though nobody was hungry. Shamime was unstrapping her high-heeled sandals. He

118

wanted to fold his hands over her feet. He wanted Minnie to be here.

'He hopes to become a sales executive,' he said.

He climbed to his feet. Shamime rose, the sandals in her hand.

'Just going to take a look around the shrine,' she said. 'I'll meet you back at the car.'

Duke stood still with surprise. She turned to go. The shrine lay behind the tomb. They walked a few steps with her; it came into view. It was a turreted building, kind of plain and small. Modern, compared to the mausoleum. Its whitewashed walls were dappled with shadow from the trees. There was nobody about but a man with a basket of flowers. Shamime bought a garland and pulled the dupatta around her face. She ducked her head to enter, her blue robes flapping.

Duke himself had never entered the place. Minnie had put it into words, saying it was their shrine. She was sensitive about that.

'Would you care to go in, Mr Chowdry?'

Mr Chowdry shook his head with a polite smile. Was this a site visit on Shamime's part, or had she gone in to pray?

They made their way down through the bushes.

'It must be a little frustrating,' said Mr Chowdry, 'waiting for the final permission.'

'You bet. Just one piece of paper. We're raring to go. I've two earthmovers contracted to Translux at three hundred bucks a day. They're just waiting for the word. And the structural steel in a high-security compound back in Karachi. It's getting to be expensive.'

The boy was following them; Duke could hear the creak of the yoke. Amongst the bushes lay a few lesser graves, you always found them clustered around the shrines. They were simple plaster blocks the size of coffins.

'These, I presume, will be shifted?' asked Mr Chowdry.

'Sure. We've entered Translux land. They'll be moved round the back of the hill where the village is — leastways those few huts. The tourist office didn't even know they were here.'

119

'And the dead, I presume, will make no objection,' smiled Mr Chowdry.

Duke tried to smile, too, at the little joke. He glanced behind him, beyond the bushes and the boy, at the turreted roof of the shrine. Within there stood Shamime. Or maybe she knelt. Was she praying for her lost virtue? Last Sunday he had sat in the chapel, in a congregation of six, and prayed for his.

'I believe they go there to pray for offspring.'

Duke was startled. Mr Chowdry had also stopped. 'And the warm water from the tanks, I believe, is also claimed to cure a large number of diseases. Every disease, no doubt. The simpler the worshippers, the more prodigal the claims. But it's mainly for the babies, I've heard.'

Minnie, with your stitched belly. Duke scratched his bites. They ringed his flesh at waist level. It must have been Saturday night they had stung. He had inflamed them with his scratching; he wanted them to get worse. At Mohurrum these Muslim men whipped themselves for their sins, until their backs dripped like meat.

They made their way through the bushes, the boy following. Duke held the paper cornets. He felt warm towards this small, precise man who had sat next to Shamime in the automobile and who was sharing this afternoon. Ahead lay the pool. It was muddy; its shores were pitted with hoof prints. Local goat herds watered here but alternative arrangements, involving pipes, would be made for them. Down this side of the water, right by the shore, stood the hot spring. Duke had been disappointed with this. It was kind of plain: a stone tank with steps leading down into it. But the water steamed, all of its own accord. Three young men wearing loincloths sat on the rim, their legs dangling. They stopped talking and stared at Duke and Mr Chowdry.

'There are two tanks,' said Duke. 'One beyond the tomb, without a pond, and this one. The first remains on public land. But this one, and the pond, is what we aim to develop.' It was easier talking without Shamime here to confuse him. He gathered momentum. A few yards up the slope the boy shifted his shoulders, adjusting his yoke, and sat down. Duke could feel his gaze.

'At the beginning, the personality factor posed some problems. At the Lahore Tranny, of course, you have the Kipling motif, with your illustrated wall-panels, the Mowgli Suite and the rest.'

'I was telling the charming Miss Fazli about the latest innovation in our Coffee Shop.' Mr Chowdry picked from a cone and started munching. 'Kim-Burgers. And for this trial month, with every Bumper Kim-Burger we're giving away a free portion of french fries and a cannon ballpoint-stand for the kiddies.'

'Great.' Duke laid down his cones.

'*Gram*, sahib?' The boy half-rose.

Duke shook his head, pointing to the remaining cones. The boy sat down again, lowering his pans. He could not be older than eleven, but then you could not tell with some of these kids. They weren't fixed as children, like the snapshots of his boys at eleven.

'So here we plan to feature the Wishing Well.'

'Wishing Well?'

Duke pointed to the tank. 'We keep the steps and rebuild the wall with fancy brickwork, same as the tomb, with coloured plastic inlay in the old style. We build a rail around, for folk to lean over, build a pavilion roof, and there's your Wishing Well. Guests will be encouraged to throw in their small change, paisa pieces like you give to the beggars, but this time it'll be in aid of charity.'

'You are a man of imagination, Mr Hanson. And the pond?'

'You're no longer looking at an insanitary puddle, you're looking at a boating lake. Six times the size – according to our expert, the natural water source can fill at least six times the capacity it's filling now. At the far end we'll have a barbecue pavilion and bandstand for local-type music – sitars and such – and displays of traditional dancing. And the opposite shore from the hotel we'll have the chalets.'

'Ah yes?'

'Sure. Lakeside accommodation with road access round the rear. Eight units, fully air-conditioned of course, with bathroom en suite and personal car port. They'll have a beautiful view of the hotel across the water and, behind them, the hill with the tomb. We have permission from the tourist office to install spotlights. I have in mind some kind of *son et lumière*.'

'Your enthusiasm is infectious, Mr Hanson. I must say, when I first looked at this place ... And the landscaping?'

'For a job this radical we've found nobody — ' Duke coughed, 'uh, can't seem to find any suitable contractors in your country, so I've flown in a team of experts — American-trained; I worked with them in the Gulf. Before that they'd been responsible for the revolutionary Abu Dhabi Translux — the one with the underground gardens. They'll be importing the top-soil, turf and so on. Astroturf in recreational areas. Plus half-mature trees and decorative shrubs. It'll be an overnight transformation. High-cost outlay, but otherwise you wait twenty years for the place to look good. And it's going to look good. Mr Chowdry, my heart's in this one.'

'It is your baby, as they say. I am right?'

'Sure. There's something about this place. I've even taken to dreaming about it.'

They gazed across the water. Shamime had told him about the fishes, swimming with their heads toward the shrine. He had imagined them like bright silver filings drawn towards a magnet. But his irrigation engineer had found little evidence of aquatic life, the place was so polluted. There was a silence. Up the slope behind them, the boy hawked and spat like an old man. Duke wanted to explain that he was doing this because he was ambitious not for money but for his homeland. He wanted to bring the best of his country to this one. He felt it like a missionary. It was the hygiene he wanted to bring — hygiene in body and spirit, in business-dealings too. A clean world unmuddied by caste and corruption. Here the water was dirty. Only in a clean world was there a chance for everyone, as there had been a chance for himself, Duke Warren Hanson. But how could he put this into words for a Pakistani, even the Under-Manager of a Translux? Mr Chowdry would be offended. And to Shamime? He did not like to tell her in case she mocked him.

Besides, she just might say: who's so incorruptible now?

They left the waterside and made their way back up through the bushes. The boy rose to his feet but he did not follow them. They walked past a food stall with its hissing lumps of batter. A family sat on the mat, eating.

Mr Chowdry indicated them, smiling: 'I think you shall attract a different class of customer, Mr Hanson.'

My hotel will be classless, Duke wanted to say. Sure you had to have the money, but who the hell would mind what job you did? Who would mind if your uncle was a minister? No sign of Shamime here. He hadn't seen her for so long that he felt clumsy and nervous again.

Both cars stood empty. The Cameron driver emerged from a tea stall. In Duke's hand, the cones were scrumpled paper balls. When could he speak to her?

He fetched two Cokes. When he straightened up from the car she was there.

'Phew. Wow. It's hot. Can't you just dome-in this whole place, Duke, like Houston or wherever, and air-condition the lot?'

He fetched another Coke. She unwound her dupatta, twisting her head to pull it off. Her hair was damp around her face. 'It's sweet, the shrine. Very kitsch, with a puce nylon shroud, all scattered with the flowers of the faithful.'

Duke grunted. Half, he was relieved that she hadn't been uttering prayers. Half, he felt she should.

'Humbugs,' said Shamime cheerfully, 'most of them. Sham miracle-workers. God I need a drink.' She took the can. 'Then we ought to be getting back, Mr Chowdry.'

'I have a reception at six,' said Mr Chowdry. 'A family wedding. But I would so much like to hear more about the hotel itself. I've had a most interesting introduction to its outdoor facilities.'

Shamime paused. 'I know. Duke, you go back with Mr Chowdry, then you can talk.' She had the can to her lips. 'I'll drive your car. After all, I know how to work the starter.'

The Coke fizzed in his mouth. She mentioned it so casually.

123

Mr Chowdry walked towards the Cameron car. She was waiting for something. She stood near enough for him to make out the stitching, small fancy coils, around her collar and down the front. She lifted her hand towards him, a half-gesture. He opened his mouth to speak.

'Duke — the key?'

'Uh. Sure.'

He rummaged in his pocket, holding his can in the other hand. She took the key and climbed into his automobile, smiling up at him for the first time. In the dashboard ashtray lay the stubs of her cigarettes from last Saturday. He disapproved deeply of smoking but he could not bring himself to clean them out.

She drove ahead. For a while they kept up with her. She had opened the window. Her hair flew loose in the wind like black snakes; they whipped and tangled. The blue sleeve billowed. Before she had looked muffled; now she looked released, with her wild hair splaying.

Her hair in his mouth. She was lying on his chest, turning her head this way and that, rubbing it against his face. 'Dook, Dook,' she murmured. She mimicked his accent; he tried to lift her face and push back her hair to see if she was smiling.

Duke rubbed his belly. The bites burned. He had not seen her body, only felt it smooth as an eel. He pictured Minnie's familiar stomach — flat, sallow skin softened by childbearing; the grey pucker of her appendix scar. 'Life has made its mark,' she had once said with that grave smile. It hadn't mattered to him, though how could he persuade her of that now, after what he had done? It would be so obvious to her: a young body instead of a known, used one. If only he could persuade himself it was that simple. Nobody would be harmed then.

Her belly was altered now. He himself had not seen its tacky black stitches. Right now he felt responsible. It was his wound.

He was telling Mr Chowdry about the proposed conference facilities. Shamime drove recklessly. Ahead his Datsun dissolved in the heat haze. He could not grasp her; she mocked him with her teasing hair and her teasing voice. He must let her drive away.

124

15

CHRISTINE had bought the seeds her first week out here. She had filled a Cameron dinner platter with soil. (British Home Stores china.) These at least I can germinate. And five weeks later some had sprouted; just a few. Cosmea: their branched leaves, feathery frail, had opened like babies' hands.

She knelt in the flowerbed. A strip of sand ran round three walls of the compound, the fourth side being the driveway which was edged with flowerpots. She dug with a spoon she had stolen from the kitchen. It was not the time for planting. *Tips for the Tropics* made it clear that winter, not summer, was the growing season. But why not, if she kept them watered? Her little seedlings must take root.

She must do something. It was all right for Donald, out at the office all day. He was part of the working city; he arrived home perspiring, drained but elated, with his briefcase full of papers. He had taken root.

She put a seedling into the hole. Three pairs of eyes watched her. These belonged to Mohammed's girls. Christine poured in the water and the seedling floated on its side. The water drained away; she held the plant straight and pressed in the soil around it.

Mohammed's wife called the children, her voice a high wail. Easy to think her fat, Christine had told herself several times, rather than pregnant. She herself had not dared go near the quarters since that visit to the doctor's a week ago. She felt too embarrassed. But she also felt obscurely rebuffed, that the woman had not given her the occasional smile since then. After all, they had sat in the surgery, two women together; they had practically held hands. Sisters under the skin.

The children did not leave. They just moved back a few steps, probably to get a better view. She firmed in the seedling. Perhaps Mohammed was watching, stilled during his morning's toil. Recently she had not spoken much to him, either. Before, there had been the odd moment of domestic intimacy — when she had tried, laughingly, to use his mosquito spray; when she had pointed out Joyce's children in her dressing-table snapshot. Since last week she had been avoiding any social conversation. Just once she had asked him where this hot water man was — 'kidder', she knew the word for 'where'. But he had taken her to the gate, pointed into the distance and gabbled a stream of words. In fact she had also asked Rosemary (Reckitts Rosemary, because her husband was in Reckitt and Colman), when thanking her for that drinks party. 'Hot water man?' Rosemary thought she was inquiring about a plumber and had gone on about their unreliability and how her shower unit was already cracked. She could not ask Donald; he would want to know why and that would make her shy.

Beyond the wall a car drove by, blaring its horn. She could see nothing from here. She must get past this wall and into the city. It was no good walking around here; it was just modern streets and chowkidars staring. And it was not getting into the place, to drive to Rosemary's or Sally's and drink lime sodas while they discussed tennis fixtures and the heat. To think that she was now the sort of woman who waited for her husband's key in the lock. Except that he did not have to open the door because Mohammed was there to do it for him.

The problem was, she had lost Sultan's card. Yesterday she had taken a taxi to Nazimabad but it must have been the wrong part, perhaps West. 'Kidder East?' He had driven her to an amusement arcade, a dispiriting place called Happyland.

126

Heaven knew what he thought she wanted. And the office buildings had all looked the same. She could not find his name in the phone book, but then it was full of misprints. Sultan Rahim had disappeared back into the city.

She gazed at the seedlings. They looked frail; some were crooked. Behind her she could hear the children breathing. Sometimes she tried to speak to them, but they just hid their faces like their mother and ran behind the house.

She stood up. The girls scattered, with muffled squeaks. She straightened a leaning seedling. She had always presumed to have children some time, at her own convenience; everyone did, didn't they. She had not bothered to put it into words. Motherhood was a glow on the horizon if she cared to turn her head in that direction. They had talked about everything else, herself and Roz and Cassie, those long smoky afternoons in the shop. More accurately: they discussed in detail the outcome — the career compromise, the child-sharing, father participation, individual fulfilment and all that. But they had never discussed what would happen if one could not have a child at all. Choice was what they discussed: women's choice for this and for that. Choice, all in their heads. They had never thought of their bodies making the choice for them.

She wiped her hands on her trousers. Donald was coming home for lunch; he sometimes did. Then he would return to the busy city where his work waited. Already her seedlings drooped in the sun. Alien, English plants; would they ever root themselves in this foreign soil? She was the same as them, wilting.

A pip-pip outside the gate. Donald was back. Mohammed emerged from the house and walked up the drive. Why could not Donald open the gate himself? It looked so silly, sitting in the car. But then he did not blare his horn like some of their neighbours; just an apologetic bleat as if his car was clearing its throat. Sometimes this disarmed her. Sometimes it irritated her. If he was going to wait on his rights ('After all, darling, it's what we pay the chap for'), at least he could do it in the Pakistani manner.

Mohammed stood aside as Donald drove in. Mohammed found it a relief when Donald returned; she sensed this increasingly. There was a rhythm between the two men, as if they had been rehearsing for this all their lives. Centuries of assumptions were taken for granted. She walked to the porch. She was the loose attachment in this machinery.

Mohammed carried in the briefcase. Donald did not kiss her, with the bearer there in the hall. In fact he seldom touched her when Mohammed was on duty.

'Phew.' He laid his jacket on the hall chair. 'Hot, eh?' He turned to Mohammed. *'Bahut garum.'*

When alone, she dismissed Mohammed and made herself a sandwich. Today the table was laid for a proper lunch. The ceiling fan turned; the cloth lifted, revealing the table-legs. Mohammed had still not learnt about the mats. Instead of the plain ones he had put out Ann Smythe's nursery set. Perhaps he was a child at heart. Today she had the elephants and Donald had the teddies. From the kitchen came discreet clinks and the smell of frying.

'Pleasant morning?' asked Donald.

'The fish-wallah came to the gate, so I bought some interesting little local fishes, I couldn't understand the name. Then I read a bit ... ' She paused. She sounded like someone from the last century. But then it was the last century here, for women. 'Then I planted out those seedlings from the spare bedroom.'

'Good. You must get mali to water them thoroughly. He's a sly old bugger, you know. Always creeping off.'

She straightened her spoon. 'Oh, I've given him leave.'

'What?'

'I told you before,' she lied. 'I'm sure I did.'

'Told me what?'

'I'm still paying him, of course. It wouldn't be fair otherwise. But I told him he needn't work here any more; I'll be doing it. He'll soon get something else because of my card at the B.W.A.' Mention of this should soften Donald; he liked her to be in touch with the B.W.A.

'But Christine ... ' He stared at her. His nose was still peeling;

128

it remained crimson since last week at that donkey place. 'You can't do that.'

'Why not? It's my household. I'm supposed to be in charge of something, aren't I?'

'I don't think you understand.' He jerked his head towards the kitchen and lowered his voice. 'They must think we're mad.'

'The mali didn't look surprised.' This was true. In fact he never did. Perhaps he was simply too old to be surprised by the English. Mohammed had translated to him, laboriously. Then he had ambled down the drive, tucking the rupee notes into the fold of his pyjamas. Mohammed had stood at the window, impassive as a plaster dummy in a catering shop.

'Christine, it's just understood that you can't give these people money for nothing. I presumed you'd realized that. They lose all respect.' He gazed at her seriously. Under the inflamed nose he was growing a moustache; as yet it was blonde stubble. 'It's not being kind; in fact it's rather cruel. They learn a begging mentality, expecting something for nothing.'

'You used to say that in England, about Social Security scroungers.'

'But here there's nothing to fall back on, don't you see? You can do awful damage that way.' He gazed down at the teddies. 'You take away a man's self-respect, and that's often all he has.'

'I'd think he'd love a hundred rupees a month. I don't want him. *I* want to do it.'

'You mustn't think about yourself. You have a responsibility to these people.'

'Don't call them "these people".'

'You're only here for a year or two. It's like ... well, feeding the birds in winter, then going away without warning. They've got used to your charity, so they lose all self-reliance.'

She gazed at him, charmed by the simile. Then he spoilt it.

'Besides, you don't know how to do it.'

'What, water a lawn?'

He lowered his voice again. 'I mean, Mohammed's work. I know you're dying to inch him out. After all, the Smythes had a

129

sweeper too, and you got rid of him. But don't you understand how nice it is to come home to a clean house?'

A silence. 'Ah. So that's it. All this airy-fairy stuff about self-respect – '

'No – '

' – doesn't mean anything. You're complaining about the way I kept the flat.'

'Oh come on, let's not drag that up. You know I longed to be able to afford someone then, so you could be free to do something more interesting ... '

'Except I just flitted from job to job and never got down to anything interesting. And I was a hopeless homemaker as well.' She looked down at the elephants, trunk to tail. And I can't even give you children. Or you can't give them to me.

'I thought it would be a relief,' said Donald. 'I used to feel so guilty, hearing you banging about in the kitchen and feeling I ought to be basting the blessed chicken or whatever.'

Mohammed entered with the dishes. They fell silent. The fan stirred the sullen air. A fishcake was put on to her plate. She had asked him to cook the fish the local way, the way his family would eat it. Grilled with spices or however they did it. This must have taken hours, with all those little bones to take out. Mohammed served the vegetables and went into the kitchen.

'He thinks', she whispered, 'that we want it English-style.'

'Perhaps he doesn't know how to cook these fish. Maybe he can't afford them. How much were they?'

'Forgotten.'

'There you are. He can't afford to be vague.'

'You're getting at me again.'

'I'm not. Don't you see, I *want* you to be able to be vague. I want you to be free.'

'To do what?' In the kitchen Mohammed coughed. She kept her voice low. 'I can't work. I'm a woman, aren't I.' She pushed the nursery food around her plate. She disliked the petulant tone in her own voice. 'Will you drop me off in town this afternoon?'

'Uh-huh. Doing some shopping?'

'No. I want to try and find this man I was talking about, this Sultan Rahim.'

'I'm looking forward to that beach hut.'

'But the job too. I told you, he said he might be able to get me one.'

'Does anyone know this chap? Is he all right?'

'He had lots of visiting cards. He was so nice and willing. I'm only going to ask a man in Bohri Bazaar. He probably won't know where he is. I can take a taxi back. Please let me do something for myself.'

She struggled with the pink blancmange. It kept slipping off the serving spoon. Mohammed waited, holding the bowl. What was he thinking, standing so near, his brown hands nearly touching hers? What could she touch in this country?

After lunch Donald had to sort out some papers. He crossed to his study. He wore a short-sleeved bush shirt, tight beige. He was gaining weight, no doubt about it. Though shorter than Duke he was built rather the same—solid and sandy, with freckled fuzzy arms. But Duke was solid, whereas Donald was soft. He had been fed by fussy women all his childhood. They had waited, like Mohammed waited now, while he helped himself. He had hardly cooked a meal in his life. Even when he had lived in his London bedsitter he had stocked up at Brinton each weekend, returning with packages tenderly wrapped in foil.

She walked around the living-room, pulling forward the chairs Mohammed always lined against the wall, as in a waiting-room. Waiting for what? The way Donald ruffled through those papers irritated her. So did his little moustache, his effort to be manly. Perhaps it was the heat. In the old days they sent the women away during the hot season. For their marriages' sake, no doubt, as much as for the women's. Then the men could get on with the real work, like moving paper from one side of the desk to the other. Outside the walls people seethed in the streets. Only the laundered ones entered, to serve the tea or flatter the English with their Balliol accents. With the weight of tradition behind him Donald had grown so stiff here, stiff and self-conscious. He had always been so in public places and here it was public everywhere — servants in the house, people in the streets. Even alone he could not really relax; he still acted upon other people's expectations of him. But then he had always clung to structures — his school, to which he still returned for reunions; Cameron's with its old reassurances.

But then she had relied upon this, in him. She had mocked it, but turned to him when she wanted to be safe. She remembered one holidays when she was sixteen. In those days it was like renting a brother for the summer. She could run off, temporarily wild, but he was always ready with the towel to dry her, ready with the handkerchief to blow her nose. She had caught him gazing at her but he had hardly touched her. Other boys had done that. Royce, in particular. That summer Royce had been camping on the Downs, Royce from Royston, or was it somewhere else? She had not even known how he spelt his name but Jesus had she wanted him. He had black hair and nicotine-stained fingers; he had driven her too fast on his motorbike. One night he had taken her into the concrete bunker on the beach, that smelt of lavatories. Why could he not have lain with her under the stars? She had been running along the surf; her bare legs were wet. He had pressed her against the wall, his zips scratching her. Give me time, she had called out silently, for me to make this all right. But he had just pushed and rutted, hurting her. On the return journey she had not danced along the sand. She had gone to Donald's house. The lights were off. She had stood on the lawn. An ordinary little bungalow, just like the others. She had looked at Donald's curtained window, thinking: Do you know how much I need you now? Only the cat came out and rubbed against her legs. Perhaps it was not for any man that she had been skipping through the surf. Perhaps it had just been for herself, a sixteen-year-old, those stars up there winking.

She had told him later when their relationship had changed. He had been so sorrowful, and furious with himself that he had not realized through telepathy. Touchingly he had even tried to make a weak joke, something about Rolling with Royce. He had been just right. Not exciting; just right. They had fitted together. She had even borrowed his clothes, him being her size, and forgot to give them back when she left for London. He was so mild; she took advantage of him.

Years later she had watched *One-Eyed Jacks* on the TV with Roz. There was Marlon Brando, packed with muscle, pushing open bar doors. Big with pride he sacrificed everything to get even with the man who had humiliated him. 'Imagine a woman doing that,' said Roz. 'Imagine a woman *minding* whether she's the biggest shot.'

'Donald doesn't mind,' said Christine. 'Thank goodness.'

But in her blood she yearned for Brando, with his slicked black hair. Donald had never been dangerous. Upstairs one of Roz's babies had started crying. Roz had sighed; her face was pale above her second-hand matted jumper. She was always wearing that jumper; it had little bunches of grapes sewn on it.

At that time Donald and herself were already trying to have a baby. She had not mentioned this to Roz; nor the fact that after the incident with Royce years back she had missed two periods.

'Penny for them?'

Donald stood there with his briefcase. She loathed that expression *penny for them*. She shook her head and rose from the sofa. Of course she had not told Donald either about the missed periods nor the unusually heavy one afterwards. It had proved nothing, and even if it had she dared not be sure, for both their sakes.

They drove down to Bohri Bazaar. It was crowded; they were pushed from side to side.

'Sahib want to change dollars?'

'What I was trying to say at lunch', said Donald, 'is that I don't think you ought to be gadding about.'

'I'm not. I'm looking for bloody work.'

'You looking for onyx, madam? Please step this side.'

'You're not in England, Christine. You're always telling me that *I'm* so unadaptable ... you must respect their ways, you see. That doesn't mean wearing their blessed clothes — it's a bit subtler than that.'

'Yes madam you like camel-skin lamp?'

'No thank you,' said Donald. 'You might be putting yourself in the wrong position. It's you I'm worried about, Christine. They'll take advantage of you, and it won't be their fault. Not entirely.'

'For you, special low price. Only fifty rupees.'

'Things that are perfectly all right in England are offensive to them here. They're Muslims.'

'I *know* they're Muslims. Honestly, Donald. Anyway I still think it's you we're talking about. Your position here, as manager. As representative Brit. You're the one who stands to be offended. It's that awful male pride again. Years ago I thought you had less than most; that was why I liked you.'

'Do keep your voice down.'

'This place has just brought it out into the open. It's made for it.'

'Do stop dividing things into male and female. *Male* pride. You never used to separate the human race like this. God it's hot.'

'But it was there. You were just subtler about hiding it.'

'Less upfront, eh?'

'You still want me to somehow be a reinforcement to you. I can be independent, but on your terms. Colonialist, you see. Like your grandad with his native troops.'

'They weren't native. *My* terms. Good grief. What about all those notes stuck into the hall mirror when I got home? *Pizza in fridge.* Horrible bought pizza with not enough cheese in it. Did I complain?'

'Frequently. But subtly. You were snide about my friends.'

'They were snide about me.'

'For you, thirty rupees.'

'No thank you. Do buzz off. Look Christine, can't we continue this enlightening discussion back home?'

'There you are—sarcasm. That's one of your weapons.'

'They couldn't call me dominating and oppressive, so they called me subversively dominating and oppressive. Or whatever. Some terrible jargon. We men can't win.'

'Sahib please step this side. Beautiful necklace for memsahib.'

'Look I must go. I've got an appointment at three.'

'All genuine silver. Beautiful lowest price.'

'What was it they said? All men are colonialists.' He laughed. 'Women are the native states, waiting to be invaded.'

'Don't make fun of it, Donald. It only shows how insecure you are.'

'Oh God.'

She watched him leave, edging sideways through the crowd. He shook his head at one man, waving his empty hands. Despite his anger, he was so well-mannered. Not for him, the pushing and blustering, Royce-style. It was sad, that even his niceness irritated her.

16

THE place smelt of sweet perfume and drains. She picked her way around the cloudy puddles. Above her rose the tall, crumbling houses of the Old City. This alley was lined with bottles — plastic bottles, whisky bottles, rows of them and all of them empty. Somebody had once mentioned this Bottle Bazaar. In one booth a man was filling scent phials. Ahead of her the nephew searched for Mr Rahim. She slowed down behind his grimy, pyjama'd figure. She seemed for ever to be following men, their clothes flapping in the breeze, like guides through the underworld.

Nearing the end of the alley, he approached a table. Would Sultan Rahim think it odd, her seeking him out like this? Perhaps, as Donald had hinted, he would get the wrong idea.

He sat with another man, drinking Pepsi. He rose to his feet and shook her hand vigorously.

'Salaam ale'icum. It is Mrs Manley, walking down our humble thoroughfare like a film star in her black spectacles.'

He was sleeker than she remembered: a handsome man in a ripe, dark, shiny way, amiable as a seal with his oiled hair. A man doing well; a man in his prime. Unlike Donald he carried his stomach proudly, the fruit of his success. He gave her a chair, snapped his fingers for more Pepsi and bade farewell to the nephew. Today he wore green shalwar-kamise pyjamas, freshly laundered.

'This is most excellent timing,' he said. 'I am seeing my close friend in half a tick. Already I have been telling him of this charming young lady.'

She paused. Why hadn't he phoned her, then? But already she knew that one did not ask questions like that.

'About the beach hut?' she asked.

'That will be in hand, but first things first. My friend, he shows much interest in this English girl with the beautiful curls on her head.'

She put her hand to her frizz. 'Oh, good ... ' The Pepsi arrived in a smeared glass. On the tray were three packets of leaves.

'You have tried our *pan*?' asked Sultan. She nodded untruthfully. 'I have ordered a special cooling *pan*. It is the most mild.'

She took the package. She had seen these being prepared on the pavements, men squatting with their little brass pots, painting leaves with lime paste and seeds, then folding them into parcels. She watched Sultan and his companion, a placid old man with white hair wispy as a baby. They popped the packets into their mouths. The old man's gums and teeth were stained red from it. She popped in hers and nearly choked.

'Good?'

She could only nod, gagged with paint and what felt like pebbles. It was sickeningly perfumed; stalks and seeds stuck in her teeth. She tried to smile. Sultan smiled back, a fond uncle, and continued his business negotiations in Urdu.

She looked at the stall. It looked one of the more prosperous, with *Bashir Bottle Shop* written in English above the door. Plastic cannisters hung in bundles, like gourds. On the ground lay a sack of scent bottles, all Coty bubble-shaped, familiar from her mother's dressing-table. In the window stood drinks bottles, clean and shining, Johnnie Walker, Dimple, empty vessels from somebody else's good times. Perhaps some were from her own. Last week a bottle-wallah had stopped outside the gate; she had found none to give him. Presumably Mohammed had brought them down here himself. Nobody could afford to waste things in this place. Rubbish belonged to the West, not to the sub-continent.

Sultan had finished his conversation. Hamster-like she shifted the package into her cheek. 'How much does someone get when they bring in a whisky bottle?'

'For real Scotch, imported Scotch, enough for a dish of *dal* and chapattis.'

'You have a business here?'

'I have business every part. My business is resembling our great mother Indus. As she nears the ocean she flows into many creeks.'

'And when she reaches the sea you'll be a millionaire.'

He laughed, slapping his thigh. The other man gazed politely. She moved the package to the other side. How could she get rid of it? Everyone else spat, the pavements splashed red as if violence had occurred.

'Come.' Sultan rose to his feet. He brushed down his pyjamas, spick and span. 'My conveyance is waiting.'

Her mouth was still stuffed with fibres. He was unlocking his car. What was this job exactly and who was his very good friend? Donald might have made a joke about this: You've bitten off more than you can chew.

She turned and disgorged the mess into her hand. She dropped it on the street. Her hand was smeared red. She could feel the faces above her, peering round shutters. Swiftly she wiped her hand on her trousers; these being black — loose native things — it did not show.

They swerved away, bumping across the tramlines of Bunder Road, the widest thoroughfare in the Old City. The street was congested and hazy with exhaust smoke. She clutched the window handle. She felt the same as the last time she had sat in this furred interior: a strange mixture of excitement and torpor. In her stomach the lunchtime blancmange, safe nursery food, mixed with the bitter juices she had swallowed. Though a middle-aged man and plumper than Royce, Sultan drove as recklessly. Is this what she wanted, a man with oily hair, foreign to her, driving her too fast?

The manager's office was panelled in fake walnut; at first glance

138

it appeared genuine. The air-conditioner was veneered to match; it hummed beneath its blistered laminate. Her clothes cooled against her skin. Outside in the corridor people waited; she had seen them when she was ushered in. Perhaps they had waited all afternoon. None of them had looked surprised to see her enter first; people never did.

It was an advertising agency. There were no windows. Upon the walls hung Superad's framed success stories. A photo showed cotton reels: *Tasneem Textiles: The Threads of Integrity*. Another said: *By The Grace of Allah We Are Now A 200-Crore Bank*.

She sat opposite the desk, thinking: there is nobody so suave as a suave Pakistani. The manager, whose name she had failed to catch, was continuing his interrupted telephone conversation and also smiling at her encouragingly. He wore a tie and a spotless white shirt; unlike Sultan he looked the sort of Pakistani she met at cocktail parties. He was middle-aged, with a heavy sculptured face and black corrugated hair like a matinée idol. His sideburns were greying.

' ... *aap sey mil kar baten karney hain Pepsi* ... '

One of the photos showed a familiar advertisement. It was a tractor standing against the sunset, with a pile of sacks in the foreground. *Bags of Success with Camerons Nitrogen-Rich H212 Fertilizer*.

' ... *samaghtey hain Superad, kidder* ... '

He put the phone down, opened a small, wallpapered cubbyhole and passed the phone back.

'My most sincere apologies, Mrs Manley. Let us return to yourself. I'm so delighted to make your acquaintance.' He pointed to the photograph. 'As you see, our little agency is proud to carry the Cameron account. And I counted myself amongst the Smythes' friends. Charming couple, charming.'

They gleamed at each other. Donald could hardly object to this. In fact it was almost too respectable. She had expected another dirty alley; she felt both relieved and disappointed. Here she was, back with the Balliol accents.

'Our mutual friend Sultan-sahib says you would like a little part-time work, something to amuse you.'

'I'd like work. I do have a degree in English, and I have done some writing.' She looked at the photo, silently adding that she could do a good deal better herself. Bags of Success, indeed. 'I sent a story to a woman's magazine once, and they wrote a very nice letter back.'

Through the wall the phone rang. The square of wallpaper opened and an arm offered the receiver. As he spoke she worked on slogans. Here in Karachi she could jump in at the top. Who needed training when one possessed the English language itself?

' ... *main chahti hun ...* '

With a new hand at the helm, Cameron will be sailing through the seventies; Donald Manley has his eye on the horizon but his feet on the ground ...

She was no longer the wife back home; she was the prop of the company, dining on expenses, like Shamime, at the Intercontinental Tandoori Room.

' ... *mujhey karney hain ... Mrs Manley ...* '

She stiffened. He was looking at her as he spoke. His brown eyes were moist with sincerity. Maybe he was already recommending her to the copywriting department and fixing up a trial campaign. She was sitting behind a desk, rotating thoughtfully on her swivel chair, tapping her teeth with her biro while the Superad Agency waited, poised.

He passed back the phone. 'I have been mentioning your good name to an acquaintance of mine. Here at Superad we pride ourselves on the up-to-date styles — our clients include the most modern hotels and the most prominent businesses. Like a tree, we have many branches reaching out in every direction — '

A knock on the door. Someone entered with an urgent message. She moved on from Cameron Chemicals to Duke's hotel. Apparently it was going to be built around some wishing lake. He had described it to her. Translux would be a Superad account; she would extol its azure waters (would they understand azure?), the mod cons, and the quaint customs of the surrounding countryside. Above the manager's desk was a giant Tourist Board advertisement. It was divided into gaily-coloured sections: a village girl looking like Elizabeth Taylor, yachts in full sail, some mellow old mosques she did not recognize, and various costumed groups in festive mood. *Welcome to Karachi*, it said. *Discover the Timeless Mystery of the Orient*. Where had they taken the photos? It was not a Pakistan she knew. After seeing that, newcomers might be somewhat surprised by this crammed, humid city with its office blocks, slums and peeling industrial developments. She must make a good job of Duke's hotel.

The man left. The manager turned back to her, making a steeple of his hands. 'Here at Superad, Mrs Manley, we say that we are in the honesty business. We do not bend the truth. I am a devout man. In the Koran, the Prophet tells each man to look into his own heart—'

The wallpaper opened. He waved the phone away. 'We do not call black white and white black. That is not our business. If it was, we would not be the most successful agency in Karachi. More importantly, we would not be sleeping at night. The Muslim, Mrs Manley, is alone with his conscience. He must shed his outer layers and be standing revealed. We are in the appearance business, make no mistake, I do not deny that, but appearances are deceiving. This is what I am reminding myself every hour of every day. Our Prophet has no image. He is not a bearded fellow in the sky, begging your pardon—he is the space where every man is facing his own soul.'

He came to rest, flexing his fingers. Someone else knocked on the door. He called out something. She wondered about the unrestive queue. The wall clock had stopped at 10.15 but the room had the air of one endless afternoon. Sultan was the same—the frenetic driving, then the relapse into timelessness. All bustle and horn-blowing, then . . . next week, next year, *insh'allah*. Beach hut? Job? Hand on the heart, eyes vague, phone ringing.

She paused. 'So you think I might be able to work with you?'

'It is great good fortune that our paths have crossed each other, facilitated by Sultan-sahib. A fruitful future awaits us, of

141

this I am sure. You have recently arrived in our country, Mrs Manley, I am right? This is our method — I put business his way, he mine. Our emblem, you have perhaps observed, is the joined hands.' He pointed to a plaque on his empty desk.

'That's marvellous.'

'Let us get down to the nitty gritty. My photographer, on the telephone, expressed a wish for the trial shots.'

'Photographer?'

'The best in Karachi, let me assure you. He has worked in Madison Avenue, New York City.' He was gazing at her over the steepled hands. 'May I speak frankly? I am fifty-six years old and have learnt the lessons. It is a question of many things, amongst them the dress.'

She sat very still.

'We are in the image business. The image does not tell lies. It is made, how shall I say,' he moved his hands, 'more so, or less so, according to the needs.'

'You mean, what I'm wearing?'

'We are fast becoming a prosperous country, but our eyes are looking to the West. In matters of sophistication and the successful life-style, that is. To put it simply: the European face means status — it is conjuring up like magic the good things — the possessions to which our people are turning their hopes and their expectations.'

'And me?'

'Let my admiration be honest. You have the beautiful peaches and cream complexion and the charming English curls.'

A Battle Frizz, Donald had called her hair the day she returned from the hairdresser's. Something about a Brillo Pad.

'Just a little work on the make-up and the clothes.' He leant forward. Over the slotted fingers his gaze took in her muslin blouse, crumpled from her bazaar wanderings; it took in the black loose trousers with drawstring waist; it took in the rubber flip-flops and her toes, as grimy as a mali's from her morning in the flowerbed.

'So you don't want me to write?'

'That is not necessary. Just to observe your good self is recommendation enough. That face, it needs no curriculum vitae.'

'I mean, write advertisements for you?'

He raised his eyebrows. 'Mrs Manley, what you possess is precious. Any person who has education can put pen to paper.'

Sultan Rahim entered. Christine got to her feet. The two men looked pleased with themselves. Was Sultan getting a cut in this? Christine said slowly to herself: I am a model, with an agent. Holding the photographer's card, she walked to the mirror and was startled to see her red lips. A moment later she realized, of course, that it was the *pan*.

17

DONALD swivelled one way then the other, the phone to his ear. The seat creaked, dipped, creaked. The first day in the office he had spent some time swivelling, his only witness the soap lady on the hoarding. Managers needed to swivel, in order to revolve the options.

Mohammed answered. Memsahib was in the garden. He went to fetch her. Had Mohammed noticed memsahib's hands at lunchtime, the state of her fingernails?

Donald gazed at the lady's painted smile. She held the soap inquiringly, her head tilted. She urged others to keep themselves as clean as she did. *Her* fingernails were not grubby with toil. She was fixed to the office building opposite; behind her rose the heavy spire of Cameron Chambers. It sat on her head like a crown.

'Sorry,' Christine's voice on the phone. 'Couldn't turn the hose off. The mali had some terribly complicated arrangement with string.'

'How did it go? I'm glad you're back in one piece. Do we have a hut?'

A pause. 'Well, not quite.'

'I thought this chap was such a whizz kid.' Dip, creak. Swivelling in his chair, he filled his voice with authority.

'Not a kid. He's middle-aged.'

'Any joy with the job?' His voice sharper, because she had run away into the bazaar like that.

The line crackled. 'No.'

'Oh dear. Are you disappointed?'

'Something will turn up.'

'Look. I'll be a bit late because I'm dropping in at Mrs Gracie's. You know, the donkey woman. Would you like to come?'

She said not. She sounded rather distant, or perhaps just preoccupied. Maybe she was going over their quarrel, as he had done all afternoon. Putting down the phone, he pictured the beach hut. The harder it was to procure the more he wanted it. Beside the sea he might recapture her – Christine Trimmer, washed clean of prejudice and preconceptions. Chrissy Trimmer; her maiden name had suited her. Sheltering in his towel; pulling her summer dress modestly over her knees. Her hair hanging wet and innocent as it used to. They would be truly alone; there would be nobody for whom she must alter. But by now perhaps she was too much altered herself.

On the wall hung the long staff photographs. The most recent were the least yellowed. *Mr and Mrs I. Grant (1969–1973). Mr and Mrs F. T. Smythe (1973–1975).* Ann Smythe looked a remarkably pretty woman in a pale summer suit. Soon the latest edition would be added to the collection. The photograph had been taken yesterday. There Christine would be printed, wearing jeans. Would they not find this insulting? She might be trying to be all democratic, as she tried so embarrassingly with Mohammed, but would they understand to take it that way? The awful thing was that however offended they felt, none of them except Shamime would in a hundred years venture to say so.

It was nearly six. He packed his briefcase. When he bent, his shirt chafed his burnt shoulders. For the first week or so he had made sure that at 5.30, when the office closed, he was fiddling around in the communal Accounts Section so that he could say goodbye, and so that they could observe himself remaining in the office later, as befitted his responsibilities. Nowadays he did not feel he had to bother, which was one step forward. In fact there had been several steps forward. Though he had not entirely got the hang of the job yet, though gazing at the figures filled him with an exhilarated fear, though he was only just adjusting to the labyrinthine contacts and to a certain tempo, or lack of it, or unpredictability of it, in business dealings here, yet for the first time in his life he felt really at home. If only he could rely upon Christine feeling at home too.

He swivelled round. The soap lady gazed back. Close up, no doubt, her painted eyes were daubed brushstrokes and her face crude. But across the street she seemed reliable. Each day she was there. First thing in the morning, an angle of shadow lay across her brow, making her more severe. During his half-hectic, half-slumbrous office days her face stood behind him, his wooden support.

He had not, for many years, stood outside a woman's house with a manufactured excuse. Despite her age Mrs Gracie was so feminine; she made him feel like a suitor.

The old bearer, whose name he had temporarily forgotten, opened the door and walked upstairs, beckoning him to follow. Up on the landing, sunlight shone through the veranda. The bearer climbed the stairs, his pyjamas tucked up like a washerman's. Donald followed the thin ankles and cracked, grey heels.

They walked along the veranda. There were few of these old houses with verandas left in Karachi. Much of the fretwork was broken; thick cobwebs hung like skirts from the ceiling. From an open door further down came the sound of singing. He had a sudden picture of Iona Gracie, years younger, dressed in a nightie and spinning flax.

In fact the song came from a radio. This was evidently the living-room as well as the bedroom. She rose to her feet, admirably spry.

'It's Ronald. How delightful.' She touched her fine red curls and went across to the radio. 'My favourite companion.' Was this himself or the wireless?

Today she wore navy slacks and an apron. Her curls were pushed back by a navy band. It seemed appealing to wear lipstick in the seclusion of this upper room; to make up her face for the voice on the radio. She sent the bearer away for tea.

'I've brought my cheque-book this time,' said Donald, this being his excuse to see her again. 'So I can join this adoption scheme. I didn't forget, you see.'

'Kind boy. Just look at this mess.'

He gazed around the room. There was no denying its untidiness — curled photos jammed into picture frames, junky old furniture that did not fit the room. A broken chandelier hung from the ceiling. The dressing-table was crammed with pots and jars; the wardrobe was so full that the doors could not be closed. Obviously the whole house had silted up and this was the last refuge. He was about to demur, politely, when he realized that she was pointing to the floor. It was spread with newspapers and broken china.

'Iqbal's too old. I should never have entrusted him with the Staffordshire. I usually don't. But as it was the Minister I thought we should bring out the best.'

'Iqbal dropped it?'

'Two cups, two saucers, milk jug and that delightful teapot. Ronald, I'm desolate. The last of our wedding set. I'm glad Morris isn't alive, he would have sacked him.'

'Can I help?'

'Oh please. Would you care to join me on the floor?'

They sat down.

'This local glue is inferior,' she said. 'You have to hold the bits together for an age. As a rule I do all my entertaining at the Sind Club. They have a little room. I'd snap my fingers and that was that. But this time there was some delegation, I.B.M. or I.T.T. or I.B.B., some footling initials. Mrs *Gracie*, I said over the phone. All regrets. Times have changed, Ronald. So in the end I had to serve the Minister out of cups from Bohri Bazaar. Perhaps he took pity on me.'

'It's the minister who controls the land permission?' In other words, it was Shamime's uncle.

'He's an old friend; he was in opposition when my husband was alive, the only chap who could beat Morris at tennis. He listened but you can never really tell what they're thinking, Ronald. There's a lot of fight left in these old bones, I told him.

147

He sat there cooing at the pussies. At least he likes them. Heaven knows if he likes donkeys.' She paused. 'He probably hates cats but he was being polite. Or religious. The Prophet had a cat, of course.' She picked up a piece of teapot. 'A slippery man. Involved in all sorts of deals, I've heard, changing sides when it suits him. Still, they're all slippery, Ronald, you'll learn. You've only been here a few months, haven't you.'

'Less than two, actually.'

'You're young, Ronald. What was it, cotton?'

'Chemicals. Cameron's.'

'There used to be so many young chaps like you. Of course they're all back home now, quelling the English natives. I wish them luck. One hears such stories nowadays. Where's the respect gone, Ronald, and the pride? Here they're delighted enough to get work at all.'

Donald lifted a handle and held it against different pieces of cup to see which fitted. It was uncomfortable on the floor; his trousers dug into him. But he did not mind. 'That's partly why I came out, actually,' he said. 'Things in England seem, well, to have come apart. Everybody's fighting for himself. I was once in the warehouse at Cameron's, the firm I work for. It was winter and fairly cold—'

'Ah, winter.' She sighed. 'Plants weighed down with frost. Tobogganing. One pines for snow.'

'We haven't had much of that recently, actually. Usually it's just grey and drizzly.' He picked up a bit of china with a pink rose on it. 'Anyway, while two men were slowly loading boxes on to a container, a third man was holding up a thermometer. I thought he was testing the humidity or something—for the stock corrosion perhaps. In fact he was waiting until it dropped just below the statutory minimum and then they were going to knock off. Just like that. Never mind if half the stuff wasn't loaded.'

'So you worked in a warehouse, Ronald.'

He laughed. 'Oh no, I was only training—on the executive scheme. Visiting the different departments to see what made them tick. But here people have worked for Cameron's all their lives and they're proud of the firm. It seems one has to travel four thousand miles to find that nowadays. I mean, our Cameron's driver would wait all day until someone told him he could go. It might be because he hasn't been educated to think for himself — my wife would certainly say so and I'd agree. She'd blame the dread hand of colonialism. Colonialism is a four-letter — is a nasty word to her. But then the less educated you are, the more you have to have something to cling to and identify with. This country couldn't be run by a democratic government, it's simply not ready yet. One's job is to make sure it's a sound thing they're clinging to. And of course educate them so they can work that out for themselves. Christine — my wife — thinks this is an old-fashioned and paternalistic idea. Or imperialist or something. We argue about this.'

He stopped. In fact, what they argued about was mostly of a more niggling, personal nature. They used to argue about large and noble topics, but recently these had shrunk to attacks upon himself. The global subjects were mainly reserved for when they had company.

'Ah, here it is.' He picked up a jagged piece. 'I know that one's partly enjoying it here through being a big fish in a small pool. I didn't have a quarter this responsibility in England, you know. But it makes things worth doing. One's decisions aren't watered down by six people above you, or argued out of existence in committees. In England one's a cog in a big machine. It sounds selfish but I'm not just talking about me. Lots of people feel this. Nowadays there's very little room for quote individual initiative unquote.' He held the handle against the piece of cup; it fitted. 'Here, well, one has an identity.' He took the glue brush and painted the edges. Then he pressed them together. 'I'm waffling on a bit, aren't I.' It surprised him, the way he was talking.

'This is much better than the wireless. Do go on, Ronald.'

By now he did not feel able to correct his name. Nor did he want to, in fact. To her he was Ronald — more articulate, more attractive, more tenderly protective than Donald, with opinions that were not criticized but listened to, her blue eyes widening as if he were the first person to say such things. She must be

149

nearly as old as his grandmother but this did not matter. In a sense she seemed younger than Christine. Despite her brittle bones she seemed softer and more receptive. More feminine, in fact. He passed her the glue. It was a Dickensian pot with the brush sticking out of the top. What was it about Christine? Nothing he said could alter her. She had the shuttered look of the safely committed. He could make no difference; she made him powerless.

He kept the handle clamped to the cup. 'My family — I mean the men — all had something worthwhile to do. They could make a difference to things. My father fought in the war.' Christine would say: he shot down three Germans. Call that an achievement? He could not answer this but he knew it was not quite the point.

In a moment he would mention his grandfather. Mrs Gracie would understand him if he said 'Proud of their country'. In Britain you could not say that any more; the words, like so much else, had been devalued. But they meant more than people realized. His grandfather, like his father, had actually been prepared to die for what he thought was right. It was not blind indoctrination or sheep-like mindlessness. It was something to do with belief. They had not sat there looking at a thermometer.

With Mrs Gracie he could use those words, but even he felt trapped by their dwindled meaning. She leant over, the newspaper creaking, and picked up the teapot spout. Christine would say it was to do with male domination. *Everyone with a prick is an imperialist*, she had said once with half the Saloon Bar listening. That Roz was there of course. Today in the bazaar she could not laugh at this. He had hoped, so much, that this place would change her.

'They were stretched and tested,' he said. 'Up to now I've never had a chance to be that. They made their mark.' He thought of the flat in Crouch End, number 144b, looking down on to other people's gardens. 'Here we have a lovely garden that's ours. I meet people who're actually making the decisions, who change things. One can change things oneself, in a smaller

150

way. My wife thinks I'm a snob and like meeting people who know the Prime Minister.'

'Charming man, of course, quite brilliant. He can talk the birds off the trees. Picked it up in Oxford, no doubt. Are you a university man, Ronald?'

'Christine went. I went straight into Cameron's. You see, my mother was only living on a widow's pension and my grand-mother got very little. I felt I had to get a job.'

'I can tell your wife's pretty. I must meet her.'

He paused, holding together the handle and the broken piece of cup. He loosened his grip; they eased. He pressed them together. 'She's rather got into this Women's Lib business.'

'Lib?' She looked up from the teapot. 'Oh yes, they burn their underwear.'

'She's always — well, been swept up into things.' He remembered her in the sixties, a clever girl with her hair wrenched into those little plaits, swaying her head to dreamy music. Now she swayed to rousing chants. She bought these movements like wholesale fitments inside her head. He considered this lazy; it meant that after the initial investment she no longer had to question them. This made him irked and stifled. But how much had she really changed inside?

'Such a beautiful teapot, Ronald. It will never be the same. The damage has been done.'

'I'm so sorry.' He paused. 'It's all to do with recognizing women's rights, that sort of thing. They say some worthwhile things; sometimes I just feel it's the way they say it. Their missionary zeal.'

'We used to have a lot of them here, of course. I suppose they've all gone now.'

'I beg your pardon?'

'From the churches. Awfully difficult to talk to because they knew they were right. We used to have these tedious teas.'

'I see. Missionaries. The thing is, my wife can usually out-argue me. She's had a good education.' He had once mentioned this — mildly, a touch humorously. If she had been a man, with a mother and Granny to support, she would have felt obliged to go straight into the equivalent of Cameron's. 'I think she's more intelligent really.'

'We had a poor little Welsh girl; she suffered dreadfully with the heat. And with us, no doubt. Couldn't teach for toffee. Miss Sopwith, probably from rather a good family. Perhaps they were the aeroplane people. *We* only called her Soppy, of course.'

'You were brought up here?'

'All over the place. Of course it was one country then. Papa's work took him everywhere—Delhi, Bombay. Summers we spent in the hills. Mama was a very intelligent woman, like your wife. You needed to be clever, believe me. Don't be fooled by what you hear, Ronald. It took a lot of skills to run a large house and all the servants. I'm sure your wife finds that.'

Unable to answer that truthfully, he nodded. The handle had stuck at last. He rummaged amongst the newspaper for the next piece. The paper lifted with his hands, it was so hot.

'So tell me about this Women's Lib, Ronald.'

'It's catching. It's infectious. Soon they'll be wearing badges saying "Women Against Everything".' He laughed, gruntingly. He found a curved sliver. This cup must be in about eight pieces. He hesitated; he did not want to be disloyal. 'About a year ago I won some money on my Premium Bonds so I organized a surprise—a romantic week in Venice. When I showed Christine the tickets—I'd put them in a box and tied it with red ribbon —she was thrilled of course, but then she looked affronted. Was her job so unimportant, she asked, that I'd presume her to take a week off, just like that, when I'd organized for my own time off beforehand?'

'Ah, Venice. Morris wanted to take me there on our honeymoon. We had to settle for Kashmir.'

He pictured Iona on a boat, her head resting against a pillow while her bridegroom pointed out the names of the surrounding mountains. He would be expected to know such things. How easy for a husband, in those days. He himself would have known the names; that was simple.

A shadow fell. Iqbal padded in noiselessly and started to lay

152

out the tea. Donald took this opportunity to stretch his legs; they were numb. He wandered over to the veranda. It was breezy out here. They knew how to build in those days, with their thick walls, high ceilings and galleries for ventilation. None of this gimcrack modern stuff; flimsy walls like Adamjee Plaza where one had to rely on air-conditioners and the chancy electricity supply. He was a romantic at heart. Even Mrs Gracie's clutter seemed more pleasing than Christine's. Christine's disorder seemed a wilful statement of her priorities. Mrs Gracie, on the other hand, seemed helpless amidst the debris of her own past.

He gazed through the broken fretwork. Down below, one part of the garden was still tended. During winter, no doubt, that bed would be full of the flowers his grandfather had described. The lawn was shaded by trees; they looked like elms except for the black pods hanging down. Through the branches he could see the clock tower of the cantonment station. The hands were missing now. He could almost hear the bugles blowing and his Granny lying awake while the trains shunted. In those days the clock worked. His grandparents had not honeymooned in Kashmir but in the Grand Hotel in Murree. *Only the best for little Dottie*, said Grandad, pointing to the photo in the album. In this house, for the first time since he had arrived, he felt near to him.

Tea was ready; he turned back. It was drinks hour really. He had lost track of the time, gluing together these frail old cups, piecing together the past. He sat down on the floor.

'Did you live in this house when you were married?'

She nodded. 'Now you're not to guess my age, Ronald. Some sugar? Dear Morris – when he was alive everything was spick and span. He had the highest standards.'

'Was he in the army?'

'Oh no. He became a judge, like Papa. He was a good deal older than me. He kept me in order. I was a wild young miss, Ronald. The servants spoiled me dreadfully when I was a child.'

He sipped the tea, trying to work out dates. There must have been some point when his grandfather and Mrs Gracie were both in Karachi. These circuit judges travelled; so did the army officers. But Grandad had mentioned her name.

He brushed glue on the third bit of cup. 'It must have been marvellous, growing up here.'

'Except for the clothes. We used to be laced into these horrible tight dresses, most unsuitable for the climate. I feel so envious when I see these young girls nowadays gadding about in their summer frocks.'

He wondered where Christine had been gadding about today in those baggy things.

'But it was marvellous, Ronald. And as you grew up there were all those nice young officers. Always far too many to go round, of course. They used to ship out the frumps from England – the Fishing Fleet, they called it – to try and find them husbands.'

Donald paused, holding the piece in place: broken rose against stalk. 'Actually my grandfather was in the army here.'

'Dear boy, why didn't you tell me? What was his name?'

'Herbert Manley.' He added modestly: 'Lieutenant-Colonel Manley, he became.'

'Manley ... Manley ... ' She gazed at the half-mended teapot. 'So many faces, Ronald. They all looked so handsone in their uniforms, but rather alike. They would ask you to dance with a small bow,' she bent her head, ' ... like this.' She pushed back the alice band, which had slipped forward.

There was a silence. The ceiling fan creaked. He imagined her brain, slowly working with the memories. 'There was that Major Marnley, of course, I dimly remember him, but he was posted elsewhere.'

'Marnley?'

'He might have become a Lieutenant-Colonel after he married that English gel. There was a certain amount of fuss at the time, I seem to remember, but it all blew over. They all did it, of course; it was common knowledge.'

'What, marry?'

'Oh dear me no. You couldn't marry them.' She laughed. 'But it was only natural. Us girls weren't supposed to know about

154

that sort of thing, I mean I was only in my twenties, but what else could the poor chaps do? Not nearly enough English girls to go round.' She stopped to think, gazing at the broken bits of china. 'Young men in their prime.'

There was a long silence. Donald held his breath. Perhaps she was just working out where the pieces went.

'Maningtree. There was a Major Maningtree. But he was a bachelor. Besides, I believe he passed away with the dysentery. One day, Ronald, you should just take a look at the churchyard. So many graves and some of them so wee.'

Donald kept the third piece clamped against the others. He tried to keep his voice casual. 'This Marnley. Was he transferred to—I think it was something to do with Pore?'

'Something poor. Rags? Ragastan. No, it's Rajastan.'

'P-O-R-E.'

'*Cawnpore*. Silly me. How clever you are. Cawnpore. No reflection, I'm sure, on what happened. I'm sure it wasn't. Just to stop—well, complications. I presume the English girl didn't know, you see. It wouldn't do for them to meet in the street. Occasionally the native woman would make a bit of trouble —even come to the house.' She dabbed the glue. 'Sometimes if there was an infant involved, as in that case. But by and large they knew their place. No doubt a little money changed hands. They behaved like gentlemen, Ronald. Even this Marnley, I'm sure, despite what they said.' She stopped, gazing at Donald. 'Oh dear, I haven't put my silly foot in it have I? It's not your grandfather?'

'Grandfather? Oh no.'

Donald was fumbling with the three pieces of his cup which seemed to have fallen apart. He had thought the handle was glued. He tried to press them together but his hands would not do what he wanted. He did not want the pieces to clatter together with his shaking. He put them down on the newspaper.

'I can't tell you how delightful it is, Ronald, to have a young face around. It reminds me how life used to be one long party. One used to think: there he is, leading a thousand men. And here he is, bringing me a lemonade fizz. Now I'm just an old woman fighting for her existence.'

'Existence?'

'Her donkeys' existence, I should say. But my own too, Ronald. I live and breathe that place. You see I don't have many friends left now – nobody who could remember what it was like then. They're my babies. I was not blessed with children. Call me sentimental; everybody else does, I'm sure. Or else mad. Can this mad old lady rely on your support, if it comes to a fight?'

He could feel himself nodding; at least he thought he was. He gazed out at the slats, blurred by the evening sun. He felt congested.

He concentrated on his surroundings. The plaster walls were peeling. *You've always clung to the past*, Christine had said.

If he touched the walls the paint would fall in flakes, lying amongst the broken china. This sandstone looked solid but the whole house was crumbling. White ants too. In the shelves the books looked perfectly all right. Then you opened one and the pages had crumbled into dust.

He must not think of his grandfather; he must think of his manners. He smiled at Mrs Gracie. Suddenly her little-girl curls seemed odd, surrounding that wrinkled face. They must have chatted about this and that, he could not remember a word of it later. She seemed to notice no difference. He attempted to put his cup together again, with no success.

18

MINNIE was scratched all over, like she'd been pulled through barbed wire. Jewels of blood criss-crossed her cheek; her arms were scraped. She was wearing the pink pants suit she had worn last time he saw her; this however was untouched, not a spot of blood on it. For some reason this did not surprise him. She seemed undisturbed. Didn't he ask her if it hurt? He could not identify the place where she was standing. She was pulling off pieces of kitchen roll. Only gradually did he realize she was not mopping herself. One by one she was offering the pieces to him.

Her face, usually anxious, was calm and she was talking in a flat voice. He could not make out the words, as she pressed the cloth, sure, it was cloth now – as she pressed it against his cheek.

Duke was awake by now and pushing the sheet from his face. He was sweating. The room was black; the air-conditioner was humming on to itself. He sat up, breathing deeply. He never dreamed; leastways he never remembered them. He had never credited his imagination overmuch. But lately he had not been sleeping too well. Himself, Duke Hanson, who usually slept like a log.

He switched on the lamp. 2.35. The sheets were twisted half off the bed, as if he had been making violent love. He climbed to his feet. He felt both heavy and drained. He fetched his bathrobe and went down the stuffy stairway, switching on the lights as he went. He went into the kitchen, opened the refrigerator and poured himself a glass of milk. Then he fetched himself a couple of coconut cookies. He was not hungry. Gul Khan kept the house well stocked; he looked after Duke as competently as a wife. Minnie had remarked on this before she left, she herself of course never having lived with a servant before. 'I needn't worry about you,' she had said, 'after I'm gone.'

Min is Minimal. Someone had said this, one of these nights. Was it Minnie, scratched? Someone in some echoing, further dream. Some of these had featured Shamime, usually altered. He could visualize Shamime saying it teasingly, turning her head to avoid his face. *Min is Minimal*. Blowing out smoke as if exhaling, from her lungs, the stirred ghost of his wife.

He munched under the bright strip light. He tried to put Minnie back into this kitchen, right here beside him. He wished to God she had not gone away. Two weeks and it still did not get better; in fact it got worse. He had kept himself away from Shamime all this time, hoping for a cure. He would keep himself away for as long as it took. He would keep phoning Minnie. Last week she had told him the nurses were teasing her about the number of calls she received from Karachi. 'And you've been married twenty-six years?' they said. 'You lucky lady, you.' Minnie herself sounded pleased but surprised. 'Honey, really I'm fine. It's all gone fine. It wasn't one bit as bad as I thought. Dear, don't worry yourself.'

She was back home now in West Boulevard. Chester was home for vacation and working at the gas station just two blocks away; evenings he was back. There were the neighbours coming round for coffee. In addition Duke Jnr's wife, Corinne, was at hand to make sure Minnie didn't overdo things. She would have her work cut out; Minnie was that active.

He could picture her in the home they had saved so many years to buy; comfortable enough, nothing fancy. He hoped she was in the lounge with her feet up. She told him she had bought a stack of paperbacks on Third World problems, so she would return better informed. The door slamming beyond the kitchen as Chester came in from the garage, staggering under the box of

158

groceries. He could picture her in each of the rooms, sunlight coming through the windows. He could see her fetching the mail and leaning, arms flexed, on her electric blender as she fixed something for her lunch. He knew every inch of that house, he had decorated it himself over the years and put up every shelf. But they were not as usual, these pictures. They were not running through his veins, all homesick familiarity. Now they had become distanced and boxed, as in a TV screen; something he had to decide to switch on. He did switch them on, but painfully.

The freezer door dug into his back; he moved his position. Inside there lay Minnie's shopping: the steaks and packs of bacon she had bought from the Commissary. She had made him pecan pie, too, knowing his sweet tooth. He had touched none of these parcels, neatly labelled and furred with frost. He could not eat them. Instead Gul Khan cooked him something, or else he went to the Intercontinental and ate a tandoori. In fact by now he preferred Pakistani food, subtle and spicy, burning him, bringing tears to his eyes.

He had not wept for years, until that night. She had not seen in the dark. She had thought him a hungry middle-aged man who did this often. She had not believed him when he said this was the first time; her voice had changed back to its old mocking tone. He realized now it was better that she thought this. By now she had probably forgotten it had happened.

He stuffed dry cookies into his mouth. He had been down to the chapel but he could not pray. He felt altered. He could not sit easy in his old chair facing his old God. Years of living away from home, and all of a sudden he felt a foreigner. Yesterday he had been down at Ginntho Pir; the first time since that day with herself and Mr Chowdry. He had gone into the shrine. He had expected something cluttered and cheap; after all, she had laughed at it. He had visited some large shrines before but never a small village place. In fact it was whitewashed and quiet. He was awed by the simple faith. Bits of ribbon and string had been tied to the railings around the tomb, each knotted with a prayer. Some were mere threads. His eyes had filled with tears.

159

Then he had heard Shamime's low laugh, mocking the pink cloth. Had she really been so amused? She had entered, after all, with her handful of flowers. He could not presume to know her feelings. She was too complex for him. Then he had thought: maybe I only came in here so I can stand where she has been.

In what did she put her faith? Shamime driving away, leaving his car keys with the chowkidar at his office. Greeting him next day as if nothing had happened, when they chanced to meet on the sidewalk. Something had amused her back at Cameron's. He could not remember the story. She had laughed, the hot wind blowing her clothes against her body.

He would not think of her. He was not going to contact her.

Next day in his office the phone rang.

'Duke? My uncle's back in Karachi. We're going to some do at the Gymkhana Club on Sunday but after that he's bound to come home with us for a drink.'

Duke sat still, listening to the traffic outside.

She paused. 'Would you like to come along and meet him? He wants to talk about your project, I think. I'll tell you how to get to our house.'

He had no need for instructions, of course. He knew every window of her parents' home. In fact on the way to the airport this past couple of weeks he had purposely not looked in its direction. How easy, those sweet and painful questions: was that her bedroom light? Whose automobile was that in the drive?

He was being impolite. He could not think how to refuse so he said sure, and thank you. He put down the receiver. Of course, even if they were the slightest acquaintances she would have suggested this meeting. It made sound business sense and it would hardly go against his principles just to meet the guy. In fact it would seem odd if at this stage he did not. Of course he would go no further: just a drink and a few friendly words.

He sat, his head in his hands. He pushed up and down the loose skin of his forehead. How much was this a business

160

arrangement, and how much a reason for himself and her to meet? Could she in fact want to see him again?

He had forbidden himself to think like this. He felt, stirring in his heart, questions that had long since lain quiet — if, that is, he had ever asked them since his youth. Why did she do this? Did she mean what he thought she did? What, oh Lord Jesus, should he do?

He looked out of the window at the shops opposite. The lunch hour was over; the metal shutters were being wound open, the doors unlocked. He could feel his heart unclosing beneath his shirt.

Punctually at 9.30 he drove there, shaved, showered, his wet hair brushed. He felt he was borrowing someone's else's automobile. He felt like one of his own sons.

Along the airport highway the homes were set back behind tall walls. A service road ran parallel between them and the dual carriageway. Sure, he knew the house. Even before that night he had connected Shamime with arrivals and departures. The constant traffic along the road and in the sky gave her a public but temporary air. At any moment she might take off herself. She often did. The capital cities of Europe were familiar to her; she mentioned them so casually. He himself had visited only London and Paris, once, on vacation. He was a hick.

Her gates were open. He parked outside. The sun had sunk and most of the bungalow was in shadow. Bougainvillaea frothed over the wall, from inside. The topmost blossoms were lit by the sunset, a fiery pink. He sat still for a moment. He had never seen it this close; only from the highway. Each day she must steer her car through those gateposts. This was her place. His reluctance to enter, he told himself, was on account of the Minister.

And of course there was also her father to meet. He had met the man months ago, and respected him. He was courteous and distinguished, the chairman of a large investment company. Duke must clasp his hand and meet his eye, man-to-man. He was an imposter; he felt weak with nerves. He had never

161

considered himself a coward. He had knocked around the world and been through some weird encounters. He had earned a Silver Star from his service in Korea. Still he sat looking at the dashboard. He had emptied the ashtray now.

One evening. If he could get through one evening of pleasant conversation, nothing special, as if they were mere acquaintances, maybe then he would be cured.

He walked through the gates. The garden was drenched. Heavy green foliage hung against the walls. The air was warm and scented. Two cars stood in the driveway, one of them Shamime's. The other carried no government flag, but then nobody turned up on time here.

He was shown into a large foyer. From one side came the sound of beat music, disco type. For a moment he could be back home, with his boys in there.

The door was opened. The drapes were drawn and the lamps lit. In the light sat Shamime and Aziz playing checkers. They looked as if they were posed on a stage.

She rose from the table and turned down the music. 'Thank heavens you've come. I've been longing to see you.'

He could not speak. She led him across the room, her cool hand in his. 'Aziz is so hopeless.'

She let go his hand. She was wearing a sari; he had seldom seen her in one before. She flicked it back over her shoulder and opened the cocktail cabinet.

'This is Zizzy's den.' She poured him a Scotch. The sari was a rich silky brown with a gold border. Her hair was twisted up in a coil. She looked older, and statuesque. Nobody could touch her.

'I'll just polish him off.' She walked back, in the slow swaying way women walked in saris. Her midriff showed. Most women bulged there. He kept his eyes off her and looked at the room. It was papered in dark stuff, like a night club. On one wall hung Baluchi guns and knives; on another hung one of those printed mirrors you found in boutiques back home. This one featured Frank Sinatra. Aziz had a heck of a lot of equipment: stereo, TV with video recorder. Wires snaked across the fine old oriental carpet.

162

Over at the table they laughed. Did Aziz know anything about that night? Duke wondered where the others were. Shamime was dressed up; they must have returned from the Club. But they looked so absorbed he did not like to ask.

Beside the cocktail cabinet stood some framed photos. Maybe some featured Shamime. When he thought of her childhood he ached. There were twenty-four years he knew nothing about; worse than this, now he must find out nothing more. It was for some other man, at some future date, to leaf with her through the albums.

Shamime did not feature. The snapshots showed formally-dressed men. Shamime's father sat at a banquet next to the King of Jordan. Another showed two men shaking hands against a curtain; they wore garlands around their necks. One was President Kennedy, the other a tall Muslim in ceremonial leggings.

'That's Uncle Bobby,' called Shamime. 'Hey, Duke, I'm terribly sorry but apparently they had to go on to some dinner. I couldn't face it, sitting around on sofas with wives going on about how expensive everything is nowadays. Anyway, you were coming.'

Duke paused, confused. Those rusty old stirrings in his heart. Had she meant this to happen? Surely her uncle was not some excuse for her to see him? It could not be; it must not be. Aziz must not leave them alone together. He drained his whisky. His hand felt large and clumsy, clutching the tumbler.

A clunk and rattle of counters. 'That's that,' said Shamime. 'Do you want to play this stupid game, Duke?'

He managed a nod. Aziz rose from the table. He was not leaving the room; affable as ever he lit a cigarette, refilled Duke's glass and went over to his shelves. 'Any requests?'

'I'm way behind the times,' said Duke. 'My boys kid me about it.'

'Zizzy's a born disc jockey,' said Shamime, setting out the counters. 'He sometimes does it at parties. It suits his exquisite looks and nocturnal habits. But you're too lazy, aren't you, Ziz.'

Aziz smiled; he did not seem to mind. He was fiddling with the amplifier. Duke thought of him playing with his stereophonic toys while the men of the family gazed down from the snapshots. In this place statesmen bred playboys.

He sat down. The table was fragile; he must not knock it with his knees. He felt he was in some sophisticated playroom with foreign rules. He did not want to understand them; he should not be here. The board was laid out.

'I'm black and you're white,' said Shamime. 'Ho ho.'

She looked across at him. Her lips were painted deep red; her skin glowed.

He moved his counter forward. 'Haven't played this since the boys were small.'

'You mean you played draughts? They didn't watch TV all the time?'

He paused. 'Well, I guess we played it some of the time.' Now he thought of it, he could not remember how often. He had bought a box one Thanksgiving; they must have played. Maybe not so many times as he had imagined. He preferred to visualize that than visualize the TV. In fact he could not visualize the boys at all.

Music was playing but Aziz kept it soft. She pushed forward a black counter. She looked smart at this game; maybe she already had a plan of action. He needed to talk about the boys.

'We have this yard back home,' he said. 'Not the size of yours but big enough for ball games. I spent time training the kids. That I do remember.'

'How energetic you Yanks are. Don't you find us indolent? Actually Father's friends keep reading articles in *Time* about blood sugar and aortas, and now they rush off to the Sind Club gym. Unwise, I feel, after centuries of ease.'

'I jog,' said Duke. 'Maybe I told you before.'

'I'm sure you're nice and firm.'

He looked up sharply but she was inspecting the board. 'One shouldn't fight this climate.' She said something in Urdu. 'What will be, will be.'

Duke pushed a counter forward. 'Minnie came up against

this.'

'Ah ha. Bad luck.' With a clunk she jumped his counter, took it and put it her side.

'That was dumb.' He concentrated on the board. Black and white checks, clear and simple. Her perfume made his head swim.

'Yep, Minnie came up against this. She was—she's always trying to make things better. Like if she sees a pigeon with a broken wing she brings it home. Which makes it kind of difficult out here.'

He paused. Shamime did not seem inclined to answer so he went on: 'Back home in Wichita she was involved, on a voluntary basis, in an Inner City Program—working in the slum areas and building playgrounds on derelict sites.'

'How fascinating. I wouldn't put it there.'

'Ah.' He put back his counter and moved another one forward. 'Well, out here straightaway she got involved in that rehousing project out at those slums—you know the place —yeah, Liari.'

'You mean on the way to the beach.'

There was a moment's silence. 'Sure. That's it.' He looked at her smooth brown forehead. She was watching the board. 'The place was full of disease, right by the sewage outlet for the city.'

'You have to wind up the car windows. Zizzy calls it Pooh Corner.'

'Yeah, well Minnie used to come home quite sick. Couldn't eat her dinner. But then she said *they* didn't have any dinner to eat anyway. She was real upset. So there's this housing project and medical centre—purpose-built new homes on the reclaimed land near by. The first phase was completed maybe four months ago. Beautiful homes, electricity, piped water.' He paused. 'And would they go? Well, they let themselves be moved, that went fine. And know what happened? Next day they were back in their slums. No reason, nothing. That organization was baffled.'

She pushed the sari back over her shoulder. 'We're deep,' she said, smiling. 'There's no telling, with us.'

165

He paused. 'I met a stewardess once, on a Saudi flight. She used to do the Haj run from Karachi to Jeddah. The planes were full of these village people, simple folk like the ones who visit the Ginntho shrine. They'd saved up all their lives for the visit to Mecca. And they'd sit on the floor because they'd never sat on a seat, they were so confused ... ' He was going to say, they perched like birds on the toilets because they had never seen a sit-down lavatory.

'And you think that can be changed by re-designing the planes? Duke dear, the gulf is deeper than that.'

She smiled, her dark lips parted. Such smooth skin, smooth and sure. He looked down. He tried to picture Minnie's face; it was always puckered with doubt. The world's hardships were sent to trouble her.

'Minnie felt helpless. I know how she feels. Like, trying to come to terms with the place. If only we could put our finger on the solution.'

'There isn't one solution. There's no little button, Duke. It's not that your computer's got it wrong, you know. How much nicer to play draughts, black and white, right and wrong ... Got you.'

With a clunk she jumped two of his counters, one after the other. That left one of her black ones at risk. He jumped it. She had four of his beside her glass of juice; he only had one of hers.

She leant forward. The sari slipped off her shoulder; she hitched it back abstractedly as if she were pushing back her hair. Aziz got up, but he was only going to the bar. Duke thought: we discuss this and that, I talk about Minnie, by the end of the evening I will be safe. We can get through it like this. Please God we can.

'Talking of black and white,' said Shamime, 'do you dream in colour?'

Duke stiffened. 'I don't remember. Colour, I guess.' He tried not to think of his recent nights. 'Sure.'

She gazed back at him, the diamond glinting in the lamplight. Was that why he had seen blood on Minnie's face? A jewel of blood.

'And yourself?' He kept his voice light.

'Of course. They're terribly vivid. I'm superstitious about omens.'

There was a silence. He did not ask her what omens she had seen.

'There's a sweet little man who does my horoscope. I'm quaintly oriental, aren't I.'

Her mocking tone had him all confused. He remembered her ducking her head, her hands full of petals. He must talk about Minnie.

'My wife's gotten interested in comparative religion. She studies a lot.'

'And you don't.'

'Minnie's the one for the books. Always has been. And she goes to these evening classes.'

'Got you.' Two clunks and she was right into his back row of whites, none of which had been moved yet. But he could not jump her counter now, it being safe against the side.

'She didn't have too much of an education either, but she minded more. We married when she was twenty years old.' He slid a counter forward.

'Guess what I discovered yesterday. Rather embarrassing really. I was chatting with Christine Manley, and it turns out that my ghastly school stood at the end of her garden. I remember muggins here being rather rude about Mill Hill. All the little semis just the same.'

'Mill Hill, London? She didn't attend your school?'

'Apparently not. Mine was horribly posh. Fancy that though. Perhaps I knocked a hockey ball into her father's potting shed. I did once, into somebody's. One seldom glimpsed the natives.'

He ached, trying not to picture her at school. He tried to count the squares, one, two, three. He paused and said: 'We couldn't afford a lot for the kids, when they were young. Not in those days. When we first married we lived in this two-roomed apartment above a drapery store.'

'Look out, I've got a king.' She leant over and took back her counter from beside his tumbler. 'I can go all directions now so watch out. I can creep up from behind.'

'She's a demon,' called Aziz. 'You haven't a chance, old chap.'

'Watch out,' said Shamime, 'I'm advancing.'

Duke moved his counter. She jumped it and put it away on her hoard.

'Guess I'll give up,' he said.

'You can't. Not just when I'm winning.'

'I seem to be kind of rusty.'

'I thought you were a fighter.'

Not at this sort of game, he wanted to say.

'It's only a game,' she said. 'Aziz lost seven hundred rupees last night, didn't you Ziz.'

Deep in his leather armchair Aziz said: 'Eight hundred and fifty.'

'Father won't bail you out for ever,' she said.

In the photo father was a grey blob. Duke moved his counter. He felt invaded by her; she moved into him like oil. He should be gone soon. He had a call booked for the States.

She leant forward, the bangles falling to her wrist. 'You must meet Uncle Bobby, Duke. I love him. I only like older men. I mean, look at Aziz. They're all so gorgeous but there's nothing inside. They've no experience of life. They've never had to weather anything, you see. They've never had to fight. I don't want them like that, brand new and wrapped in cellophane. I want damaged goods.'

Duke placed his counter with care. But her tone was light.

Aziz climbed to his feet, looking at his watch. 'Habib and that lot said they'll be at the Excelsior by now.'

Duke scraped back his chair. The table rocked.

'We haven't finished,' she said.

'You've won. I have to go. You see, I have a call booked for eleven.'

'Ah,' she said slowly.

His first lie to her. In fact the call was booked for twelve midnight, but he must leave now. 'It's still afternoon in the States.' Or was it morning? His head was confused. Soon Minnie could tell him which it was.

Aziz shook hands and left. Duke picked up his keys and the seersucker jacket in which he had expected to meet the Minister. Tall in her sari, the hostess, Shamime stood up to see him out. He prayed for her not to speak.

In the foyer the bearer waited. Beyond the open door an engine revved up and Aziz drove off. They went outside. The foliage was damp still, and spotlit. The air was heavy with the scent of blossoms and exhaust smoke. Beyond the wall came the drone of the highway. He turned to shake her hand.

'Thank you again for a mighty enjoyable evening.'

'I'll come to your car.'

They walked out through the gates. If only she would stay home. He wondered when her parents would be returning. The chowkidar saluted and went back to his quarters behind the shrubs.

He unlocked the car door. She stood on the other side. He hesitated.

'Can I get in?' she said.

He took the keys and went round to her side. The car hood was a large, wide object that had to be negotiated. He unlocked her door, opened it, walked the journey back to his door and let himself in.

'Let's drive,' she said.

'I must be getting on home.'

'I need a cigarette.' She fiddled with the automatic lighter.

'After that I'd better escort you back,' he said.

She pressed in the lighter. Her voice was low. 'Why haven't you phoned me, Duke? I kept on staying in and making excuses.'

He stopped breathing. There was silence in the automobile.

After a moment the lighter popped out. Neither of them moved in the darkness.

Another moment passed. 'I didn't know you'd been doing that,' he said.

'What do you think, Duke? What have you been thinking?'

'I don't think. I've gotten so confused.'

Down the highway, far ahead, a neon sign switched on and

169

off. BUBBLE UP. Except it was only half working. UBBL U.

'Duke, don't you understand?'

He could not speak. He shook his head.

'You don't want to understand. Oh Duke, I can see that.'

UBBL U. Blackness. UBBL U. She leant forward; the silk shifted. She pushed in the lighter.

'What do you want with me?' he said.

'I don't want anything *with* you. I want you. That's the awful thing.'

There was another silence. The lighter popped out. Neither of them moved. He could not look at her. He looked at the dumb red letters, off, on.

'I know I shouldn't talk like this,' she said softly. 'You're too old. You're far too married.'

He said at last: 'I am.'

'Could you light my damned cigarette?'

This time he pushed in the lighter. They waited. He could hear her breathing. Seconds passed; the lighter popped out. She tried to take it but her hand was shaking. He took it from her and tried to press it against her cigarette but his hand was finding this hard too.

It was managed. She blew out smoke. 'Please let's go. Please.'

He turned the key. They drove in silence. By the time they arrived at his house she had finished her cigarette. It was nearly eleven o'clock. She did not touch him but followed him upstairs, close behind.

It was Sunday: Gul's day off. His bed was in a mess, all disordered in the electric light. He felt ashamed and asked her to wait in the chair while he straightened the sheets but as he bent down she gripped his hand. She was down on the bed with him, pressed against him, kissing him over his cheeks and his eyelids. Her sari was bunched about her waist; his hand kept meeting warm skin. He held her; she felt so slender he must hurt her, the way he was holding her now. He closed his eyes against the glare.

'Have you been thinking of me?' she whispered into his hair.

'Don't ask me that, honey.'

170

'Have you?'

As he gripped her the table moved. She had kicked it with her foot. The phone tinged.

'What's the matter? Oh Duke keep me tight. Sweetest, sweetest Duke, my sweet old man, I haven't lived since that night, I've just been waiting. I could hardly bear it that day with that other man too, I had to leave, it killed me that you could sit so calmly and talk about your hotel, Duke I wanted you so much. Last week I kept driving past your office, round and round those shops, I drove past eight times and I could never see you. Duke I thought I'd go mad.'

He must be going mad. His chest felt it would break.

'Don't move, Duke. I don't care about the light. I want to see you this time.'

But he had only moved over to lift the receiver off the phone.

19

THE STALLS were piled with clothes. Christine tried to squeeze past. They were heaped with pullovers and with creased velvet party dresses, cast-offs from childrens' cupboards the other side of the globe. It was stiflingly hot; men jostled her. She drew her dupatta across her mouth. She did it like a Pakistani girl now.

The old clothes bazaar was full of men; the few women wore bourquas. Shamime had told her about this place the first time they met, when Christine was wearing one of her Rags frocks. It wound along an alley near the Bottle Bazaar. She staggered; the crowd closed in behind her. Since Juna Bazaar she had learnt not to panic. Up above hung brassières; they wore the chewed look of countless launderings. Were the women who washed them now dead? They hung like giblets over the men's heads. According to Shamime the stuff was shipped here in bulk – ships from Japan, the States and no doubt Britain. The clothes were manufacturers' rejects, garments from jumble sales and from international aid programmes. The alley was piled with debris from the West, such an assortment, who would ever be wanting that emerald-green taffeta gown? Some of the clothes had been darned, long ago. Some pink dungarees hung up there, patched with *Beach Boys For Ever*. Below the empty legs some men were bargaining, their voices raised over the music which played from a transistor, balanced on a mound of shirts.

She thought of Roz rummaging here. Roz went to all the London jumble sales — places jammed not with men but with housewives. She was sharp-eyed, grabbing this piece of lace, that satin slip, and stitching them together to make the unique and pricey garments sold at Rags Period Frocks. They were bought by women who double-parked their husbands' cars outside. Camden Passage itself was hardly wider than this alley. Narrow old city houses just like these. No, not just like these.

She nudged through the crowd. She was more belligerent nowadays. When men touched her she elbowed them away. She leant across and lifted up a torn, gold-lamé dress. There were some beautiful things here. The older and frailer these clothes were, the more marketable they would be in London, and the less marketable here. In London women were rich enough to be seen in rags.

She stopped. She had seen what she wanted.

'*Kitne?*' She pointed. It was hanging above her.

Up in the shadows, in the interior of the stall, a turbaned Pathan sat on a pile of clothes. Shamime said Pathans ran this place. He leant slightly forward to look.

'*Das rupea,*' he said flatly and leant back. He had a face like a hawk. Instead of mountains, he gazed over hillocks of clothes. His eyes were darkened with kohl. He closed them in a cloud of charas smoke.

'*Das?*' She stared. 'Ten?'

His friend unhooked the dress. 'Tip-top for memsahib. Very good dress — look, see.' He pointed to the label. Men gathered round. The label said St Michael Polyester/Cotton, her size.

'Six rupees,' she said. Other clothes here were being sold for one rupee and less. She was no fool. She had lived here for two months.

'*Das.*'

'Mark and Spencer,' said the friend. 'All womens they goes crazy with the Mark and Spencer.'

'Seven.'

'*Das.* Ten. Last price.'

'These is not good.' The friend shook his head, pointing to her

173

loose kurta. 'This the best.' He held up the dress. It was a yellow-checked shirtwaister, the sort of dress she had not worn for years. She must look English, however, for her photograph.

She sighed loudly. 'Okay. Ten.'

The dress was perfect; it even had white piping around the edges of the pockets. She bundled it under her arm. She could not bargain; she still retained the British habit of feeling obliged to someone in a less pleasant position than herself. Last week she had met Shamime buying a length of cloth in Bohri Bazaar. At least, not buying. Pointing to this and that, Shamime waited for the old man to get them out and shake them loose in front of her. She chose one; he cut her the length. Then he named the price and she threw up her hands. Far too much, she cried. He would not bargain and she left the shop. 'But he's cut it off,' said Christine. 'How can he sell it now?' 'Chrissy dear he'll find some other dum-dum. They're all crooks.' Undoubtedly Shamime knew — after all she was Pakistani, so she was mysteriously right. But it also helped one's conscience, in this disturbing country, to believe the poor were crooks so they need be given nothing. Whatever the logic, however, in that cloth stall even Shamime seemed foreign.

She rode home in a rickshaw. It was nearly midday. Upstairs Mohammed was squirting the landing curtains with mosquito spray. Like a spy he seemed to linger just where she wanted to go. She closed the bedroom door and switched on the air-conditioner. The dress did not need ironing. An old, unreadable cleaning ticket was still pinned to the hem. She put on the frock and buckled the neat little fabric belt. She opened the wardrobe. Beside the mirror her chart stirred; she must re-Sellotape it.

She stood back, staring at the mirror. It was a changed woman who stared at itself, clapping a hand to its mouth. Trim, pretty, utterly British. She had a shape — waist, hips. She looked like some of the girls from her class at school — girls she used to see pushing prams along Mill Hill Parade. Her mother would be proud of her now with that Peter Pan collar — white next to the face, as Mummy had repeated, was indeed flattering.

She put on some sandals and stood up, smoothing down her

174

skirt. Unlike her ethnic muslins it looked as good as new. She had bought some lipstick from the Intercontinental Drug Store. She made up her face. On the floor lay her old clothes, shed skins from which had emerged this Young Conservative. A new recruit, hatched from a slum bazaar. She peered closer in the mirror. The pretty face smiled at itself – faintly freckled, floury with powder, eyebrows raised.

As she closed the door Mohammed emerged from the guest bedroom. Something, just a flicker, passed across his face. Either admiration or amusement, gone too quick to tell.

'This okay?' She blushed. She felt awkward, being a woman and drawing attention to the fact when so many identical Mohammeds jostled her in the street and put their hands up the crotch of her jeans.

He pointed to his head. 'I think ... I see Memsahib Smythe.'

She was thinking how to reply to this when there was the noise of an engine in the drive. She ran downstairs, followed by the bearer. It was Donald.

'Didn't I say I was coming back for lunch today?'

He spoke in the stagey way they talked when Mohammed was around. Mohammed must have remembered because the table was laid.

'You've done something to yourself,' said Donald. 'Good Lord.'

'Wait till I brush my hair.'

'I'm most impressed.' He paused. 'Goodness. Yes.' He gazed again. 'Good Lord.'

It was nice to see him alert. He had seemed preoccupied these last few days. It was probably something to do with his work, which he knew she would not understand. Nowadays his job spread into far more of his life than it had done at Crouch End.

They sat down to eat.

'I'm awfully glad you're going,' he said.

'What?' She stiffened. She had not told him, of course. There was no point, yet. But she had written the time and the place in her diary. Had he looked?

'I've been feeling it's time you got down to something,' he

175

said.

She hesitated, and then let out her breath. 'So have I. That's why I've done it. It's the only thing I seem qualified for, and I must do something here.'

'It foxed me, that dress, till I remembered it's Tuesday.'

She paused, a bean hanging from her fork. 'What?'

'Tuesday. The day for the fair Brits.'

'Ah. The B.W.A.'

There was a silence as her mind worked. This was tricky. She had presumed not actually to deceive him. Her absence should not have been missed because he was supposed to be at the office. To put it into words was so much more committing, for herself as well as for him.

Instead of speaking she grunted. This could be taken as an assent.

'What did your mother say in her letter?' she asked, a diversionary tactic.

'Let me see. Granny's had a date for her hip.'

'Marvellous. When?' All of a sudden she was interested in Gran.

'They're operating late August.' He relapsed into silence.

'It wasn't this place that gave her arthritis was it?' she asked, keen to continue this.

'Everyone gets it when they're old. But she suffered, you know, being out here. She didn't talk about it, not to me. But she suffered, Chrissy. Like not being able to have any more children after my father was born. They should've sent her back to England to have the baby.' He gazed at a radish, cut out with fancy petals. 'You know, I often think about them. Her and Grandad.'

'I know you do.'

'But I've usually imagined him. I've never imagined her. What it must have been like to come to India, a journey taking weeks, and marry somebody you hardly knew. And there was no one else around, no family. Just this man.'

She laughed. 'Like you.'

He paused. 'Whatever you feel, or find out about him, there's nothing much you can do. You've met this man on leave; he's looking for a wife and he's only got a few months to find one. You meet him over tea at someone's house, that's what Granny did, at her friend Aggy's. He seems rather dashing, sort of restive and manly amongst the dainty cucumber sandwiches. He's tanned, he's in charge of a whole battalion out East. You can't get to know him well, you couldn't then, you'd always see him in company. Then you're sailing out and that's that.' He put the radish into his mouth. Mohammed, waiting for this, whisked away the plates. 'And whatever misgivings you felt, you wouldn't talk about them — people didn't, did they, marriage was marriage, you didn't analyse and dissect and criticize ...'

This sounded heartfelt. She let it pass.

'And the hardship,' he said, 'and the illness, and you'd expect to lose at least one child even in my grandmother's day. And the heat — no air-conditioners ...'

'And the boredom.'

'Perhaps. I doubt it. They had their circuit — Mrs Gracie was telling me about family life — and their occupations.'

This could lead back to the B.W.A. She gazed at her yellow lap, thinking how to change the subject. After lunch, would he try to give her a lift to the B.W.A.? Then she heard his voice.

'You know, I loved Grandad a lot.'

'I know. I always liked the way you admired him.'

'You thought he was a pompous old fool, didn't you.'

'Of course not,' she lied. 'Anyway I hardly knew him. He died before we got married, remember.'

'How do you remember him?'

'Tut-tutting at me in the garden when I was wearing my red bikini.'

'Ah, that bikini.'

'When I was swotting for my 'A' levels behind your shed. He thought my bikini was a portent of social disintegration. He was very upright, wasn't he. Rather old-fashioned standards, even then. It was easy to sneer at him but actually I rather liked it. In retrospect anyway. It made him so solid, like a grandfather should be. I'd never known mine so he did instead.'

177

Donald did not reply.

'I thought he was very straight and honest,' she said, 'when people were proud to be that. A pillar of the Empire. He brought you up strictly and you're rather like him in some ways.' She stopped. 'Goodness, what's the matter? I mean, you look incorruptible. I'm sure that's why they sent you out here. You must have inherited it from him.'

He still looked startled. 'Inherited what?'

'Your integrity. That frank open gaze, the same blue eyes, as if he had nothing to hide.'

To her relief Donald could not have driven her to the B.W.A. anyway; he had an appointment straight after lunch and she made a delaying excuse. She kissed him goodbye. Today she felt tender towards him, partly because he had not forced her to lie, or to decide not to do so, and partly because he had talked so thoughtfully. Recently so pompous, today he had seemed humble and uncertain. As if for once open to change. Besides, they had talked. Usually their meals were eaten in silence, broken only by hushed bickering. She had presumed they would have more to talk about here, in Pakistan, but it had been just the same as usual.

Half an hour later she was sitting in a rickshaw. She unclicked her compact. In the powdery circle of mirror her face jogged, already beaded with sweat. Despite herself she had been flattered at Donald's reaction to the dress. In fact, in a secret, niggling way she was flattered by this whole business. What would Roz say? In the Tube, Roz plastered 'This Degrades Women' stickers over midriffs of underwear advertisements. She herself had not; she had just trooped along, half-giggling behind her gloves. Now she was out here, in fact, the whole thing seemed dwindled and rather amusing though she had not been disloyal enough to say this to Donald. This place certainly gave it a new perspective. Roz's insistence on calling Rick her 'comrade and co-parent' seemed quaint when in this city women walked around draped like furniture.

She would not mention this outing to Roz. What the hell. The

178

wind tossed her hair. She smiled. Out here she was free. Under the tassels the verges bounced past. Part of the reason she had not told Donald, of course, was that he would mock her. After all she had always gone on about women being exploited for their looks. And in this case, exploited for the colour of their skin, too. And she could hardly say she was being used when she had so readily agreed. Still, these were only trial shots. She was committing herself to nothing, and indeed nothing might come from them. It was just a jaunt, an exploration. She could not lounge about all day writing air letters. And here, when it came to jobs, one did not have the luxury of choice.

She was nearly an hour late for her appointment. The studio lay in one of the many commercial suburbs and the driver kept getting lost. He would stop to ask people who bent down to get a good look at her. Just down this way, they gestured. Everything was just down this way, just one minute, just one mile. People always wanted to be helpful by saying the thing that would please. Donald, sometimes amused and sometimes aggravated, complained about this in the office. It is ready directly, they said. Directly after directly, stretching into the mists of the endlessly possible.

Of course she need not have worried. Mr Pereira, a mild, polite man, did not seem to realize she was late. As at Sultan Rahim's, here she sipped sweet tea and chatted to him about the climate, yes indeed it was most humid but not so humid as upcountry, Karachi being blessed by the sea breezes. She wondered if he even knew about her appointment. He himself had cousins in Hainault, Essex, a very pleasant part he believed – his cousin and his family, they owned a small newsagent's business, she herself was perhaps acquainted with this Hainault? In fact, until now she had never known how to pronounce Hainault; no doubt Mr Pereira had got it right. He himself had never visited Britain. The British people, at his cousin's they could purchase their household requirements also, the groceries and soap powders, his cousin's shop remaining open until the late hours of the evening. She replied that such places were a boon for people who worked all day, increasingly so, as

179

the British shopkeepers were too lazy and unimaginative to extend their opening hours beyond five-thirty p.m. to suit the changing circumstances of society. In fact, she added, it was the Asians who had become essential in the liberation of the British women, releasing them from the tyranny of trying to shop during their working hours and thus enabling them to carry out two jobs, one at work and one in the home. As in fact her husband's firm was doing in this country, helping to establish supermarkets where everything was to be found swiftly under one roof, thus liberating the Pakistani housewife from the picturesque though lengthy daily grind of shopping at six different stalls. He replied that his cousin's business was becoming most prosperous and that now his cousin was hoping to purchase the lease on adjoining property, with residential units above to rent to the persons who worked in the surrounding commercial area. Himself he hoped to visit Britian in the near future, he had heard that it was most pleasant at this time of the year, resembling the winter months in Karachi. She agreed that indeed June and July would be the best time to visit Hainault, Essex.

Minutes ticked by. She gazed out of the window. The sign opposite said: *Dr Ravi's Revitalization Clinic*. It was like sitting in Sultan's office, and sitting in Superad. She could not tell whether this leisured politeness was due to her presence, an English woman, or whether Pakistanis always worked like this.

She cleared her throat. 'Mr Khan, from the Superad Agency, sent me here, I think I mentioned it in our telephone call. Just for some trial shots, I think, for their files.'

She paused for him to register this and perhaps to be impressed. After all, he could not have many British models coming to this bare, shabby studio little larger than a cupboard. He seemed unsurprised by this, either because he had been informed and did not think it noteworthy or because he had not been informed at all. Nobody reacted quite as she presumed. You arrived expecting something you had built up in your mind and then it melted away. The studio did not have the benefits of air-conditioning; in this heat she too gave up trying to find the

180

answers.

'I'm a bit hot,' she said. 'Shall I just powder my nose?'

At this he rose from his seat and started fiddling about with the equipment. There was a basin in the corner, and a mirror. She re-applied her lipstick. Her aunt Midge used to say: 'Horses sweat and men perspire but women only glow.' She was sweating. She gazed into the cracked glass. She did not resemble a model. Her hair stuck to her forehead in squiggles like question marks.

She climbed on to a stool. Behind her hung a white sheet. She felt ludicrous up there. In the unaccustomed short skirt she had to arrange her legs; she kept them pressed together but slanting sideways and crossed at the ankle as the Queen was supposed to do. She should have worn this dress for the office photo; what an easy way to please Donald. Why did she not bother to please him any more?

He was standing beside her, tilting her head. 'You permit me?'

She wanted to say: in England I would never have been a model, even if I'd wanted to. I am neither sufficiently lovely nor sufficiently professional. But here the standards are different.

'And ... just so.' Hand on her ankle, he moved her legs slightly more to the side.

She kept herself rigid, staring at the left-hand wall. An advertisement hung there; no doubt one of his own photos. It showed a Pakistani girl with permed hair. She was sitting on a car bonnet as those girls did at the Earl's Court Show; this girl however was decently clothed. *Our Brake Linings Are Your Life.* Would an English face like her own project even more reassurance about the quality and proven safety of the commodity? The girl was dressed in a trouser-suit, western-style. This made her more advanced. Modern expectations might be troublesome in a woman but when it came to a product, that was a different matter. Shamime had mentioned that only tarts, girls from lower-middle-class homes and non-Muslims modelled for a living – the sort of girls who became air-hostesses.

The shutter clicked. Out of the corner of her eye she saw him approaching. With light fingers he turned her face the other way. Her legs slid round, to slant demurely to the right.

'A profile now, if you please.'

On this wall hung a certificate, perhaps from his unlikely Madison Avenue days, and the photo of a baby advertising powdered milk. It was a Pakistani baby, rather fetching, dark-eyed and fat. Probably they liked them fat. She did not move her mouth until the shutter clicked twice. Then she asked: 'Have you, by any chance, heard of some saint or other – a hot water man?'

'Please to wait a moment. Do not move your head.'

She stayed rigid, eyes locked with the baby's. He gazed back at her. His glossy limbs were creased and bendy. Three clicks.

'Sorry,' she said.

'Now, please to turn the head this side and look into the camera. A smile please.'

'That's difficult. Can you say something funny?'

'My only joking it is in the Urdu. My English it is solely for the courtesies and the business.'

She kept her gaze steadied into the camera. She stretched her skin into some sort of grimace, perhaps a smile. He clicked several times and lifted his head.

'I am sorry. You were speaking?'

'I said, is there a shrine somewhere near Karachi where women go to offer prayers? Something to do with warm water.' She remembered the word. 'A *pir* used to live there. A sacred place, apparently, for ... ' she cleared her throat, 'your people.'

He gazed over the glass eye of his camera. 'I am a Christian. I am in the dark, concerning this, the same as yourself.'

She clapped a hand to her mouth, blushing. 'How stupid of me.' She tried to laugh. Of course, with a name like Pereira he must be Goan. She kept on thinking of them as all the same.

'Ah, do not move please.' He started clicking fast. 'Excuse me, but for the first time you are looking natural.'

20

IT HAD always taken Donald some time to work things out; he was made this way. During the days since the news about his grandfather he had been trying to organize his feelings. He was still confused; in a way he wanted to be. It was like the aftermath of an explosion when the haze and dust has yet to settle. When they did the damage would be revealed. He preferred to postpone this.

In the daytime it was hard to concentrate anyway. There was business to attend to, faces waiting for an answer and traffic to be negotiated in his sweltering car. The days felt different now, since Before. They had lost their transparency. But he could ignore this, as one ignores an ache by being constantly on the move. And in the evenings there was Christine, whom he had not yet told. Once he told her, in words, it would be confirmed. He would no longer be able to talk about other things and ignore the misery.

Yesterday Iona Gracie had phoned. The call had been about the Ginntho development but at the end he had asked if she knew more about this Marnley chap. The Indian woman had died, said Mrs Gracie, some years later. She had been thinking about it since Ronald's visit – after all, she had little enough to think about except this blessed hotel, and her memories. As it happened, someone's bearer was this woman's cousin and she, Iona, had heard a few more facts some years later. The woman was a local girl, a Sindhi, and had returned to her village with the baby boy. Soon afterwards she had died. For the life of her she could not remember the name of the woman or the baby, even if she had known at the time.

'Whose bearer was that?' asked Donald, trying to sound conversational.

She could not remember, it must have been—oh, fifty years ago. Some bungalow in Clifton—yes, it was painted pink now. Opposite the Dutch Consulate. A British family lived in it then. She had often played tennis there before she was married. Now it was all changed, of course, but the buildings remained.

Donald told himself: it was a long time ago; half a century. Attitudes were different then, there was a different code of behaviour according to your class and your race. He remembered from school—he had always remembered that line from some play: *But that was in another country, and besides, the wench is dead.*

But he could not settle his grandfather comfortably and forgettably into history. Even there he did not sit easy. He had not just gone along with the rules; he had exploited them. Mrs Gracie had admitted as much. It was one thing to take a native mistress and have her bear his child; it was another to treat her in a way which, even by the standards of the time must be considered cruel, cold and mean. Bad enough, in fact, for his grandfather to be transferred, no doubt for everybody's sake.

Looking back now and trying to remember Grandad, his memories were smudged. He did, in fact, remember him as tight-fisted. But that had seemed like Grandad's personal resistance to a shoddier modern world; part of his noble oblivious-ness. What other traits had he himself seen as more heroic than they were? Must he go back, painfully pick them up, and turn them over? Feel them disintegrate?

He would only picture Grandad during those last few years of his life. He would not creep right back into the past and ruin it, rendering valueless everything Grandad had shared with him, and everything Grandad had stood for. But the very word

'Grandad' now sounded inappropriate. Too false, too cosy. What words to replace it? An old man? A cruel old man?

As an old man what had he been like? Someone more tender with plants than with people. Towards the end of his life he had treated his wife, by now frail and querulous, with a belligerent gallantry. Constricted by the narrow doorways, he shooed away others to let her through. He would snap at her but not allow anyone else to do so. He guarded her with fierce exasperation. Donald had presumed that their marriage had been quite happy. They had rubbed along; in those days one did not inspect the bond with the intricate vocabulary one did now. It was to Donald that he told all his jokes.

Had Granny known? Surely not. The woman could have lived in the house and Granny would not have noticed. She seemed too absorbed in herself and her husband's comforts, too preoccupied with the small moments of day-to-day life. (Had the native woman offered him something better than this?) Besides they had moved away from Karachi the moment they married, or soon after.

What did it matter, something that this old man had once done, long ago? It did matter, of course, most dreadfully. It mattered that his grandfather had told nobody. Whether the reason was that he was too ashamed, or too uncaring, thinking it of no account – both mattered in their different ways and now Donald would never know which it was. Back in Brinton his grandmother, aged eighty-eight and bedridden, obviously had no knowledge of it; even if he wished he could find out nothing from her. Part of the horror of it was that his grandfather probably had had no moment, during all that time in India, that he would have needed to lie about any of this; not really. After all, a native woman was not the same as an English one; she was not part of one's life in the same way. Perhaps she had meant more to him than that; but perhaps one did not recognize, even to oneself, that such a woman could.

It was partly for this reason that he had not yet told Christine. She would wade in with all the arguments about injustice, racism, women's roles, imperialism, all that. Which indeed was a point, but not *the* point. Besides, she had always accused him of hero-worshipping his grandfather. Through her indignation (aimed at Grandad) and genuine sympathy (aimed at himself, Donald) there might just be a faint taste of justified come-uppance. And he did not care to discover this.

That afternoon he had to drive out some twenty miles to visit a Government of Sind Fertility Station. This was a new project with experimental strip-testing of various compounds, a drainage scheme and a new legume crop being planted. The road led out past Ginntho Pir into the desert beyond. A few villages were visible from the road. They all looked the same: obscure, mud-walled huts hemmed in by piled-up scrub. From the distance they scarcely showed — mere dun irregularities, blocks and tangles natural as rocks in the landscape. In the nearer ones you could see, through the thorn scrub, penned goats and the women who rose from their haunches with earthenware pots on their shoulders. Cattle dung had been slapped on the walls of the huts, to dry in the sun and burn for fuel. Behind the walls, what went on was as closed and incomprehensible as in another century. *And besides, the wench is dead.*

Here he sat behind the khaki shoulders of his driver. In a village like that a boy had crouched in the dust, years ago, as those children were squatting now. His surname should have been Manley. Donald would never know who he was. Perhaps the man still lived in a village like that; he must be over fifty-five years old now, a little older than Donald's own father would have been, had he lived. Perhaps the man had died or gone away. Perhaps he had moved to Karachi. One of those men past whom Donald had pushed in the crowded streets — one of them could have been his own half-uncle.

'Sahib is all right?'

Donald managed to open his eyes, and sat up straight. Jalal the driver was looking at him in the mirror.

'Fine. It's just a little hot.'

At the Fertility Station Donald stood in the concrete porch, asking the director the correct questions about chemical mix and crop results. In front stretched the fields edged with raised mud walls, like the plasticine models he had made as a child. Water had been pumped along the ditches; the earth was damp as putty. Green shoots grew in the various strips, some sparse, some thicker.

'Soon I hope we are having some rain,' said the director. 'Generally in August there is a little rainfall. You are feeling the heat, Mr Manley?'

Donald nodded. 'Just a little.'

'And you have a family out here?'

'A wife, yes. No children.'

He could have added: but my grandfather had a child here. Somewhere he sowed a seed. One child grew, perhaps paler than the others. Lost now.

On the return journey the car approached Ginntho Pir. From this side the mound rose above the small collection of huts. As yet Donald had not visited the place; he was waiting to do so with Christine. On top of the hill, shaded by trees, the shrine stood behind the large old mausoleum. As the car passed, it slid slowly behind the larger building, its white walls disappearing from sight. These people went there to pray. For what? For a child to be born, for a child not to die, for some impossibility to happen. Perhaps the woman had knelt in there, once. He himself would feel like an intruder. The humbler the place, the more private it seemed. He turned to look out of the back window; as the car drove down the road, past the bushes and the bazaar, the little shrine again slid into view, smaller in the distance. He felt oddly moved by its absurd plaster turrets. Somebody had tied flags around them – flags showing loyalty to no country, only to faith. Why? He knew nothing; he must try to understand.

Back at the office there were some telephone messages on his desk, left by Mary. One said 'Please ring Mrs Gracie.'

He sat down. It was six o'clock; he could quite reasonably put it off until tomorrow. He knew what she would say – that she had thought out a tactical plan of attack and that she was relying on him to do a, b or c. She still had no idea who he was, or his connection with the proposed development. If it came to a confrontation the whole thing could be extremely awkward. His loyalties should lie with Cameron's, of course, but he would prefer this not to be tested.

She answered. 'Ah Ronald dear. I just had to tell you, I've been rummaging through my desk trying to find the lease as I promised and you wouldn't guess what I found instead.'

A pause for effect. He could picture her breathless in that sombre hall, her hairband askew. 'What?' he asked.

'A bundle of my mother's letters. They were written to her friend Annie Kershaw in Surrey. Annie must have returned them to us after Mama's death, they're absolutely riveting. I want to read you something. Ready?'

He grunted, nodding, and pushed his swivel chair round. The Tibet lady faced him, holding the soap. She looked dumb, suppliant and beautiful. Perhaps his grandfather's woman had looked at him like that.

'It's about your grandfather's friend, that Marnley. You said you wanted every scrap I could find for the book.'

He sat up, alert. 'That's right.' He had forgotten that he had told her his grandmother was writing her memoirs, hence the need for information. He loathed lying; he had managed to forget this one already.

'Here it is. There's a bit about some regimental parade, who fainted and so on, then this: "The usual rash of confinements this winter, Winnie Atwood had a girl, Mrs Herrick a big bouncing boy, eight pounds, and scandal scandal, I know you like all the tit-bits Annie dear, on the servants' grapevine this morning I heard that the native so-called sweeper of a Major in the Kentish Fusiliers, a woman called Moni, had a boy born last week. Ayah's aunt was the midwife. Ho hum, nothing unusual here, men will be men, my dear." Then she goes on about a garden party. The dates fitted, Ronald. I just thought you'd like to know, so you can fit in the woman's name. If indeed one wants to include such things.'

'Thank you so much,' he said. 'Most useful. Moni.' He put down the receiver.

Moni. He gazed at the hoarding. He sat still for some minutes, rubbing his forefinger from side to side, across the surprisingly dense hairs of his new moustache.

He did not drive straight home. At the Sind Club junction, the boy who usually sold him *Newsweek* waved a copy, grinning, as Donald turned the car left, towards Clifton. It was the only clue he had and he was unlikely to get any more. It was a miracle he knew this much after all these years, when so many things had been changed out of recognition.

The road to Clifton, for instance. In his grandfather's day Clifton, built upon the only hill for miles, had been an elegant residential suburb. The sea had not been drained then; Clifton had been something of a resort, with an esplanade, a telescope and the sedate amusements of an Indian Brinton. In the days of the Raj the British families had lived there, and it was separated from the city by a stretch of causeway.

Now the sea had been drained, leaving miles of salt-bleached desert. All along the Clifton Road apartment blocks were being built, below them the empty canyons of garages and future supermarkets. The bleak buildings were softened in the evening light. Cameron's, amongst others, was helping push this country into the twentieth century. Surprisingly, he was a part of this. Between the blocks you could still glimpse vacant land marked out with posts. Goat herds picked their way around the cars parked by the Mid-East Medical Center, with its sprinkled lawns. Soon Clifton would be joined to Karachi. He negotiated the roundabout, with its Islamic Progress Monument, bright steel gleaming with hope, pointing up to the sky.

He drove into Clifton. The street was wide and empty here, lined with trees which were now casting long shadows across the road. The old bungalows resembled those near the Sind Club where Mrs Gracie lived. He drove up the hill and stopped outside the Dutch Consulate.

Across the street stood the pink bungalow. Its gates were open. Outside stood a huge tree with creepers hanging; perhaps this was a banyan, his grandfather had spoken about boys swinging in the banyans. Perhaps this too was a lie. Behind it

189

the building looked unreal in this radiant light, like a pink, pillared wedding cake left outside too long.

He rang the bell. Closer, the paint was blistered. In this climate nothing remained new for long. The door was opened by a moustached bearer in white shirt and trousers. Donald paused. The furnishings looked sumptuous. He did not know how to begin.

'I'm looking for a woman,' he said. 'I wonder if you could help me.'

'I will fetch memsahib.'

'No, not memsahib. This was a long time ago. It concerns the servants, you see.' The bearer could not be over forty, but Donald felt reckless. For once he did not mind what anyone thought. 'Is there an older servant here perhaps, who has been in this residence a long time?'

'I do not understand. You are wanting sahib?'

'Er no. There was recently perhaps an older bearer here, or perhaps a cook?'

A Pakistani woman appeared, glittering with jewellery and very plump. No, on second glance pregnant. She shook his hand. 'Good evening.' She paused. 'I believe we've met before. The Boat Club, perhaps? You are the new man at Cameron Chemicals. We were acquainted, too, with Mr Frank Smythe.'

He introduced himself. For a moment he had forgotten his job.

'Yes, and my husband he works for Ciba-Geigy. That will explain it. We met at the reception. He will be returning in a moment. Please do come in and sit down.' She turned to the bearer and seemed to be ordering drinks.

He hesitated in the hall. 'Actually, I really wanted to talk to your servants. I know it sounds funny.' He looked around at the various open doors. 'Have any of them been here for a long time?'

She raised her eyebrows. 'We have been here since nine years. I don't understand.'

'I'm sorry. I know. Have any of your servants been here long?'

190

'The servants? You are wishing to know about the servants?'

Donald rubbed his moustache, nodding. His face was hot.

'The cook, he has just arrived from another residence. The bearer, Mumtaz, he is here when we shifted to Clifton. You are wanting a servant perhaps? You need a cook-bearer?'

Donald felt like a private detective, a shabby intruder fired by the chase. 'Well no, not quite.' He turned to Mumtaz, who had not gone for the drinks. 'You have worked here a long time?'

'Since eleven years, sahib. Before this, in Lahore sahib's residence.'

'Ah. Not long enough.'

The bearer coughed. 'But mali, he is working here for very long years.'

'Ah.' Hot with embarrassment, Donald looked at the hall sofa. It bore a row of plump silk cushions. They too seemed waiting for him to make himself plain. 'Is he around?'

'Not until tomorrow,' said the woman. 'He is gone now.'

'You don't by any chance know where he lives? I'm terribly sorry to be such a nuisance.'

'He has done something wrong? I have never quite been trusting him.'

'Heavens no. I'd just like to visit him to ask him about some-one.'

'I see. He has a friend you want as mali. I don't know where he is living. I don't know his name. I am just calling him mali.'

'He lives backside.' The bearer pointed through the lounge door. This could mean any distance. The three of them stood there for some moments.

'Mumtaz, *jao*. Take Mr Manley.'

Donald muttered his thanks to the pregnant lady, whose name he had not caught. She must think he was mad. But the English were mad, weren't they. This did not ease his blushes.

They walked out of the front gates. As they turned the corner, a silver Mercedes drove in behind them. He heard the car door slam, and raised voices speaking in Urdu. By this time he was out of sight down a steep path between the two compound walls. The ground dropped sharply here. He stooped to avoid the thorn bushes.

The path smelt of excrement. Ahead of him, dazzlingly white, walked his guide through this jungle. The earth was scattered with rubbish and dung. A pariah dog yapped at his trousers. The bearer walked swiftly; Donald hastened to keep up. Through the thin bushes ahead he could see some huts. He realized that a settlement clung to the side of Clifton, hidden from the houses above by the drop of the hill.

Now he was closed into a narrow lane, picking his way along a ditch that ran down the centre. It was sickeningly smelly. A radio played. Evening meals were being prepared, with cooking odours and clatter. On either side rooms were full of families; faces turned to stare but he did not like to pry too closely, they were so exposed. But then so was he. He hurried after Mumtaz who had turned up another lane. A hundred yards up the hill this man would have been serving him whisky and soda.

The huts were packed along either side. Children ran after him; a man shouted. In the twilight he slipped in the mud.

The bearer had moved into a doorway. Donald followed him. He blinked in the electric light. He was standing in a small room. Two women and some children disappeared through a fringed plastic hanging. An old man remained, lying on a rope bed.

Whether this was the mali he did not ever discover; he might just have been an old man with the longest memory. Donald cleared his throat and smiled. The bearer acted as interpreter, though how much he understood Donald could not guess. Donald told the old man how many years it was. Would they think in the same span as he did? Time altered according to your expectations of what life had to offer. He told him about an English army sahib called Manley, and the woman's name, Moni. Speaking it now, he realized that it might be a Hindu rather than Muslim name; after all, this was years before the separation of the two countries. If she had been Hindu the family that survived her would certainly have fled to India. If the family still existed; if indeed anyone still possibly knew.

He sat on the edge of the charpoy, sipping tea. The wooden frame dug into his thighs. The old man was sitting at the other

192

end. He seemed to weigh nothing; it was Donald who sunk the thing down. Perhaps none of them understood what he was getting at. Did they realize they had something he needed? The women and children had returned to squat in the corner. Another man, also elderly, had arrived. His voice joined in the conversation, which sounded more like an argument. The women were talking now. *Moni*, he heard, their voices rising. They were too young; they could have no idea whom he was seeking. The argument seemed to be taken out of his hands. His legs had become numb but he did not like to move. By now other men were crowding the doorway.

With a scrape, someone dragged in a chair. They gestured that he should sit on it. Somebody shooed away a child. He rose with difficulty, stickily, and sat down. Everyone's eyes were upon him. He felt both the culprit and the honoured guest. He did not know which he was supposed to be. He addressed the second elderly man, who wore glasses and who seemed the most respected voice in the discussion.

'Moni is dead,' he tried to explain. 'I look', he pointed to his eyes, 'for Moni's son.' He had forgotten the word for 'son'. He could hardly indicate someone small, when his uncle would be over fifty years old. If indeed he was still alive. He looked around for the bearer, but Mumtaz had gone.

More men had arrived. With the rise and fall of the voices he felt his own hopes rise and diminish. Fifty years in a settled country was long enough but fifty years here seemed beyond any reckoning what with wars, and poverty, and families scattered like matchsticks over three countries on the tide of events his grandfather had helped to promote. Little shanty towns like this grew up overnight and then were destroyed without a trace. Up on the hill, in the big bungalows, nobody would even notice.

Men gestured and shouted; perhaps they just wanted him to get out. The light caught their wrist watches. What were they talking about? The room was filled with cheap cigarette smoke. Some of the words might be names, for all he knew. He felt like a child listening but not comprehending, back in Brinton at the

193

beginning of his ignorance. Perhaps he should not have listened then.

Somebody touched his arm. It was the old man in the glasses. He pointed to Donald's chest. Donald inquiringly pressed his hand to his heart. The man wanted his pen. Donald took it from his breast pocket and gave it to him; the man passed it to someone else. Donald thought: perhaps they want my wallet. The talking grew louder. Another man leant down, pointed to Donald's knee and tapped it. The old man said something he could not understand, leant forward and fingered the sleeve of Donald's bush shirt. Donald sat rigid.

Another hand reached out and pointed to Donald's buttons, one by one. Donald buttoned up the top one, which was undone. He tried to keep smiling like a guest. Perhaps they were going to tear off his clothes. Perhaps they were going to get their own back. His shirt stuck to him damply.

A piece of paper was put into his hand. Mumtaz was pushing his way back through the other men. The man in the glasses nodded. The paper read: *Saleem Beg, Near Petrol Pump, Commercial West Colony, Karachi.*

'This is son of Moni,' said Mumtaz. 'This,' he pointed, 'his location.'

The old man pointed again to Donald's shirt, then made looping movements in the air. At last Donald understood.

'Each day,' said Mumtaz, 'he is sitting here. He is tailor.'

21

'AH, THE fair tones of Mrs Manley.'

'I was just phoning ... you never seem to be in your office.'

'My deepest apologies. I am going hither and thither.'

'I was just wondering about the beach hut.'

'No problem. I have the beautiful beach houses in my files.'

'Oh good.' She felt the usual bafflement. Had he forgotten that she wanted one, then? She said: 'And there was just one other thing. You are really the only person who might know. I've heard about a sort of shrine. I think it's a shrine. A place with hot water.'

'You are wanting the sightseeing jaunt? This will be my pleasure.'

'Well, sort of. Do you know the place?'

'Any place you want, I will be taking you.'

Mohammed, waiting for his cue, took the receiver she passed him. He was, she hoped, going to explain the directions. He spoke in Urdu, seemingly for a long time but then it always seemed a lengthy process when the language was unknown, as a journey seems endless when the road is unfamiliar and the destination expected around every corner. Besides, as Donald remarked, in Pakistani conversations ten words will always do instead of one. Mohammed stood with his back to her. Perhaps instead of road directions he was discussing herself. He must know her secrets—he emptied the waste-paper basket, he brought her bed-tea in the mornings; he was the true inmate of this house, rather than their temporary, rented selves.

No problem, said Sultan. She went upstairs to change.

Last night she and Donald had quarrelled. She had made a fuss about going to some cocktails at the Weatherbys', saying how boring all the people were.

'You don't have the wives,' she said.

'You needn't have the wives. We're not Muslims.'

'But the division's just the same. All you men talking about your work.'

'Back home all your friends were women.'

'Not women like these.'

'Christine, I wish you'd learn to adapt.'

What she really meant, though had not said, was how boring they made Donald seem to her. How little any of them had been changed by this place. The English were so closed, hemmed in by their fixed beliefs and their fear of germs.

'They just see this place as a threat,' she had said. (*They*, not *you*.) 'Everything's conspiring against them, it's all falling to pieces in their hands, the biros aren't like the English ones.'

'They aren't.' Donald shook his pen. It was after dinner and he was sitting at his desk.

'It's a wartime mentality; they're locked in. No room for doubt or change. Duke getting all his stuff from the Commissary. I bet he couldn't tell a tandoori from a Toblerone.'

'That's English. He eats Hershey Bars.'

'Don't be pedantic.'

'And he eats curries. He was having lunch today at the Welcome Tikka House.'

'You know what I mean.'

Did he? She had looked at Donald's face in the lamplight. Before you could not have described it. Now, with his new moustache it was defined; he was a man with an identity. He looked heavier.

'They bring their cultural baggage with them,' she said.

196

'But isn't that what you're doing?'

She had ignored this. 'I try to be open, Donald. I want this place to change me through my bloodstream. You see these hippies just sitting and experiencing.'

'Darling, it's something else that's changing them through their bloodstream.' He had sipped his coffee and remarked mildly: 'Anyway, I don't really see what's so ethnic about working for an advertising agency.'

She had shifted in her armchair. She wished he had not put it like that. 'It's only because there's nothing else. Anyway probably nothing will come of it. It's a week since I saw them and I haven't heard.' She meant: it was a week since she had been photographed, but she had not yet informed him about the precise nature of the work. That nobody had phoned both relieved her and rebuffed her vanity.

He had gazed down at his pile of *Scientific Americans*. He had become so preoccupied of late. Near by smoked a mosquito coil; it gave the desk a sacred air. No doubt he was getting more involved in his work but could speak less of it, now that it was growing daily more complex. She felt the same about her letters home. After the first few wide-eyed ones filled with local colour and travelogue cameos she had relapsed into near silence. Her life had become both more ordinary and more subtly different. She could no longer remember what was unusual about this place.

She had gazed at the lamplit profile. 'Anything worrying happened at the office?' she had asked. 'You've been seeming so withdrawn.'

He paused and turned, rubbing his finger back and forth across the moustache. This was a new habit, grown wih the growth. He had said gently: 'Nothing for you to worry about, darling.'

She had tensed to speak, but she stopped. Nothing, in other words, that she would understand. Don't bother your little head about it. She had not replied. They must not quarrel. If they did, they would feel too drained and sad to in all decency make love later. And they ought, tonight being marked with a star. A trivial squabble would have been all right, in fact often proved pleasantly inflammatory—both of them, she suspected, realized this. A spirited discussion about whether she fancied David Weatherby despite his booming laugh had resulted in a playful start to something which could otherwise be far from ecstatic. Could be, in fact, a barren rubbing of flesh against stubborn flesh; the polite mutual moans, the damp separateness and private griefs.

To avoid more words she had gone into the garden. The lamplight shone across the lawn; from the bushes came the whirr of some insect or frog she still could not identify. The sky was bright with stars in foreign configurations. Travel sounded so liberating. From England, Pakistan seemed a blood transfusion of the spirit. But here they were, the two of them 3,500 miles from home, damper and hotter but heavily mortal.

Even out here you could smell the city. It was always with you; it was in your nostrils as you stepped off the plane. It was indescribable. 'Humanity' was the nearest you could get. Behind the house a baby cried. She looked into the sky. Two bodies rubbing together in the dark. Stubborn flesh. Between them no chink of infinity; no other life beginning.

An hour later that morning she was standing at the gate while Mohammed waited in the porch, grave as her father seeing her off on a doubtful date. If Sultan was so busy, had he broken appointments to arrive so promptly?

The sky was overcast today. After two months of unbroken blue this closeness was almost more uncomfortable. In August the monsoon weather arrived. This did not necessarily mean rain; just a weighed, pregnant grey.

On an impulse she had put on her yellow dress, obscurely both to please Sultan and to keep him at a distance. She sat down beside him. Today he wore crisp cream pyjamas. He was freshly scented. The doll bounced as they drove down the potholed streets of Phase Four; beside the doll jigged a spangled motto sewn on to cloth—no doubt a Koranic saying. In England she would have considered such things vulgar toys; here they

198

were magic talismans, bouncing and jigging and leading them there.

He was in high spirits. He switched on his radio; a woman's voice warbled and swooped. He pressed the police siren. A bearer, wobbling on his bicycle, regained his balance. They passed the familiar bungalows of Phases One and Two and the Chief Minister's residence with its sentries outside. There had been riots again yesterday, Sultan informed her. These had not been reported in the newspapers, the spaces being reserved for the Prime Minister's hand-outs, but Sultan said that there was increasing trouble at the top; reshufflings were about to happen, with ministerial replacements, even imprisonments. They drove into town, past the hotels and the Playboy Night Club.

'Young lovebirds come, with their slacks, and do cheek-to-cheek dance.' He leant to point, scattering her lap with ash. She glanced at him, picturing being pressed against his cheek. They were driving down the highway now. Up above the kites were circling. (Not buzzards, she had learnt this.)

'Are we going to the shrine or the beach hut?' she asked.

He lifted both hands off the wheel. 'As you wish.'

'You've found us a beach hut?'

'Ah yes, no problem.'

She persisted. 'Do you have a key?'

'No key. If you are wishing, we go to shrine.'

He did not change direction; this must be the route to the shrine. She tried to relax and accept. He had no plan about this; his voyage was not her voyage. In all their shared journeys it never had been. Like the kites, the usual vague questions circled in her head. Did he want her company as a business venture, herself a female kind of real-estate to be leased for her looks? Did he perhaps want her sitting beside him for the status she gave him, or for her unique self? Perhaps it was not prestige but lust. Inflamed by magazine stories and reports from Kensington Market he knew that English girls, even married ones, were only good for one thing. The car had slowed down behind a lorry; he revved the engine, his baggy leg pumping, and swerved to overtake. Or perhaps he was just being kind: the diligent host showing her his country at some inconvenience to himself. Ashamed, she realized this was the one motive that had not yet crossed her mind. She wondered, as always, what he looked like under his clothes. She had touched no Pakistani, except to shake hands.

The woman sang, eerily high. The sitar, weaving up and down, cast a spell on these dingy factories. Ahead lay the hills, flat against the pewter sky. She imagined vaguely that the shrine was in some cave, as in *A Passage to India* – that book haunted her, it was written for her. A hole where little would happen but where some change, oh at last some change, would take place. She would emerge from it altered through the blood and the spirit. She felt grateful to Sultan for knowing her destination and taking her there without question; likewise she herself should not keep querying this disappearing trick with the beach hut. Sentences rolled around her head. The arrival is the beginning, not the end. Or: it is the voyage, not the destination, that is important. Did that make sense? These voyages with Sultan through the sprawling, centreless city were the nearest she had felt to some inner reshuffling. Each time her destinations had not been as expected. Nothing had arisen from her meetings with Mr Khan and the photographer. But the voyages and the waiting had been somehow more dense than their supposed result. A journey without an arrival; it was like walking into a mosque, with just an empty niche to face you on the innermost wall.

They were driving across the desert. She recognized this as the highway that led to Duke's hotel site. The shrine must be beyond. Those hills ahead might be near or far; they rose up as sudden as theatre props. You could not tell the distance. In the summer they used to send the women up into the hills.

They passed the asbestos factory. A little further, in the shade of some bushes, Sultan stopped the car.

'This is the hotel site,' she said.

'It is more far, you are thinking?'

She paused, the car door still closed. 'You mean it's here?'

He indicated that this was correct, and switched off the engine.

'But I've been here before. Duke — Mr Hanson, an American — he brought me here last week. He's building a leisure complex. We walked around.' She gazed at the scrub.

'You have already been visiting the shrine?'

'He didn't mention a shrine. He mentioned a boating lake. It was all a great hurry.'

Ginntho Pier, he had said. She had presumed he was mentioning some sort of jetty. Pier?

'This is the Ginntho Pir,' said Sultan, spreading out his hands.

She tried to connect the two places: her misty vision of hills, and this. Her head ached as she tried to pull them together into one. Last week four of them had come here — Duke, Shamime, herself and some ministerial aide of Shamime's uncle. She had met them by chance at the Intercon Coffee Shop and they had invited her along for the ride. Duke, unusually formal and abstracted, had escorted them to the water's edge, talking in square metres. She had felt intrusive; this was obviously the last and most tense stage of negotiations. They had only stayed a few minutes. She had also felt embarrassed, having just heard from Donald of his involvement with the donkey place.

She climbed out of the car. The haze had cleared and the sun was shining, as blistering as ever.

'This is where the hot water man is?' she asked.

Sultan was standing the other side of the car. He raised his hands and shrugged: as you wish, his hands said. He is where you care to find him.

From here she could see the hill with its domed old monument, or shrine, or whatever it was.

'That's the holy place?' She pointed.

He nodded — at least, the oriental equivalent of a nod, a sideways movement of the head, a shrug really. *Acha*, people said. *Acha, tikka, okay.* If you want it to be yes, then it's yes. Either the shrine was there, or he did not know, or he thought she really should not be here, it was too scruffy, or she really should not be here, it was a place sacred to Muslims, perhaps to

201

himself, and she was an intruder. Now they had arrived at their destination he seemed strangely detached.

She hesitated. 'You are coming?'

'If you wish.'

'I'll go. I won't be long. Are you terribly thirsty?'

'*Gee-han*. You are thirsty? I get us drinks, okay?' Again the sideways nod.

She walked up past the stalls, the air wrapping around her like flannel. There were stirrings and rattlings as the beggars climbed to their feet and organized their tins. Squatting on the ground, women stared. A turbaned mullah glanced at her coldly, like a robed master who finds a pupil coming to the wrong school. How could you forget yourself in this country when all those eyes reminded you who you were? She pulled out her dupatta and wrapped it around her head. The topmost stall sold garlands. Ignoring the crowd which had gathered, she fished for some money and bought a string of blossoms. Someone tittered.

As she walked on the footsteps followed. Ahead stood the large old building. This must be the shrine; there was only one other building up here, a little whitewashed modern place that did not look important. She must not hesitate too long; several people were giggling now.

She went up to the building, slipped off her sandals and stepped in through the high arched doorway. She could hear nobody following her.

She had expected a grave of some kind; some monument to the hot water man upon which the faithful could scatter the flowers and votive offerings so copiously on sale down in the bazaar. The saint had died, but surely he would have left something to touch? There was nothing: no garlanded tomb. Nothing but a high, domed interior, an empty stone floor and a crumpled chewing-gum packet. There were arched doorways looking on to the bushes outside, with the people blocking the one behind her. There were chipped, crumbling walls and vandalized bits of mosaic. She stood still, willing herself to feel something. She had come so far for this. Only now did she realize how much she had relied upon this place.

Still nobody else came in. She remained for several minutes, her flowers dangling. She had expected a holy stillness; instead there was this graffiti'd vacancy. She hesitated, gazing at the cracked plasterwork and the litter swept into one corner.

Outside she put on her sandals and made her way down the slope, past the stalls with their incomprehensible trinkets. Her throat felt tight. Ridiculously, tears pricked her eyes. Her belt and the prim little sleeves chafed her. It was midday and there was a cloying smell of frying. People were no doubt watching her taking her string of blossoms in the wrong direction.

Sultan's car was there, but no Sultan. A couple of rickshaws waited with their sleeping drivers. A drinks seller cycled past, his box rattling. She searched around, absurdly disappointed.

Just then a hand touched her arm. Turning, she saw a young boy. He was bent under a yoke, with tins hanging at either end.

She shook her head. 'No. Non. *Nahin.*' She could not even remember the right word. She felt as weary and baffled as she had been in Juna Bazaar, before she had met Sultan. Weeks ago, that was, and she had come nowhere.

He said something in Urdu. '*Nahin,*' she said, shaking her head and pointing to the nuts in the tins. She tried to shake off his hand but now he was pointing down the road and beckoning her to follow.

She started off behind him, following his dusty feet. They were walking towards the hills. His back was bowed under the pole that sagged as he walked. He could not be more than twelve years old. They passed the monument and the huts down the other side of it. After a few yards the bushes stopped and the desert road stretched ahead. He halted and pointed.

There, set back from the road stood a solid little whitewashed building, its shutters closed. Above the door a sign said *Government Rest House*. Formerly, no doubt, it had been a dak bungalow for the British. It was shaded by one large tree. Nobody seemed to be about. The only sign that anyone looked after it was a rope bed standing in the veranda.

She paid the boy a rupee and watched him walk back down

203

the road, his load swaying. She felt hot and dizzy. The building was freshly painted; it made her wet eyes ache. The door stood ajar.

Trampled sand led up to it, with trampled thorny plants. She walked slowly. Did the boy presume that this, in fact, was her destination? As she neared the door she heard music from within. She felt both torpid and alert.

'Hello?' She stood on the veranda, speaking rather than shouting. There was no answer.

She stepped through the door, blinking in the gloom. It was a narrow little hallway. Sultan's radio stood on the floor, playing music. There was a chair, made of woven plastic loosened with use, and a wooden table. On it stood a tray with two bottles of Fanta and a dish of nuts. Sultan's shiny black shoes lay on the floor. She was still holding the string of blossoms. She laid them over the back of the chair.

The inner door was ajar. She hesitated, hitching the dupatta around her neck. Was somebody in there? She stepped through the threshold.

It was darker in here. She stood still, waiting for her eyes to adjust to the gloom. The room was close and stuffy. After a while she could make out detached shapes in the darkness: a cupboard, a chair and a bed, with somebody lying upon it.

She moved closer, quietly. In here it was as still as a shrine. For a moment she thought he was dead. He lay motionless on his back, facing upwards. Sleep made him dignified; his face was calm, its talking ceased. She knelt down beside him, easing off her sandals and laying them on the floor.

He did not stir. Only his lips moved, opening and closing; she heard the small puffs of air from the dreaming life within. One of his hands hung down near her. The other lay across his chest, closed around his packet of cigarettes.

Her eyes were accustomed now to the shuttered dark. She tried to make her mind a blank, and not to wonder if he had expected her to follow him in here. She just remained, hardly breathing, kneeling on the warm concrete. She gazed at his blind face and listened to the sighs of exhaled air. He seemed so saintly in repose. He was no longer Sultan Rahim, he was all Pakistani men, at last oblivious of her. She leant closer; she could smell his hair oil.

In the front room the singing stopped and was replaced by the announcer's voice. Still he did not stir. Just the lips pursing and the hand, over his heart, barely rising and falling. A fly landed on her cheek; she did not dare raise her hand to wipe it away.

Another song began, liquid and eerie, higher and higher, like a bird nobody has ever seen. She thought: I did not find my hot water man. She gazed at the swell of his stomach, shadowed and mysterious, and at the loose folds of his trousers.

She swallowed with difficulty; her throat was tight. Just then he mumbled and shifted over. The cigarette packet fell to the floor. His clothes rustled as he rearranged himself, with a grunt, on to his side facing her. He still slept. His hand hung down, touching her dress. She leant against it.

His hand started moving on her hip. She inched closer, pressing herself against the bed. When she moved, she realized she was wet with sweat. His face was half-buried in the pillow; his hand moved round her, rubbing gently up and down her buttock.

He mumbled something in Urdu. Still asleep, he probably thought she was his wife. She tried to swallow again.

He mumbled again in Urdu. His hand moved more firmly now. She closed her eyes. His hand moved up, and stopped at her belt.

It remained there a moment. He hooked his fingers around the fabric. She did not breathe. Nor, it seemed, did he. She kept her eyes closed. He unhooked his fingers. His hand moved up and down her damp back.

'You are staying with Sultan.'

It was neither a question or a command; just flat words. She nodded. She could not move to get up and close the door. If she climbed to her feet she would come, clumsily and humiliatingly, to her senses.

She remained kneeling, her face pressed into the thin scratchy wool of the blanket. Something must happen; at last it must. His eyes must be open now; he was unwinding her dupatta. He laid his face on the top of her head. She felt his nose pressing into her hair; he was smelling her, rubbing his face to and fro. Both his arms were around her now, pulling her in so she was jammed against the frame of the bed.

His hands moved quicker now, fluttering over her back and touching her here and there. She shivered. She was wet all over. Still kneeling she moved back and undid her buttons, fumbling with the tight little holes. She took his hand and pushed it down the front of her dress, pressing it against her slippery breast.

22

SHAMIME slept with her face in the pillow. She fell asleep so quickly afterwards. Duke could not bear to look at her body when she was oblivious. He leant over and gently pulled up the sheet around her shoulders. He picked up her clothes from the floor; she always presumed that there was somebody to pick them up and there always was, himself included. He folded them carefully and laid them on the chair — her office clothes, loose chiffon kamize and shalwar trousers, that clothed her with such Muslim seemliness in the company of others.

Above the bed hung the studio shots. Three boys, taken years back. They'd all worn crewcuts then. Grinning, they looked beyond their father into the shadowed room. It was midday and the drapes were closed. In the past Duke had never needed to close them. Though nothing could stop Gul Khan closing them in the evening, he himself had always opened them before he went to bed. He liked seeing the dawn, he always told folks that this was the best part of the day. Soon after that he would be jogging. Except that he had stopped jogging recently; inertia had been creeping up. So I get fat, he thought, so I get a coronary? So, why fight it? So what? So he no longer cared for this body that had betrayed him.

He parted the drapes. Unusually, the day had begun muggy and overcast, monsoon weather. Now the haze had cleared. He looked down North 6th Street. Pleasant modern homes not so different, he had once thought, from West Boulevard, Wichita. A gate opened and a car drove out; in the back sat two Pakistani women, residents of the house. The women here had changed, now that for the past two weeks he had loved one, her black hair catching in his mouth. He did not want to touch these other women; he just knew them. They were familiar to him. In some way he even felt that through them he knew the men too.

Gul was out for the day. There was some family celebration; his sister had produced a boy. That was the reason Shamime and himself had come back here, rather than drive in the evening to the beach hut, the only other place they could be alone. His mind had grown cunning. It dismayed him, that the moment Gul spoke his own thoughts had sped to this room. Gul's gratefulness when given a whole day's leave had sickened him still further. Gul made him feel guiltier than he had imagined. He was very fond of his old bearer who, he was sure, knew nothing. Still Gul carried out his routines, rubbing the beach sand off Duke's shoes and leaving them ready in the wardrobe. Gul had the innocence of the devout, unlike the beach chowkidar who was on to something. This man was a swarthy Makrani; he hung around Duke's car when they arrived at dusk. Duke tipped him generously with soiled notes.

He had always considered himself so straight, but how doggedly he now lied. Once you had told one falsehood, it was so damned easy. He thought sin was punished but nobody found him out. He said to himself: I am an adulterer. He was like everybody else now; most men of his age had experienced that which, ludicrously, bore the same name as what was happening between him and Shamime. Could they possibly feel the same? Young Javed, the Translux architect, had not questioned him when Duke had phoned this morning to postpone their lunch. No thunderbolts had struck. To other folk nothing appeared to have changed — he did his work, he made phone calls, he made conversation with Shamime while other people were in the room. He had arrived in this country thinking he could change the way things worked, like Minnie believed she could change herself by the books she read and the classes she attended; he thought that he had the fibre to do this. Do-It-Yourself Hanson, they called him in Kuwait. He had never betrayed his wife, though Jesus he had been lonely. Even he knew there had been opportunities should he have wanted them. Pleasant career girls on planes; in foreign bars, in foreign cities, women who sat next to him and talked about themselves in flat smokers' voices. Now he could not recognize that man. The voice on the phone to Javed was still oddly his. It sounded the same as it always had, but he was not the same inside. And he was starting to think: what difference does it make? As if he were being sapped by something in the air of this place.

He rubbed his eyes. Her smell was on his fingers. She stirred. He did not want her to wake up. If anything could be simple she looked simple now: just a black tangle of hair. His cool, wily child.

He should have stopped after that first time. He could have forgiven himself that one night. Shamime would have been spared this. Minnie would have understood; it was a moment of passion, not the steady betrayal it had since become. That second time, after the checkers, they had lain here in the terrible intimacy of speech. *When did you first notice me? Was it when I thought it was? Remember when you opened those groceries? I knew you knew I wanted you then ...* Luxurious, murmured words, painful beyond bearing. That was when the true betrayal had started. One stage worse would be when he allowed himself to compare her with Minnie; this was the one way he had not yet succumbed.

He took his clothes into the shower room. He was normally a hygienic man; today he could not be bothered to take a shower. What had she said that day? *Cleaning the clothes by day and the souls by night.* He sat, slumped on the closed lid of the lavatory. On the shelf Gul had placed his shaving-cream tube in the mug next to the toothbrush. His toothpaste, on the other hand, had been put away into the cupboard. Gul always did that; Duke no longer corrected him. He would always do it. Duke sat there for a moment. There seemed no point in action, if he were going to sin again. He had no will to wash.

He dressed and walked quietly through the bedroom and downstairs. It was one-thirty. He poured himself a glass of bourbon; he was drinking more heavily. Upstairs he heard a gush of water in the bathroom. She was awake. Maybe she had only been faking sleep. She was too complicated for him.

He finished his drink and poured another. Footsteps across the ceiling. She would be sitting at Minnie's dressing-table now. Minnie herself never sat there; she just rubbed some cream into her face at night. Her hair, cropped short as a boy's, never needed attention. But Shamime always spent time over her toilette. He was charmed by this — everything she did charmed him once he had allowed himself to be charmed — once he had fallen and, in falling, pulled her down with him. But a small corner in him was irritated when she was late at work, although she was more efficient than most once she had started. But really he was aching to see her; she tantalized him by her delays. That was the reason he was upset. He was fooling himself to think otherwise.

Up in the air-conditioned bedroom it had been cool. Down here he sweated. He looked at the spines of Minnie's books along the shelves. *Modern Parenthood. The Mid-Life Crisis.* One of them had a set of instructions to repeat to yourself. She had read them out to him, half-jokingly, a little self-conscious: 'I can change myself; I am what I make myself; I am in my own hands.'

Shamime was coming downstairs. Her high-heels tapped. She looked ready for the office; she had pinned up her hair on top of her head.

'You old boozer,' she said.

With her a Muslim, the censure had a cultural weight behind it, a disapproval beyond herself. It was not like an American woman chiding him.

'Don't say I'm driving you to drink,' she said.

'Honey, it's got to stop.'

'I know, it's ruining your liver.'

'I mean, us.'

She smiled. 'You're always saying that. It's called post-coital guilt.'

'I mean it now. Please let me mean it.' He pressed his hands to his face. His fingers, that belonged to her. His whole body belonged to her.

'You didn't seem to mean it an hour ago.'

'Honey, forgive me. I've got no excuses. I've behaved in a way I wouldn't have believed. I don't know what to say to you. I'd do anything in the world to make it all right. Sammy, tell me what I should do.'

She paused. 'It's only because your wife's coming back. Three weeks isn't it? Enough time to tidy up. Oh you look so simple and uncalculating. Don't be fooled, folks.'

He could not look up, with her face like that. He rubbed his eyes. 'I mean it.' His voice sounded choked and theatrical. 'Shamime honey, it just can't work.'

There was a long silence. He heard the click of her lighter. 'You mean, I've been your bit of fun on the side.'

'Fun? You think we've been having fun?'

'Actually I thought you meant it. Me, muggins that I was.'

'Of course I meant it. That's the terrible thing.'

Her voice was low. 'You meant it, with an eye on the fucking calendar.'

'Oh don't swear. I can't bear to hear you swearing.'

'Sorry to offend your delicate sensibilities. You think you can fuck me—'

'Don't, please.'

'What on earth do you think we were doing? Having a little cross-cultural communication? East-West dialogue? Getting to know the natives? You Yanks always have a nice way of putting things, you'll say a device was detonated when you mean a bloody bomb's been dropped. You call *us* devious.'

'I don't talk like that.'

'But you *think* like that. Fooling yourself, but you're even less honest because you believe it through and through.' Her voice cracked. 'That awful self-righteousness. I thought there was a reason for it once, but you're as shoddy as the rest.'

Her voice rose. It was all happening so quickly. She was so passionate. He could not believe that this was them; it seemed unreal, himself slumped in the chair and this young girl, trembling in her cloud of smoke.

'I thought I could trust you,' she said. 'I thought you were the one person in this place who wouldn't be corrupted. I didn't realize you would be, but deep down where it didn't show.' She started to sob. A black tear slid down her face. 'Oh you look so straight, you all-American good guy, but it's all worked out.'

'Honey don't.' His chest ached. He was sobbing too, in jerks.

'You even said you loved me. Remember that time in the middle of Chundrigar Road with all those other people around? You seemed so wonderfully unfurtive. Large-spirited. As if you really were swept over.'

'You think I don't love you?' He buried his face in his hands. He could not bear to look at her like this, her face breaking, with that black stuff sliding down it. Her plainness moved him more passionately than her beauty. It had happened that first time in the beach hut when she had looked so lost, and his breath had stopped.

'I don't know what to say.'

'You always were the strong silent type.' She tried to laugh; it came out wheezingly. 'Oh it's all so humiliating. Why did I have to fall for you? There's everything against you. You're no oil painting. I just thought you were a good man. You didn't use people. I even thought you weren't using me.'

'You think I was?'

'Well it's all okay. Bobby told me last night. You've timed it perfectly.'

'What's that?'

'It's all coming through.'

'What's coming through?'

'Oh Duke, don't look so flabbergasted. It doesn't convince me any more.'

'Please don't talk like that. Please be anything, but don't be cynical.'

There was a silence. She stood with her back to him, running

212

her fingers to and fro across Minnie's books. She said lightly: 'He told me last night. He said he'd granted the permission and the documents would be coming through this week. On Monday you can get the earthmovers in. I didn't tell you because I didn't want to harm your precious self-respect. Your innate integrity. I wanted you to think *you'd* done it.' She paused. 'Most people do it with money. You're too bloody pure to do it with money, you've always been superior about that. Us corrupt Pakistanis. So you do it with me instead. It's all going your way, isn't it.'

He felt choked and sick. 'Shamime, I didn't realize. Can you believe that?'

She turned round and picked up her handbag. 'I don't think I believe anything any more. I'm going.'

He got to his feet. 'You can't just walk out into the street. I'll drive you to the office.'

He found his car keys. They did not speak. She blew her nose, opened her compact, grunted at her smudged make-up and wiped her face with her handkerchief. He, too, blew his nose. They tended to themselves, side by side in the large lounge. She would not let him help her. He wiped his eyes. They were not fierce tears like hers; they were the rheum of grief. Today he had become an old man. Nothing he could say would help her because he no longer knew what he believed.

They drove into town, Shamime sitting beside him. At the traffic lights by the Sind Club, with the car at a standstill, he leant over and put his arm around her. She continued staring ahead.

'Mustn't let your darling project suffer must we,' she said. 'Don't worry, I won't let you down.'

'I wasn't meaning that,' he bellowed in despair. Behind them cars hooted. On the pavement, emerging from the Club, stood several men he knew. If he had cared to think of such things he might have thought it ironic, that the one time he and Shamime looked really compromising was the moment it was no longer true.

'HELLO,' she said. 'I'm awfully sorry to intrude.'

He turned slowly to look at her. He shook his head, smiling, and turned back to gaze at the water. Nobody was around. Down here by the shore, bushes screened them from the bazaar and the road.

She said breathlessly: 'I saw you once, I think, sitting outside Bohri Bazaar.' Wearing apparently the same clothes he wore now: flimsy, grimy orange kurta and trousers.

He raised his eyebrows.

'The place with the trinkets,' she said. 'Down in Elphinstone Street.'

'Elphinstone Street ... ' He seemed to find that amusing. He had a flat Midlands accent.

She sat for a moment, trying to catch her breath. Running in this heat made her pant. She had spotted him near the tea stall when she was hastening from the sleeping Sultan. She had followed him down to the water's edge.

He did not seem inclined to engage in small talk. Nor did she. They sat in silence. Flies buzzed around them. He scratched his bites; his ankles were even whiter than her own.

'You know this is a magic place,' he said. 'You can feel it.'

She nodded.

'Like, you've got to be open, see. Be still.'

'I know.'

She sat looking at the muddy water. She was dirtier. This rickety little place was shabby but she was shabbier.

'You're emptied now, right? Your mind is pure. Just pure and blank.'

She nodded. If she nodded she might feel it. She smoothed down her crumpled yellow skirt. It did look second-hand, now. She had pushed it up and held him pressed against her. So quick, it had been. Then the juddering—his spasm, not hers. And then the breathing, as deep and regular as before. He had sunk back into sleep as blindly as he had emerged. Perhaps he would never recollect his humiliation.

'You just sit here. You accept. Like it kind of flows through you. People who come here, they don't learn this. They try to fight it.'

'I've been trying to learn.' She looked at his grey bony face with its soft moustache. You did not see many people like him in Karachi. 'Have you lost your way to India?' she asked. 'Karachi's a bit off the route.' What, she wondered, was he finding in his own passage to India?

He wagged his finger at her, slowly up and down. 'Once you're lost, it's then you begin to find yourself.'

This sounded wise. She felt terribly lost.

'I don't know how to get back,' she said.

'Turn right at Tesco's and it's second on the left after the Curry Inn.' He giggled like a schoolgirl, alarmingly high.

'There isn't a Tesco.'

'You can get lost when you're right back home.'

'Are you going back to Karachi? I want to get back quickly.'

Get back before he wakes up. Who was that Sultan Rahim? She made him a saint for her own gratification. She made him mysterious, for her own foreign *frisson*. Who was he? A genial businessman, a generous-hearted host who bought her a drink and lay down for a sleep. A family man no doubt, a diligent Muslim.

And how she had used him. She had confused and inflamed him; oh pray to God he would think it was a dream. She had raped him. As the British had once invaded this country, so she

215

had invaded him. She herself, of all people, was the worst colonialist of all. She had used him for the colour of his skin.

'There's a bus. There's always a bus. You wait, and there's a bus.'

He spoke like Sultan: you want a shrine? You wait, you'll find a shrine. Wherever you are looking, that will be the holy place.

She rose awkwardly and went down to the water. She squatted in the liquid. It seeped up over her sandals. She splashed the water on her face. It was as warm as soup. Perhaps this was the hot water she had heard about. She would believe it was; it was the faith that counted. Words rolled around her head – racism, sexism, tinny catch-phrases she had mouthed without feeling. She had been so strident and innocent.

Even after the wash she felt sticky. They walked up the slope, through the bushes. Sultan's car had gone, but there were tyremarks in the sand.

Families were standing around waiting for the bus. It was true: when you wanted a bus, so you saw other people waiting for one too. You would not have noticed them otherwise. They were poor people, women carrying tiffin tins wrapped in cloth and children carrying babies. They seemed to have sprung from nowhere; when she had visited the shrine it had been so empty.

She did not look at them. She had misused them all.

24

FOR A week Donald had kept the piece of paper in his wallet. *Saleem Beg, Near Petrol Pump, Commercial West Colony.* He knew the place; it was the other side of the city, a run-down business suburb between the industrial sector and the beach road slums. He had driven through it several times on his way to the Cameron factories beyond.

He had to go in working hours, of course; the tailor would not be there when the shops were closed. Twice this week he had tried to drive there. The first time he had been stopped by a frantic phone call from Mrs Gracie. The permission would be coming through at the end of the week; could he get up a petition at the Sind Club? Highly embarrassed, he had gone there for lunch. They would think he was mad – a crackpot Englishman instead of the sober Sales Manager and fellow sport he had been trying to appear. It was tricky, to campaign against a minister when not only did Cameron's need the man's support but when most of those who propped up the bar were the same minister's friends and relatives. Out of loyalty to Mrs Gracie however he had cleared his throat and approached some of them. It fell flat. None of them had heard of the Donkey Sanctuary. Worse than this, few of them seemed to have even heard of Mrs Gracie. Since her day a new generation, and a new race, had arrived at the Sind Club. Then he had been obliged to break the news to her, blaming himself and his lack of contacts and charisma to divert her attention from the painful fact that she herself, as well as her cause, was in truth extinct.

The next day he had left work early and driven to Commercial West. He had been stopped, however, by a cordon of police. There was another riot in the area. Afterwards he had read about it in the paper – just a small paragraph on the back page. Discontent was growing. What had originally started as a protest against the rising price of *ghee* was being fuelled by the few members of the opposition not in prison. The shaky presidency was shakier than ever; the Prime Minister's bungalow in Clifton was now permanently guarded by a reinforcement of troops. There were rumours of corruption in high places and a ministerial re-shuffle; no doubt the risky members of the government would be replaced by those who toed the party line.

Today he was going there. At five o'clock he was concluding a talk with Shamime about the paints brochure. He rose to leave.

'One small thing, Shamime. I was supposed to meet Duke Hanson for a drink at the Intercon, and I can't put it off because his line's been engaged. Could you possibly have another bash when I've gone?'

'Me?' she said sharply.

'I'm awfully sorry. It's just, with Mary being off sick ... ' Meaning: I hope you don't think I'm treating you like my secretary.

'No, no, of course, that's fine.' She looked composed again. She was a tricky girl, with her moods. He wanted to say: sorry, my mind's a bit confused today. You see, I'm off to find my uncle. But then again it was not much to ask. After all she was a friend of Duke's. Only yesterday she had lunched with him; he himself had seen her climbing out of Duke's car when he was parking his own.

He put her out of his mind. He was outdoors now in the suffocating heat of the car park, tipping the old man who polished his windscreen. He had always preferred this man to the small canny boys who ran this way and that with their cleaning rags, calling him sahib and giggling, making him feel foolish and younger than they.

The old man bowed without a smile. Donald unlocked the door and waited while the man fumblingly opened it for him. Nowadays he looked at the man differently. Somewhere in this city a member of his own family was surviving on small coins such as these. Each time he realized this his stomach shifted.

He drove through the traffic. Billboards advertised airlines and insurance schemes. Below them people squatted in their pavement camps. A barber cut someone's hair; bundles slept on rope beds. Christine complained of being watched but she could retreat. It was only the humble who, year in and year out, had to suffer in public the indignity of their private lives. He himself had taken snapshots of the more picturesque amongst them.

Lodged in his heart, he had a snapshot of his half-uncle. There was the petrol pump, exhaust fumes and a stall. They usually sat at junctions, for maximum trade. The setting was as primitive as these: just a tailor's space on the pavement, a heap of clothes and customers being measured as people jostled past. His uncle must be the lowliest of the low, a half-caste with no place even in the humblest society, his mother dishonoured and dead. Spawned from two races you belonged to neither. At least he had an occupation, albeit that of street tailor. Like the discarded wrappings that littered the road, the man was the debris from his own father's career.

How could he make amends? He was driving down the highway now, tense and tacky. He still had not decided. It would be cowardly not to identify himself. But even if he made himself understood, which seemed unlikely, the man would probably think that the most tasteless joke was being made at his expense. They had their pride; however poor, one could retain a measure of that. In Donald's wallet lay 2,000 rupees, about £80, the sum of his savings so far. Though little enough for himself — for the first time in his life he could actually afford this — it was large enough to set up the man in a better place. By Mr Beg's own pitiful standards this would be a fortune. Or they could perhaps work out some kind of provident fund, or subsidy. Better late than never.

He drove into the commercial colony, today cleared of the

riot troops. Passing through on previous occasions he had noticed a small petrol station; he did not remember a tailor nearby, but then he would not have noticed one anyway. He parked a block away from the petrol pumps; he did not care to draw up there in his polished vehicle like a sahib.

He remained in the car. Now he had arrived he wanted to turn around and drive home. Nobody would know. He half-wished Christine were beside him telling him what to do. It was only through his reluctance to tell her that he had realized the rift that had grown between them. He sat fiddling with his car keys and trying to ignore the glances of passers-by; few Europeans came to this place. Outside stood some grubby stalls dealing in spare parts — in one lay a heap of carburettors, in the next a pile of exhaust pipes. The keys dug into his hand. He could not believe the words he repeated to himself: *I am making a family visit.*

Outside it was dusty. Men walked with cloths pulled across their mouths. Squatting amongst their rusting machinery the shopkeepers looked at him. Someone familiar to these shops had a paler skin. Perhaps he had Donald's own blue eyes. How did Christine describe his grandfather? *That blue gaze, as if he had nothing to hide.* One of the few remarks she had made about him without irony. Until recently he had never really inspected the people who walked in the street. There were so many of them, you did not have the energy to distinguish one from the other. They were the masses; his old books called them the natives. You stopped your car to let them stream across the road. Mr Beg — Uncle Beg — might have children, of course. These would be near to his own age. One of those young men with his mouth covered, or those shrouded females shuffling past, might be another member of his own family.

His stomach clenched. He unstuck himself from the car seat and climbed out. He walked around the corner, past what they called a hotel — in fact, just a tea stall. Men sat at the tables. He searched their faces. No doubt his uncle was known here; he must have sat on one of those wooden benches for years, even decades, pouring his tea into the saucer before he drank it, as they all did.

At the road junction ahead stood the Burma Shell sign and the two pumps. A rickshaw waited there, being filled. There was no sign of a tailor this side; the only other possible place for him would be around the corner in the next street.

Donald lingered for some moments. What he must do was place one foot in front of the other, walk past the pumps and turn left. That pavement was more solid than it seemed. He told himself: you can simply walk past him. He need never know. You are just a foreigner passing by on business of your own; he will hardly expect you to stop.

He felt his jacket pocket; the wallet bulged there. He made his way around the pumps, and turned the corner.

This place was busier than the street of Spare Parts; its pavement was crowded. He stood still, searching. Some men squatted in front of the shops; their cloths were spread with soap, plastic combs and Johnson's Baby Oil. Another man sat beside his boxful of *pan* leaves and cigarettes. Somebody tapped his shoulder. Donald swung round.

'Very nice hairs clip, sahib.'

He stared into the man's face. After a moment he managed to shake his head.

He could see no one resembling a tailor, or even selling cloth. It took some time to search, with all those men in twos and threes, holding hands and blocking the view. The nearby factories had closed for the day but the shops were still open; everybody seemed to be in the streets. And there were no tailors, as far as he could see, on the other side of the road either. How near, exactly, was *Near Petrol Pump*? The man must be within sight.

Rickshaws and taxis were parked along the street, jammed at all angles. Alongside him a lorry pushed past a donkey cart, blaring its horn. The donkey staggered and regained its balance; both drivers shouted. Donald turned his attention to the buildings.

He moved nearer. It was a large new emporium with a window stretching the length of three shopfronts; luminous pink stickers were pasted up saying *Fully Air-Conditioned*. The sun glared on the glass; Donald moved, and saw inside the shop tiers of folded cloth. At the back, beyond the shelves, some steps led up to a platform with a cash booth and, on either side, men bent over sewing machines.

He stood still. Of course, the man must have meant a tailor's *shop* near the petrol pump. There must be thirty men up there on the platform, hard at work. In their midst was the glassed-in booth where the proprietor sat in state. They were bent so low that Donald could not see their faces. Mostly they looked old, but then the poor aged quickly here. Some had grey hair; some had dyed their hair orange with henna. He did not know what to do.

'Yes sahib — you are pleased to enter?'

Donald jerked round. The door was being held open. An assistant waited.

Donald backed away, trying to smile normally. He shook his head, backing further. He bumped into somebody.

'Sorry.' He must stand at a distance and try to collect his thoughts. If this was the place — and there was nowhere else — then it needed some adjusting to. He had not expected such a large flourishing business, a factory really. He must face one of the assistants, or else that man in the booth. He was enormously fat; he sat above his toilers, his head and shoulders lit by the fluorescent light. He looked like a besuited Buddha up here; a plump god of commerce. Should he, Donald, go in and ask him for a Mr Beg? He hesitated. Perhaps there was more than one Mr Beg in there; it was a common name.

He had not expected this meeting to be conducted under so many eyes. This would be even more difficult than he had imagined. Somehow he must get Mr Beg out of there. Perhaps he should take him back to his car. He must go in. He glanced up. The plastic sign said TIPTOP TAILORING.

He felt dizzy. It was unreal. He was not here; he was standing outside Selfridges in an oddly stuffy winter. It was hot for Christmas, out here on the pavement. Behind the window sat the puppets, worked by electric, their little machines clacking

222

up and down though he could not hear a sound.

Again the door opened.

'I'm looking for a Mr Beg,' said Donald.

Without hesitation the assistant said: 'Please to come this way.'

Donald followed him up the stairs. He could still turn back and run. One more step and he was at the top. His heart thumped in his ears. This close, some of them looked younger. He searched the older faces, with their greased, red hair scraped back over their skulls. Few looked at him; they continued their work, their heads bent. They seemed so aged and shrunken. Which one would raise his face?

The assistant was tapping on the door of the booth. He opened it.

'Mr Beg, there is somebody to see you.'

The man rose to his feet and held out a pale, soft hand.

25

'I'M AFRAID he's rather pissed,' said Donald.

'So are you.'

'At least I got back to home sweet home.'

He leant against her, partly to steady himself. They stood looking at the car; in the passenger seat Duke lay slumped. In the dark garden that frog went scrape, scrape.

'Where did you meet?' she asked.

'At the Intercon Bar. I was supposed to meet him earlier and I turned up just in case. He couldn't have got the message.'

'Was he as bad as this?'

'We both got worse. He kept on mumbling about his wife, as if he was trying to speak to her on the phone and he couldn't get through. It was exciting driving back. He kept falling on me round the corners.'

'Did you keep mumbling about me?'

'I needn't, need I. You're here.'

'You're not allowed to be so prosaic when you're drunk.'

They gazed at Duke, illuminated by the porch light.

'It's so unlike him,' said Donald. 'I always thought he could take his drink. He seemed so impervious.'

Duke's head was propped against the window. His big face was crumpled like a baby's; a snail's trail of saliva glinted down his chin.

'Perhaps he's been terribly lonely,' said Donald.

'Perhaps he's been having an affair.'

'What, Duke? Not him.'

'Does seem rather hard to imagine. We can't lift him can we?'

'He's like an ox.'

Christine fetched some cushions from the house and wedged them around Duke's head. She closed the car door.

Leaving Duke, they went indoors. 'One step here,' she instructed, 'easy does it.' He protested. She liked him best when he was drunk; he improved with loosening up. Unlike many men he never became belligerent, just emotional.

In bed he clung to her.

'You're everything I've got, Chrissy.'

She was so moved, tears pricked her eyes. She had wronged him. Since yesterday she had said nothing, but he must know. With guilt like hers the other person could surely tell. She was an adulteress. Blind in the dark, she felt his face with her fingers.

'Nobody else matters, do they,' she whispered, making him understand.

He shook his head, his hair rubbing across her face. His body felt warm and known. 'Nobody. Here, darling. I want you so much.' A moment later he said, 'Safe and sound.'

She pressed her face against his cheek. He hardly ever talked like this.

'Home safe and sound,' he murmured again.

She opened her mouth against his. Was it just the drink?

Afterwards they lay drenched. On either side the mosquito coils smoked, like twin spirits rising.

26

NEXT morning she came downstairs early. Donald still slept. Down in the living-room she found Duke slumbering on the sofa; a large creased object, like a parcel that had been too long in the post, propped against the cushions from the car.

'Did you do that?' she asked Mohammed who was entering, sober in his starched white.

He shook his head, a muscle twitching in his jaw. This meant, she thought, amusement rather than disapproval. She sat down. He put a papaya in front of her. She opened the newspaper.

Her own face gazed up from the page.

She slapped the newspaper shut. An inch from her hand, coffee was poured into her cup. Two mats were moved an inch nearer. Upon one was put the coffee pot; upon the other the milk jug. He had finished.

A pause. 'Papaya is okay?'

'Oh yes.' She picked up the piece of lime and tried to squeeze it on to the fruit. It slipped out of her hand.

'Fine,' she said, picking it up.

'Madam is liking toast?'

'Yes,' she lied. She waited. Then his plimsolls squeaked as he went into the kitchen.

She opened the page. It was a head shot, grey and slightly

226

blurred. But not blurred enough. *The Smile of Confidence,* said the advertisement. *I need feminine protection. The very best. And the Most Safe. Join me by use of Tahira, Pakistan's first Tampon.*

In the next room the sofa creaked. A grunt.

Quickly she took her knife and slit the page along the fold. Her hand was trembling; the cut was torn. She gave this up; instead she pulled out the whole two-page spread of news and shuffled the rest of the paper back together. Nobody would notice the page numbers. A screech as she scraped back her chair and hurried over to the wastepaper basket. She screwed up the paper and put it at the bottom, under the rest of the rubbish.

27

NEARLY noon, and Duke was back in his office. He put his head in his hands; the sick bulk of his body punished him. Never, even in the army, had he made himself that senseless.

He had drawn down the blind. Out in the street stood the shops Shamime visited and maybe would be visiting again; he could not see them now.

I had five sittings for some shoes at Faizuddin Leather House. I kept on finding something wrong with them, just so I could sit there and see your window. Me, Shamime, behaving like that! Up there in your office I thought you could tell. Once I saw you standing and stretching. Your shirt lifted up and showed your furry gut. How can I love this man? I thought. My love.

Since the news about the site thanks to God he had been busy. Yesterday he had spent hours on the phone trying to contact the cement contractors, the shippers and the Port Authority. His business seemed to function beyond him, in an overdrive of its own. He seemed to make sense to these people when he spoke.

He lifted his head from his hands and phoned the ministry, but the Minister was not there. It was a minor formality about land tax, the last small detail that needed settling.

He spoke to Mr Kasim, who had accompanied Shamime and himself to the site a week or two ago.

'Pardon me,' said Duke. 'I'm not getting you clear.'

The line was faint and crackling. Through it he heard Mr Kasim clear his throat.

'Still not getting you,' said Duke. His head ached this morning; the crackling was amplified in chambers through his brain. He caught 'delicate' and 'unexpected'.

'Delicate what?' he said.

'…grave matters…all most unfortunate, Mr Hanson…' More crackling.

'Shall I call you back?'

'I am trying to make myself clear, you understand…'

'It's fading again.'

'It is about permit.'

Duke sat still.

'Mr Hanson?'

'Yeah. Still here. The permit.'

'It is rather difficult to make this into words for you, Mr Hanson. Let me be blunt. I will not shilly-shally. Permission has now been refused. It is a change of circumstances.'

'Refused? Who the heck's responsible for this? I must speak to your Minister.'

'Please, Mr Hanson. As I said, the Minister is not in office.'

'When's he coming back? There's been some God-awful misunderstanding. Pardon my language.'

'I can understand your distress. Please, it is not my business.'

'Yeah, of course. Pardon me.'

The man could say no more. Duke tried a few more times to get him to give some reason but with no success. He put down the phone.

He did not move for some time. Down in the street a woman laughed, shrilly. The clock ticked on. At one o'clock there was a rattle as the shops rolled down their bars and closed for lunch.

He did not know what to do if he moved. He did not want to think too hard either. Two days ago his life had stopped – the reason he breathed each breath had stopped. But at least his work had gone on.

Her uncle loved her, of course. *I'm his favourite niece. I say the things he doesn't dare say himself. He calls me his Fire-cracker. He'd do anything for me.*

Anything. Even, it appeared, this.

He would say this for her. She had sure taken her revenge in style.

28

MOHAMMED has put the room into rightful order. He has tidied settee, he has plumped the cushions, Memsahib Smythe having told him the method of this, and he has placed them in the correct positions, two on settee, two on chairs. He has opened doors and aired lounge. Smythe-sahibs, they were giving many parties, they had high spirits in plenty. In the morning there would be sometimes a sleeping English sahib lying on this settee after making whoopie. This is foreigner's way. It is to his liking too. He himself is getting large tip, and he is bringing also his cousin and his sister's husband to join their work to his, they also receiving baksheesh. In addition there is plenty of booze, many glasses not empty, it being his duty to dispose of them in suitable manner.

With Manley-sahibs it is different matter. They are having no big parties in the buffet style. When they are holding small dinner, memsahib she is purchasing food and filling kitchen with soiled pans. Next day it is she who is going to Bottle Bazaar, this dirty place is to her liking. She returns with money for himself but this is not so large a sum as he himself purloins, bottlewallahs giving her small price as she is ignorant foreigner.

Mohammed is emptying wastepaper baskets. And Memsahib Manley, she is not buying the imported tins of good quality; she is purchasing bazaar goods like low-class Pakistani. There are no pleasant surprises in the throw-aways. In his quarters he has many tins and jars that he has put to good use but these are in the main mementoes of Memsahib Smythe's residence.

He is throwing rubbish into the box. There is ball of paper. He picks it up and then sees picture printed upon it. Sahib and memsahib are not at home; he smooths newspaper piece on floor. It is Memsahib Manley with the happy smile.

He cuts around picture with the scissors. When work is finished he takes it to his quarters. Reena asks what her husband is holding in his hand. She too recognizes the features of memsahib. She too is proud that her memsahib is featured in national newspaper. Memsahib Manley has new importance; Mohammed's heart is swelling.

Around wall is one shelf holding the beloved possessions. There is kangaroo Memsahib Smythe has given to baby. There is Marmite-jar in which his wife is keeping the marriage *tikka*, gold throughout. There is ballpoint pen Manley-sahib has thrown out, still in working order. There is picture of the Qaid-i-Azam and Mr Bhutto, and snapshots of Smythe family in green compound of bungalow in Wimbledon, Britain. Beside them he is placing picture of memsahib with the happy smile.

He cannot read the English words. He does not know the reason for the smile of confidence. Nor can he read the remainder of the scrumpled newspaper, also unread by the other occupants of the bungalow this morning, Manley-sahib and American sahib.

Minister Replaced. Government spokesman said that senior minister has been replaced, in internal re-shuffle, with effect from today. Police last night arrested five men under Section 26 of West Pakistan Maintenance of Public Order Ordinance. A senior government official denied rumours of more riots in Nazimabad and said: 'These are routine actions necessary to the continuing peace and prosperity of our country. There is no foundation in rumours put about by scandal-mongers and traitors to our national progress.'

29

PEOPLE had seen the photograph, of course, though her Pakistani acquaintances were both too polite and no doubt too shocked to mention it. Donald saw its second appearance in the newspaper the next day. He seemed to find it incomprehensibly funny; this was startling, but a relief.

'The Cameron manager's wife,' he said with a wild laugh. Who was he laughing at, Christine or himself? His responses nowadays were taking her by surprise. He seemed to have changed, but like most changes it had not come when expected – at their removal to this country, or at some notable crisis – but had crept up recently. He seemed both harder and more tender. Stiffer in company, he was more intense and wayward when they were alone, as if the public nature of life here built up pressures that had to be released.

'At least you went and did something,' he said, 'instead of moaning. Seems we've all been off on our voyages of discovery.'

'What do you mean?'

'I'll tell you, but wait until my suit's finished.'

'The one you're having made? What on earth's that got to do with it?'

But he just rubbed his moustache. Then he put up his feet and flung back his head, his eyes closed, frowning as if his very spirit clenched. You come out East, she thought, and the most mysterious person is the one who has been beside you all the time.

A cheque arrived, with a compliments slip, from the Superad Agency. Perhaps she had misunderstood about the photo; perhaps they were not meant to be test shots. On the other hand, maybe she had been exploited. She could not phone Sultan to hear his reactions. Besides, who had exploited whom in all this?

In town later that day she met Shamime. At first it surprised her, seeing Shamime at a *pan* stall. But the man was reaching under his box to produce a *Vogue*.

'He gets it from the airline crews,' said Shamime, in answer to her question. 'Twenty rupees, what a con. Talking of which, cover girl, you're in *Herald* too. Saw it at the hairdresser's.'

'Oh no.'

'I thought: and here's the girl who said she didn't need protection.'

'What?'

'*Tahira, for feminine protection*.' She smiled. 'When we first met, you were saying you didn't want to be *safe* here, like the others.'

'Oh I see.' Christine smiled reluctantly. After a moment she said: 'I keep wondering why they used me for that. I suppose for silly prestige.'

'They used you because, dum-dum, no Muslim girl would let herself be seen dead in a photo for that. Her family would never speak to her again. She'd die of shame.'

Christine paused. So she was not at the top of the heap, she was at the bottom.

She looked at Shamime. She had not realized how brittle and unkind she was. But then it might be grief. After all, sadness seldom improves people. Instead of languishing pitifully they become harder and more irritable — less able to be helped, rather than more so.

'I'm awfully sorry, by the way,' she said. 'I only heard yesterday. You're very fond of him, I know.'

'What do you mean?' Shamime's sharp voice.

'Well, I mean you always said you were. You said that he was

234

the only man who made you laugh, and all the young men seemed so weedy.'

'When did I say this?'

'Goodness. Sorry, I can't remember. I suppose we asked you – we were interested, him being a minister and all.'

'Oh. *Bobby*.'

There was a silence. Christine said: 'He's not in prison is he?'

'Heavens no. They wouldn't dare. He's all right; he's writing a book. He'll wait his time. Things are going to change.'

Everyone was saying this. But they usually added: not for a year or two, not until the opposition gets organized. Probably it would happen when Donald and herself had gone back to England. She would have missed the action again.

'I'm sorry for Duke, too,' she said.

'Why?' That sharp voice. The diamond winked as she turned to Christine.

'His hotel. He's put up a fight, Donald says, but it's no good. Apparently at the beginning he thought your uncle had changed his mind. He rang up Donald in quite a state. But Donald had just heard the radio news, so he told him.'

She paused.

'Go on,' said Shamime.

'Well, that's it. At least Duke knows it's not your uncle's fault. Not that it does him much good. He's paying off the contractors. In a couple of weeks he's going back to the States.'

'To his wife.' Shamime turned and hailed a taxi. '*For better or worse.*'

It was a dented taxi, plastered with stickers. '*Till death do us part*,' she said, climbing in. She did not offer Christine a lift.

The back window was decorated with red lights. As it pulled away from the kerb they chased round and round, as if demented.

30

'I'M REALLY a thirty-six waist?' asked Donald. 'I didn't like to believe it last time. I used to be thirty-four.'

'Move a little forward please,' said Mr Beg. 'I have three branches in Karachi and two branches more in planning stage.' He wagged his finger, smiling. 'You think I am doing this by making the incorrect measurements?'

'I know. I just don't like it in black and white, that I'm putting on weight.' They were becoming quite chatty this second visit. 'I suppose it's having everything done for me here. You know, in Karachi.'

He looked at Mr Beg, who filled the fitting-room. Neither of his grandparents had been fat. But then Mr Beg had other people to do things for him too.

'Now the trousers.' Mr Beg turned to the tailor. '*Lao*. Please take your own off, Mr Manley.'

Under the strip light of the fitting-room Mr Beg had a certain pallor, as if in ill-health. Otherwise his features, sunk in fat, bore no resemblance to anyone Donald had known. His eyes were brown, his lips thick. It was obviously an honour to have the proprietor in attendance like this. Wedged behind Mr Beg stood the tailor himself, an emaciated old man hung with measuring tapes and a pincushion on a string. He held the tacked-together pieces of cloth.

Donald took off his trousers. Mr Beg took the new trousers

236

from the tailor. 'Feel this cloth, Mr Manley. You have chosen well. When I saw you I said to myself: this Englishman will choose the best. Feel the quality.'

Donald, standing in his underpants, did as he was told. A fawn lightweight weave, it was the costliest in the shop. After all he had arrived with a full wallet. No doubt people like Mr Beg could tell. That was how they expanded to three branches and two more in planning stage.

'Now, please.'

Donald lifted a leg. 'Sorry.' He hopped, once, and steadied himself on Mr Beg's shoulder. It was soft as a sofa, upholstered in the nylon shirt.

Mr Beg helped him pull on the trousers. The tailor knelt at Donald's feet and started to pin up the bottom seam. Mr Beg gave him instructions in Urdu. Donald stood as still as a dummy. Mr Beg was perspiring; so was he.

Mr Beg bent, with difficulty, and straightened the fall of the trousers. He pinched in the cloth at Donald's thigh.

'Just half an inch, Mr Manley, here.' His fingers held the cloth against Donald's skin. 'I will pin it myself.'

He pinned one thigh and then the other. 'Now please bend your legs. Comfortable?'

Donald flexed his legs, feeling foolish. Even if he had not become fatter, this place made him feel so.

'Fine.' He paused. 'Have you always been a tailor?'

He nodded. 'I have worked my way up from the bottom,' he pointed to Donald's feet, 'to the top. Next year, *insh'allah*, I will also be leasing made-to-measure shop in new Hilton Hotel, soon to be completed. All the businessmen are arriving to Karachi, our country develops its prosperity. And the Arabs are arriving from the Gulf. Myself, I prefer the English customers like yourself.'

'Were your family tailors?'

'Maybe yes, maybe no. Mr Manley, I am poor orphan.'

'I'm awfully sorry to hear it.' Donald waited but Mr Beg did not continue. 'Your English is very good.'

'You are kind. I take correspondence course. At the night-

237

time, while the city is snoring, my own light is shining. I determine to make my way.'

And you have succeeded, thought Donald. You must have far more money than I will ever earn. Mr Beg spoke like Christine's descriptions of her real-estate friend Mr Rahim. He wanted to ask Mr Beg so many questions but he did not dare in case he became suspicious. Close up, in the flesh, it was impossible to believe that this man was his half-uncle. Perhaps he did not want to believe it. There was simply no connection; nothing familiar to which he could attach himself.

'You are always dressing on left-hand side?'

Donald's face heated up. He nodded.

'Excuse me please.' Mr Beg pinched the crotch of the trousers. 'One centimetre,' he murmured.

Donald stood still as he inserted the pin. He was seized by the same panic he had felt in that hut in Clifton. He was a sacrifice; the man was going to puncture him with pins, in retribution.

The panic passed. Mr Beg was behaving perfectly normally. 'Okay,' he said, 'please take them off now. Take care please, with the pins.'

The tailor came forward and eased down the trousers. Donald stood revealed again in his underpants, his shirt flap hanging down. His legs looked bald with the black shoes at the bottom of them. He felt more nude than if he had been undressed. Soft and bald and silly and English.

'Man to man,' Mr Beg lowered his voice. 'I also was making very good marriage. My wife, she was rich widow-lady. She liked my get-up-and-go. Also my pale and distinguished complexion.'

'I see.' At least Mr Beg had been given one advantage.

Mr Beg winked.

'And you have children?' Donald asked casually.

He shook his head. 'I have no little ones, to care for me when I have grown old and feeble.'

Donald started putting on his trousers. Perhaps, like fat, this too ran in the family. Their family.

His legs and crotch were tacky. He was drenched with sweat,

despite the air-conditioning at TipTop Tailoring. If this man was simply his tailor he would have rather liked him. In fact, he had the feeling that next visit Mr Beg would appear more ordinary than this time, a large affable stranger: either an obsequious master or a bossy servant, Donald was not sure which. After which no doubt he and Mr Beg would part for good, their transaction completed.

Today he had parked on the other side of the road, next to a tall stucco wall. A school must lie behind; he heard high Pakistani voices singing:

> *'The farmer wants a wife,*
> *The farmer wants a wife,*
> *Ee-aye, ee-aye, the farmer wants a wife ... '*

He fiddled around for his keys. On the opposite side of the street, a driver opened the door of the black Mercedes. Mr Beg climbed in. No doubt he was off to another of his emporiums. The whole afternoon had such an air of unreality that Donald felt helpless.

> *'The wife wants a child,*
> *The wife wants a child,*
> *Ey-aye, ee-aye, the wife wants a child.'*

He sat in the car, limp. If somebody else were here, he might have smiled. He laid his head against the steering-wheel.

31

THEY drove Duke to the airport on a Saturday afternoon. Christine sat in the back, Pakistani-style, behind the men. She had always been fond of Duke, but in the ebb and flow of friendship they had only really come together this last couple of weeks. Since his overnight stay he had spent a good deal of time at their bungalow, bringing lavish gifts of food and bourbon from the Commissary. He was not a man for disguises; he did not hide his need. It must be losing his project like that. He had come to this country to change things and been defeated. She thought: why have I come? To *be* changed. And Donald? To find a lost, old order. For changelessness, in fact. Do any of the things we seek actually exist? They seem to lie only in our heads.

The last day or so Duke had worn the preoccupied air of the traveller, but you became used to this here. Amongst their sort of people, above the forever trapped and static poor, arrival and departure punctuated their daily life. Already several of their European acquaintances had left, to be replaced by others who arrived, pale from a tepid summer and alert to all the sights Christine and Donald now took for granted. This airport road was the most familiar in Karachi.

'That's Shamime's house,' said Christine, pointing it out to Duke. 'We went there once for cocktails. Isn't it huge.'

Duke nodded.

She leant forward. 'Aziz is just off to New York, on some business thing of his father's. He's actually going to do some work.'

'You've seen her?' asked Duke.

'Just at the office.'

'Talking of whom,' said Donald, 'I forgot. I've got you a memento. Can you pass me my wallet, Christine? Just some snaps from that beach party.'

Duke thanked him and took them.

'You look so startled in that one,' said Christine. 'It makes people look startled, flash. Like rabbits in the headlights.'

Duke studied the photos a moment, said thanks again and put them into his pocket.

'Just think,' said Donald, 'only three months ago we arrived. Remember that camel cart, Chrissy, looming out of the dark? It seems like a year. I suppose it's not the same for you, I mean you being here anyway.'

Duke mumbled something.

'What?' said Christine.

'Pardon me. I said it seemed a long time too.'

'Poor Duke. You must be dying to see Minnie again. And your enormous sons. She's going to be amazed when she gets that present.' Duke had bought his wife an extremely expensive set of gold and sapphire jewellery. He had gone off and done it by himself. Secretly Christine could not picture the necklace around the neck of Minnie, whose photo she had seen and who looked decent, but peaky and boyish, not that sort. She remained silent. She felt car-sick.

They drove in silence. There seemed nothing left to say. Donald and Christine could not repeat how sorry they were. After some months' leave Duke would probably be going to Oman to set up the Muscat Translux.

They parked the car amidst the usual press of porters, and climbed out.

'You okay?'

Christine swayed in the heat. Donald gripped her arm.

'I seem to get less and less used to it,' she said.

241

'Guess what,' said Donald as they followed the porter. 'When Christine and I arrived that night, I thought we were standing in the Boeing heat outlet.'

They said goodbye. Christine kissed Duke's tired, leathery face for the first time. Afterwards she could not face climbing to the roof to watch him take off.

She lolled in the passenger seat.

'When did all the memsahibs come back?'

'What?'

'From Simla and places?'

'Pretty soon now. September.'

'God.'

'Are you all right?'

She nodded. They drove down the dual carriageway. Flags were flying for some state visit or other. Donald told her it was Nigeria. Hoardings, facing the incoming trade, told them to book rooms at the Agha 3 Star Hotel and to rub their hair with Purinoor Pomade.

The car swerved and squealed to a halt. They faced wooden scaffolding. Donald grated the gear and reversed backwards at speed. Dust and exhaust fumes blew about in the windscreen.

He stopped the car. The dust dispersed. They gazed up at the hoarding.

The painter had altered her. The giant curls were now a brassy yellow. Her face, despite creamy skin and scarlet cheeks, was softened and sensual, with the thickened pouting lips of an Indian film star. Her eyes were lined with black paint and there was a black beauty spot on her cheek.

Underneath this oriental blonde, so horribly recognizable to the thousands of people driving past, was written: *Join Me with Tahira Protection. So Safe. So Sure.*

She pushed open the car door, struggled out on to the verge and was sick. Donald hurried around the car and held her shoulders.

'Good Lord, Christine.'

She moved back to the car and sat, wedged sideways in the

passenger seat. She did not meet his eye, but gazed at the dust.

'Look, I know it's frightful ... ' he began.

She raised her head. 'And actually, I think I'm pregnant.'

32

NOT LONG after the announcement under the billboard they found a beach hut. Reckitts Rosemary and her husband were posted back to London and they passed the lease of their hut over to the Manleys. No estate agent, no Sultan. In this place things did not happen as you expected, one logical step after another. You took these steps and what resulted? It all dissolved away.

'Viz Duke,' said Donald, 'at Ginntho Pir.'

He was doing the crossword and raised his head. 'I've just realized. Know what Ginntho's an anagram of? Nothing. N-O-T-H-I-N-G'. He shook his head. 'Nothing ever came to anything there, did it.'

She could not speak, thinking of that empty, littered tomb. Thinking that nothing might have indeed come to something there. He did not remark upon her lack of response; any curious behaviour he put down to her condition.

During that strange autumn she wondered if in the future she would remember this as their Beach Hut Period, the last, elegaic phase of their marriage when they sat on the sand together and gazed at the waves. They spent a good deal of time there. During the first three months she was almost continually ill. Donald fetched her book, which she pretended to read. Anxious and proud, he fetched her towel when the evening wind blew and laid it around the shoulders of his lethargic wife, for the first time helpless. They were so gentle with each other – he because she was pregnant, she because she had betrayed him.

He talked lyrically of their early days at Brinton. 'Remember when you twisted your ankle and I carried you all the way to the bus stop? All heavy and sandy?' His arm tightened around her shoulders. 'When will it show?'

It was agony to hear. She felt so painfully loving towards him; she had never loved him like this. How dominating she had been before; selfish and self-righteous with her untried opinions. Now she was humbled. Many times she rehearsed the words with which she would tell him about Sultan. On one or two occasions she almost started to speak, but she could not begin. She could not bear to ruin his pleasure. She kept saying to herself: Sultan might not be the father. One scrambled five minutes. What was that compared to the many times with Donald, lying afterwards so careful and still, a vessel filled with precious liquid that must not be spilt? Once she had a niggling feeling: how unfair this is, that a woman's moment of weakness must have such a result. If a man had done what I did, nobody would ever know. Once she might have said this to Roz, but Roz seemed far away now; tinny and shrill, the complaints they had discussed decades ago. She wrote to her mother, putting in exclamation marks with her false biro.

Just as Donald put down her strange moods to her condition, so did everyone else. Her pregnancy gave her a place; overnight she was accepted by Europeans and Pakistanis, for the first time they knew what to talk to her about. At last she had done the right thing. They included her. Once when they were discussing names – Emily, Jonathan, what was Donald's middle name, Frederick, why not Frederick? – she had broken down and cried. She's pregnant, they murmured; had not they all had babies? It was bad superstition to talk about names, like buying clothes before it was born. Oh yes, they all understood. 'We understand,' they said, and she sobbed more violently.

Mohammed appeared pleased too. His own wife grew plumper in his quarters. Christine could sense his achievement, having two swelling ladies under his care. Perhaps, though it was never mentioned, he assumed his own hot water man had given fertile blessings to his memsahib. Perhaps indeed he had. She could not face curries; Mohammed cooked her the English food he had always wished her to prefer. She ate the mounds of mashed potato.

'I used to do this when I was a little boy,' said Donald. He flattened the potato with his fork, lifted a knife-full of peas and sprinkled them on the top. 'We plough the fields and scatter the good seed on the land,' he sang.

And it was such beautiful weather. Now that winter approached people emerged into the climate. The rain that had threatened in August never arrived, though there was flooding up in the Punjab. Each morning dawned fresh, deepening into the blue of a perfect English summer's day, one of those summers before our time, Donald said, in those old photos; a golden age. She sat in the veranda, mocked by the sunshine. Looking back later she could not imagine how she passed the time. She read little. Donald said she looked broody. Once a pariah dog limped past the gate, her dugs dragging in the dirt.

Out on the airport road the hoarding, advertising the product she no longer needed, grew shabbier. Dust was thrown into her face by the passing taxis; her complexion blistered. Donald laughed at the painting. There was a gaiety about him nowadays, he had loosened up. As if his stiff anxieties had melted in the face of their own shared miracle. One day he told her about his half-uncle; in fact they went together to collect the suit. In the car afterwards he said: 'I'm never going to keep any secrets from you.' He touched her knee; she burst into tears.

He wanted to talk about hospitals. She kept putting off a decision. Did she want to have the baby in England? he asked. It was so much safer. On the other hand Dr Farooq had his own private rooms in the Jinnah Hospital. Several English women had had their babies there, it was not like his grandmother's day. He had phoned Muriel Landsbury and she had nothing to complain of, all the latest stuff imported from the West, all mod cons. Christine herself made no inquiries; she did not want to put the birth into words. He presumed this to be a natural fear.

'I'll be with you, of course,' he said, 'I'll rub your back.' Then he had seen her face. 'Darling, I won't if you don't want me to.'

In the end she decided to have the baby in Karachi. Her mother would be flying out. She could see the relief on his face, that he would not lose her for several months and that he did not have to fly to England himself. She thought: but will he send me back there when he finds out? He bought a book and they looked at foetuses, growing larger each page they turned. 'He's like that now,' he exclaimed, pointing to one, pale and curled. 'Or she is.' He laid his head against her belly. Inside lay the baby, thrilling them with its thuds. She thought of it: part of her, forever hers, curled and brown.

Donald was so lighthearted, but awed too. She did not want the months to pass. He made jokes for joy. She grew large. Her fuzzy perm was growing out. She had to buy a loose dress for Shamime's wedding – Shamime had decided with surprising suddenness to marry her cousin's business partner, it must have been an arranged union, even Shamime seemed to have succumbed to the society around her. As they left for the ceremony, their bearer stood beside the door of the car. 'Look,' said Donald, 'I'm bringing the mountain to Mohammed.'

It was a charmed time. Unbearably so. She was a secret sufferer who has been told she has only a few more weeks to live. But for her these strange, heightened days would be ending not with death, but with birth.

33

SHAMIME heard the click of the bathroom switch. She lay still. Across the floor she heard the tap of his slippers. Fancy embroidered things, he had picked them up in Bangkok ('along with something else', she had heard him laugh in the Gymkhana Club Card Room).

The bed creaked. He eased himself down beside her. He did it purposefully, but not quite loud enough to waken her should she really be asleep; already she knew these movements so well. Eyes closed, she lay facing the wall. She kept her breathing regular.

'Sammy-ammy,' he whispered, not too loud; he was still doubtful. And he did not want to actually wake her up; he was decent enough.

He ran his finger over her shoulder. He was pressed gently against her nightdress, cupped around her back. His breath smelt of whisky and toothpaste.

'Sam the sham,' he murmured. It saddened her, that he already suspected. He was moderately witty really, considering the company he kept. She should be grateful that he had turned out such a generally pleasant surprise. Girls adored him. With his looks he must never have had trouble like this before.

He touched her hip. There was a pause of some minutes. He did not try to push closer. He was gentler than he appeared in public.

248

'Darling?' he murmured.

There was a long silence. A minute must have passed. She did not move, her cheek pressed into the sodden pillow.

Each night she lay here talking to Duke. *You can't reach me, not now. Did you ever feel you could? You reached me all right. But see? Nothing's changed.*

He moved back. The sheet moved with him but she did not dare pull it back. She heard the rasp of the match as he lit a cigarette.

34

S HE TURNED her head to and fro against the soaked pillow. Her insides were being dragged out.

'We must push.' Dr Farooq's voice boomed, as if spoken through a metal tunnel.

'More gas,' she grunted.

'Just a little. We must push now.'

She grabbed the rubber mask and clamped it against her face, snorting it in. Deeply, but not deep enough. Voices echoed. Reddened shapes burst inside her head. She sucked into the mask. A hand tried to pull it away.

'No,' said the voice, far off.

She gripped it greedily. Someone got it away this time.

'Push, darling.' Donald's echoing voice. 'Nearly there. Dr Farooq, is she okay?'

'She's doing fine, just fine.'

Crimson explosions. Blackness, and burning pain. She was breaking.

'One more push.'

'A big one this time, darling.'

'*Now.*'

She pushed. She was splitting. She yelled.

'*Now.* Again. Hold her back, Mr Manley.'

She pushed. Between her legs the head pushed out; then a slippery gush.

There was a rustle of movement. She lay emptied and the others got busy. They had cut the cord so quickly. She could not see it, the doctor was in the way.

A faint creak, then a cry. Her heart kicked against her ribs.

'Can I see?' She tried to sit up.

'Mrs Manley, it's a beautiful girl.'

Her mother seemed to be there too, in a mask. How long had she been there? She and Donald could see the baby.

'Oh quick,' cried Christine.

They pulled down their masks. They were smiling.

'Bring Mrs Manley her daughter, nurse.'

Christine held out her arms. Tucked in a towel, her baby was given to her. Enough was showing to know.

Tears ran down Christine's cheeks.

'What's the matter?' Donald's face swam in front of her. He turned to her mother.

'Everyone does this,' said her mother. 'I did. It's the great happiness and the relief. Am I right?' She looked at Christine, who nodded.

SEESAW

Take an ordinary, well-off family like the Prices. Watch what happens when one Sunday seventeen-year-old Hannah disappears without a trace. See how the family rallies when a ransom note demands half a million pounds for Hannah's safe return.

But it's when Hannah comes home that the story really begins.

Now observe what happens to a family when they lose their house, their status, all their wealth. Note how they disintegrate under the pressures of guilt and poverty and are forced to confront their true selves.

And finally, wait to hear all about Hannah, who has the most shocking surprise in store of all.

'Provocative, enthralling, bang-up-to-the-minute... truly, Moggach gets better and
better' Val Hennessy, *Daily Mail*

'A delight to read' *Daily Telegraph*

PORKY

At school they called her Porky on account of the pigs her family kept outside the bungalow near Heathrow. But she felt no different _ not until she realised she was losing her innocence in a way that none of her friends could possibly imagine. Only a child robbed of her childhood can kuow too late what it means to be loved too little and loved too much...

'Deborah Moggach conveys with chilling skill the process by which a fundamentally bright, decent child becomes infested by corruption' *Spectator*

'Illuminates with great compassion how love can so easily go off the rails' *Daily Mail*

'At once eerily exuberant and bleak, this is a compassionate, tough book' *Observer*

'Extraordinarily skilful' *Anita Brookner*

DRIVING IN THE DARK

Desmond never did have much luck with women— except in getting them through their driving tests. Now a coach driver, he is at the most crucial crossroads of his life. His wife has thrown him out. The crisis serves only to deepen his despair over another failed liaison — until he elects to steer his coach on a spectacularly reckless quest for the son he has never seen.

'Disturbing and witty... a deftly-described odyssey that places the battle of the sexes in a new arena' *Sunday Times*

'Moggach, for the purposes of this book, has turned herself into a bloke. His monologue throughout strikes me as totally authentic, but not only does Moggach get his lingo right, she thinks through his head, dramatizing his confusion, decency, wit, pain and determination. This is not just ventriloquism, but empathy so complete as to be phenomenal' *Irish Times*

'At once acutely funny and sad... a woman's protest at the inequality thrust on men by the worst excesses of the women's movement' *Mail on Sunday*

'Poignant and funny... Deborah Moggach is brilliant at capturing just the right voice for her characters' *Cosmopolitan*

CLOSE RELATIONS

The three Hammond sisters have each chosen their own paths. Louise leads a seemingly perfect existence in Beaconsfield with her venture-capitalist husband, messy teenage children and Smallbone kitchen. Prudence, who has successfully forged a career in publishing, is having a fruitless affair with her married boss. And Maddy, always the square peg in the round hole, has just met and fallen in love with a lesbian gardener.

When their father, Gordon, has a heart attack and then runs away to live in Brixton with a young black nurse, Dorothy – his wife – is released like a loose cannon into her daughters' lives.

As passions run high, relationships break up and dramatic developments look set to change them all for ever. For better or for worse.

'A compassionate family comedy... Moggach writes of the calamity of love and the devastation of divorce. A novel of comic appeal and topical wit' *Times Literary Supplement*

'Moggach is a skilful narrator, deftly weaving together the threads of each family member's life, creating an instantly recognisable world' *Daily Telegraph*

ALSO AVAILABLE

ALL ARROW BOOKS ARE AVAILABLE THROUGH MAIL ORDER OR FROM YOUR LOCAL BOOKSHOP AND NEWS-AGENT.

PLEASE SEND CHEQUE/EUROCHEQUE/POSTAL OR.DER (STERLING ONLY) ACCESS, VISA, MASTERCARD, DINERS CARD, SWITCH OR AMEX.

☐☐☐☐☐☐☐☐☐☐☐☐☐☐☐☐

EXPIRY DATE .... SIGNATURE ....
PLEASE ALLOW 75 PENCE PER BOOK FOR POST AND PACKING U.K.
OVERSEAS CUSTOMERS PLEASE ALLOW £1.00 PER COPY FOR POST AND PACKING.
ALL ORDERS TO:
ARROW BOOKS, BOOKS BY POST, TBS LIMITED, THE BOOK SERVICE, COLCHESTER ROAD, FRATING GREEN, COLCHESTER, ESSEX CO7 7DW.
TELEPHONE: (01206) 256 000
FAX: (01206) 255 914

NAME ....
ADDRESS ....
....

Please allow 28 days for delivery. Please tick box if you do not wish to receive any additional information ☐
Prices and availability subject to change without notice.